Love's Tender Prelude

Love's Tender Prelude

Caught in the crosscurrents of history, Chloe Celeste is determined to make her dream come true. But will war tear away the brother she loves?

Kay D. Rizzo

Pacific Press Publishing Association
Boise, Idaho
Oshawa, Ontario, Canada

Edited by Bonnie Tyson-Flyn
Designed by Tim Larson
Cover photo by Sinclair Studios
Typeset in 10/12 New Century Schoolbook

Copyright © 1994 by
Pacific Press Publishing Association
Printed in the United States of America
All Rights Reserved

Library of Congress Cataloging-in-Publication Data:
Rizzo, Kay D., 1943-
Love's tender prelude / Kay Rizzo.
    p. cm.
  ISBN 0-8163-1224-9. — ISBN 0-8163-1219-2 (pbk.)
  1. World War, 1914-1918—United States. 2. Young women—United States. 3. Violinists—United States. 4. Family—United States. I. Title.
PS3568.I836L68   1994
813'.54—dc20   94-5442
                                                              CIP

Contents

Prologue 11

1. Dear Emily 25
2. Shilly-shally 41
3. Light Conversation 57
4. From Little Girl to Lady 73
5. Facing the Music 89
6. Ostrich Feathers and Saffron Silk 103
7. Booked, Beleaguered, and Bailed Out 117
8. Trouble Comes in Bunches 135
9. Diary, Dear Diary 149
10. Days of Innocence 163
11. Caught in a Whirlwind 179
12. A Call to Arms 195
13. A Call to Faith 213
14. We Gather Together 227

Dedication

To Ann Miller,
a friend to the end,
and beyond

Characters

It is a time in America when hope is green, when all things are possible. It is a time for old wounds to heal and for new dreams to flourish, a time to remember the past and look to the future, a time to inhale the heady aroma of freedom and to defeat the enemies within, as well as those beyond her shores.

CHLOE CELESTE (CEECEE) CHAMBERLAIN—A high-spirited spitfire of a girl, she dreams of applause and fame on the concert stages of Europe. But when her life gets caught up in the world of debutantes, dilettantes, and war, anything can happen.

CHLOE MAE CHAMBERLAIN—A woman of determination and courage, whose heart is torn between her family's needs and her own, she looks for strength and guidance from her heavenly Father as new beginnings beckon, new horizons call, new frontiers await.

CYRUS CHAMBERLAIN III—A quiet man of steel, tempered in the fires of heartbreak and duty, he must uproot his family in order to better serve his country, not on the battlefield, but in the boardroom. He struggles to hold his family together despite the raging winds of change.

JAMIE MCCALL—An eager, dedicated medical student, he must dig deep within himself to choose between his passion for medicine and his patriotism, a decision that may cost him his future, his family, and possibly, his life.

CYRUS (RUSTY) CHAMBERLAIN IV—A scrappy, fearless ten-year-old, he is his mother's son in every way, but a plunge in the Atlantic's turbid waters might sever his taste for adventure—forever.

ASHLEY MCCALL—The daughter of Ian and Drucilla McCall, and an irrepressible coquette of seventeen, she looks fragile and pretty, but her petulant will leads her from one daring fling to another—and possibly, to the escapade that will destroy her and those she loves.

JULIA MCCALL—The proud matriarch of the McCall fortunes watches helplessly as her comfortable and secure world unravels, threatening to destroy all she treasures most.

JAMES E. MCCALL—The wealthy McCall patriarch who supplies the quiet strength that binds his family to his side must once again search within himself for the necessary faith to survive the pending crisis.

THADDEUS (THAD) ADAMS—The son of a Cape Cod shopkeeper, Thad hears the rumblings of the conflict across the sea as the call that will fulfill his wildest dreams, dreams that might destroy his future.

Prologue

A bitter wind blew off the ocean, bringing with it the cold sting of salt on Chloe Mae Chamberlain's face. Grateful that the January rains, a downpour since dawn, had momentarily stopped, the Nob Hill matron gave the burly cab driver her hand as she alighted from the automobile. Once her feet were secure on the irregular cobblestone street, the man released her gloved hand.

The darkness of the night couldn't hide the lines of worry on the man's face. "Ma'am, I don't like leavin' you alone in this part of town." His frown deepened. "I often pick up men from your part of town at this hour and bring them to Chinatown, but not ladies like you."

The fine cut of Chloe's plain, dark cloak hadn't escaped his notice. "Please, Mrs. Chamberlain, let me take you back home."

The woman smiled, hoping to allay his fears as well as her own. "I can't say that I like being left alone here, but it can't be helped. Are you sure this is where the child told you to bring me?"

"Oh, yes, ma'am. This is the spot." He glanced about nervously. "She looked to be no more than ten or eleven, but then, who can tell with those people?"

Chloe grimaced. *Those people.* The shadows of the night cloaked her disgust. The man shifted his weight from one foot to the other while she slid her hand inside her cape to her jacket pocket. "Here, this should compensate you for your trouble." Chloe extended her gloved hand toward him and dropped three shiny coins into his hand.

"Are you sure Mr. Chamberlain knows where you are at this hour?"

The woman inched into the pool of light from the street lamp and raised an eyebrow, successfully squelching further questions. "Please, don't wait with me. The girl should be along any minute."

The cab driver hesitated, stroking the tips of his bushy mustache. "If you're sure you'll be all right. I'll tell you what, if I don't get a fare in the next ten minutes, I'll check back here to see if you need a ride home."

"Thank you. I'd appreciate that." Adopting an air of confidence that didn't reach the rumblings of fear in the pit of her stomach, Chloe smiled up into the man's distressed face. "Now, you go along. You don't want to keep your next fare waiting."

The man touched the brim of his hat, nodded, and rushed to the other side of the cab. The heels of Chloe's shoes clicked on the cobblestones as she picked her way around the puddles and floating gutter debris to the curb.

Once safe on the other side of the street, she turned to watch the taillights of the cab bounce down the block and disappear around the corner toward California Street. Except for the soft pools of light from the evenly spaced street lamps on the main street, the dark, raw night engulfed her. Chloe took a deep breath, squared her shoulders, and peered down the unlit, narrow alleyway. The stench of rotting fish, damp straw, human waste, and the nauseating aroma of opium accosted her nose. *I may grow accustomed to seeing the rat-infested hovels and treating disease-ridden children, but I'll never get used to the putrid odor.*

She sighed and stepped out of the circle of lamplight into the shadows. On the banner stretched across the front of the corner butcher shop, she could barely make out the words "Gung Hay Fat Choy."

"Happy New Year to you too," she murmured, glancing down the alley once more. The wind bent the black ostrich feather on her dove gray felt hat, tickling her nose. Brushing the feather aside, she tucked the loose strands of fiery red behind her ears and up under the hat.

Chloe Mae, this was not one of your most intelligent decisions.

You should have waited until Cy got home—or at least awakened Buckley and asked him to drive you. Then she remembered her mission. *Right! As if babies wait on tardy businessmen and aging butlers. If I waited for either of them, the infant would be celebrating his second birthday before I reached my patient.*

Across the narrow alleyway, she could see the crumbling brick walls of a toppled building disappearing into the shadows. She took a deep breath. *How many years and how many tremors will it take before the memories fade?*

In the ten years following San Francisco's big earthquake, much had changed in the wealthier sections of town, but little had changed in Chinatown. Rubble from the quake still lay strewn about the neighborhood. Shells of buildings housed families too destitute to rebuild.

The rebuilding of the business sections of the city and of Nob Hill started as soon as the earthquake and resulting fires had died. The wealthy San Franciscans had chosen to ignore the radical changes suggested by architect Daniel H. Burnham and rushed ahead to rebuild the city. The result was less beautiful and more susceptible to future quakes than the city he had envisioned.

By the 1915 Panama-Pacific International Exposition, the city sported a façade of wealth and commerce. But the lingering evidence of the catastrophe could clearly be seen in Chinatown's back alleys and steep, narrow walkways. Chloe's new women's clinic, like the mythical Phoenix, sprang from the ashes of the old. Her husband Cyrus had thrown himself and his money behind the building project. Built to accommodate twice the number of patients as the original clinic, it operated at capacity only two months after it opened its doors.

While Chloe knew she'd gained the trust of the people of Chinatown, she also knew that she hadn't changed their habits. Young Asian girls of thirteen and fourteen, in order to feed their families, still sold their bodies to sailors on shore leave and to visiting businessmen. As a result, the women of Chinatown still conceived and birthed half-breed babies, uncared for by either culture. These rejected children grew up to be pickpockets, prostitutes, and pimps. And the women still died at an alarming rate from disgusting social diseases and self-induced abortions, in spite of Chloe's efforts to educate those who came to the clinic for medical attention. *If only I could make a real difference.*

Just that morning she'd examined her first second-generation pregnant girl. Chloe closed her eyes and pinched the bridge of her nose. *Oh, dear God. How do You stand it, year after year? Don't You ever get tired of us?* Her shoulders slumped. She sighed and leaned her head against the shop's window. *I'm just overtired, I guess.*

Straightening her shoulders, she clutched her medical bag and scolded herself for thinking negative thoughts. Her heart quickened when, through the gloom, she spied a kerosene lantern bobbing toward her.

Just as she stepped out of the shadows, somewhere between her and the lantern light, she heard a door slam, followed by the discordant voices and the unsteady shuffle of three distinctly inebriated men. "If a body meets a body, comin' through the rye, should a body kiss a body?"

Drunken sailors! Chloe clicked her tongue in disgust. *I'm probably in this God-forsaken place due to the lusts of louts such as these.* Her scorn didn't keep her from shrinking farther back into the shadows.

The sound of boots scuffing and a child's terrified cries interrupted Chloe's musing. "Let me go."

A man laughed. "Come on, Chinky gal. Let's have a party."

Chloe peered around the corner in the direction of the voices. The sounds of a struggle ensued—men laughing and scuffling in the darkness, a girl crying, "No, no. I no do things like that. Please, let me go!"

One of the men growled, "You want to play rough, we'll play rough, right here on the street, OK?" The sound of a jarring slap followed by the girl's scream of pain echoed along the alleyway.

Chloe started. "Oh, dear God!" Her free hand clutched her throat. *I can't just stand here and let those brutes rape that poor child. If I don't do something—* She thought for a moment. *I could scream for help.* She laughed at her own naiveté. *If the girl's screams don't bring help, what do you expect yours will do?*

The girl screamed again. Almost as a reflex, Chloe unclasped the metal buckles and slid her hand inside her medical bag. Her fingers brushed past the new stethoscope her son Jamie had given her at Christmas, past the bottles of medicine and disinfectant strapped to the sides of the case, and across the top of the rolled bandages. As her fingertips grazed the handle of her sheathed scalpel, her stomach knotted. Her husband's frowning face flashed into her mind. *Sorry, Cy, but I have to do this. Please forgive me—*

Down the alley, the struggle intensified. While the girl begged for mercy, the men argued about who would get her first. Taking a deep breath, Chloe wrapped her fingers around the instrument's bone handle and slipped the razor-sharp knife from its sheath.

A cry of pain from the girl jolted Chloe to action. The woman set her open case against the storefront and tiptoed down the garbage-strewn alleyway, praying that the men's drunken state and the child's sobbing would cover the click of her heels on the wooden walkway. Suddenly her foot bumped into something soft. A startled yowl filled the night air as a cat scurried under a stoop.

"What's that?" one of the men asked. Only the terrified child's sobbing could be heard. "Shut up, Chink!"

Chloe held her breath. *Oh, dear God, help me.*

She released her breath when she heard one of the men say, "Aw, it's just some cat! Let's get back to business before this brat wakes the entire neighborhood with her bawling."

Chloe inched closer. In the light from the discarded lantern, she could see the child quivering on the ground, pinned down by her assailants.

Just as I thought, sailors in dress blues. Stepping up behind the nearest man, she pressed the steel blade against his left ear.

"Let the child go!" she demanded.

The man froze.

One of the other men swung his face around toward Chloe. "Hey, what the—" The third man looked up from the child.

Chloe's captive lifted his hand to stay the action of his partners in crime. "Leave her alone, Archie. The lady's got a knife."

In a low, even tone, Chloe continued. "Don't get any ideas, just because I'm a woman. I know how to use this thing. Tell your friends to step away and to stay where I can see them."

Instead of obeying her command, the man named Archie whispered to the other two, "Hold still. I can take her."

Chloe jabbed the point of the knife into the tender flesh behind her victim's ear. "I said, let the child go."

"Ow, you cut me." The man's hand flew to his ear. Chloe pushed it away with her free hand. "Not so fast. That was only a pinprick, sir. Tell your friends to back away quietly, or I shall be forced to do as you suggest."

The two free men flattened themselves against the nearest peeling plastered wall. "Yeah, crazy lady. Whatever you say."

The girl scrambled to the opposite side of the alleyway, leaving the lantern to light the middle of the alleyway.

Chloe dared not look away from her captive. One careless move on her part, and the six-foot man could easily overpower her. Out of the corner of her eye, she detected a slow, stealthy movement from the man called Archie. She tapped her victim's ear. "Son, your friend is making me nervous. You'd better advise him to stand still, or my hand might begin to shake and, well, that might be a trifle painful for you."

Without moving his head, the sailor shouted, "Hey, Archie, Deaver, the lady means business."

All right, Smarty, you have them where you want them. Now, what do you intend to do with them? The sudden sound of excited voices and woven-straw sandals slapping against the wooden walkway answered her question. Around her, people poured out of the rickety shacks. In broken Cantonese, she shouted over her shoulder, "Would someone find a policeman, please?"

At her shout, the child bolted, sobbing, into an old man's arms. Archie and Deaver took advantage of the distraction and broke into a run, only to be caught by the crowd and dragged back. Chloe heard, rather than saw, the two police officers break through the excited crowd. "What's going on here?"

A man's hand gloved hers and slipped the scalpel from her grasp. "It's all right, ma'am. You can let him go now." Chloe looked up into the grinning faces of two officers of the law.

"Oh, am I glad to see you."

One policeman clapped a set of handcuffs on the terrified

sailor. "Just what is going on here?" he repeated.

The sailor named Archie, restrained by two Chinese men, shouted, "We were minding our own business when the little Chink pickpocketed my friend, Deaver. She tried to run, but I caught her. Then this insane female jumped us and threatened to butcher us all right here in the street."

A cry of anger swept through the crowd. Chloe shook her head. "Sir, that's a lie! The three men attacked the child and wrestled her to the ground. I heard everything from the corner." She gestured with her head. "Go up to the corner and check. You'll find my medical bag by the butcher shop on the corner."

The first officer jerked Chloe's arm. "What's a lady like you doing down here at this hour, anyway? Does your husband know where you are?"

Chloe's lips narrowed and tightened. "Sir, I operate the women's clinic down by the wharf. I was called here to—"

"Missee tell truth!" The old man with the terrified child clinging to his waist stepped forward. "The lady tell truth." He waved his hands toward his neighbors. "We hear. We see from behind our windows, but—" The man bowed low before Chloe. "We afraid to stop them. The lady put us to shame."

The officer in charge eyed Chloe suspiciously. "Just who are you? And what, pray tell, are you doing out alone at night in this part of town?"

"My name is Mrs. Cyrus Chamberlain. I am a midwife, answering a call. And I suspect that, before these sailors accosted her, the girl here was coming to take me to her mother or sister."

"Oh, Mrs. Chamberlain," the policeman sputtered. "I didn't recognize you. I, uh, stop by your clinic regularly for the free doughnuts your cook whips up, and—" He squirmed uncomfortably, "—and I, uh, stop by to see Margaret, your, uh, helper."

She grinned. "Oh, yes. You must be William. Margaret has mentioned you."

With her identity established, Chloe suggested, "If I am finished here, there's a woman badly needing my services."

"Here's her satchel, Will, just like she said." The second policeman handed the case to the first policeman.

He grunted and handed the case to Chloe. "We'll need you to

come down to headquarters tomorrow morning to press charges."

A cry erupted from the sailor whose ear Chloe had almost pierced. "Press charges? If anyone should press charges—"

The policeman named William whipped about and shook his fist in the man's face. "One more word out of you, and I'll let this mob have you!" Turning back to Chloe, he continued, "You're free to go, Mrs. Chamberlain."

"Thank you, William. And come by the clinic any time for more doughnuts."

William touched the visor of his cap. "I will. And thank you, ma'am."

The child took Chloe's hand and led her down the walk to a shack in the middle of the block. Chloe stumbled up a flight of rickety stairs behind the girl and into a tenement room. As the door opened, the reek of fish and cooked pork mingled with the aroma of incense made Chloe gag.

"My sister," the child explained, pointing to a moaning woman on the other side of the room.

Chloe hurried across the room and bent over a terrified young woman. Chloe patted her arm gently. "I'm the midwife. I'm here to help you."

By dawn, a wriggling, wailing baby boy announced his arrival to the poverty-ridden community. As Chloe watched the young mother cuddle the tiny boy, tears filled her eyes. *Poor little mite.* Chloe stood up and arched her back to ease the stiffness. *How long will it take before your spirit breaks? How long before you're out on the street begging coins from tourists or hawking your aunt for grocery money?*

Chloe glanced at the burning candles standing on the washstand and at the tiny altar set with a New Year's feast of rice, melon seeds, and wine to propitiate the household gods. Her eyes brimmed as she returned her instruments to her case and prepared to leave.

The old man, the infant's great-grandfather, bowed and grinned. "I have pretty good rickshaw. I take tourists through Chinatown. I take you home."

Chloe hesitated. The idea of having a human being assume work as a beast of burden repulsed her. Remembering the uncomfortable walk home, she relented. "If you will allow me to pay you."

The man shook his head and bowed again. "No charge for missee. No pay. No pay for ride." Reluctantly, she agreed.

After checking the mother and the baby once more, she packed her instruments in her case and allowed the man to ferry her in his red-and-black lacquered cart over the bumpy cobblestones to her graystone town house on Clay Street.

"There, there." She pointed. "That's the place." The rickshaw owner stopped at the curb in front of the house and lowered the poles to the ground. Before Chloe could disembark, Cyrus, her husband of ten years, charged through the front door of the house, fury snapping in his deep-set brown eyes.

"Of all the crazy stunts to pull, going off like that in the middle of the night! Chloe Mae, this one takes the cake. Don't you care about your own safety?" He grabbed the medicine case from Chloe. "Did you stop to think of how worried I would be? Don't you know that your son and your daughter need you here, alive and well? I do too." He took her arm and helped her out of the cart. Jabbing his free hand into his pocket, he extracted a coin and offered it to the rickshaw puller. The old man bowed, shook his head, and without a word picked up the cart poles and trotted down the street.

"Good morning to you too, Cy dear." Chloe glanced at her husband then up at the second-story windows. One panel of the Belgian lace curtains fluttered into place. She waved her gloved hand toward the window. "Good morning, children."

Cyrus grasped his wife's elbow and guided her up the steps into the house. Chloe glanced toward her husband. "And how did your meeting with the company vice-president go last night?"

"Don't try to change the subject, Chloe Mae! Going to Chinatown alone at night is incredibly irresponsible of you. When I discovered your note last night, I almost went wild. I don't have to tell you how many tourists have wandered into those alleyways and been found floating in the bay, having been bludgeoned to death."

"Cyrus, listen to yourself. I've been going down there almost every day for the last twelve years."

"Day, yes. But not at night by yourself, woman."

"Good morning, Buckley." Chloe greeted the white-haired man who stood at the door, wringing his gloved hands. A tiny Chinese woman stood behind the butler, sputtering in the Hunan dialect. Cy handed the man the case and reached for his wife's cape. "Why didn't you ask Buckley to drive you?"

"Ma'am, I would have been pleased to do so." Lines of worry creased the man's patient face.

Chloe patted his arm. "I know. I would have, but you were already in bed for the night and, well, the cab driver was here, ready to take me where I needed to go."

Cy placed the cape over Buckley's extended arm. "And what about the two policemen who stopped by this morning?"

She turned in surprise. "Policemen?"

"Yes, policemen! They stopped by to see if you made it home safely." Cy glared at his wife. "You can imagine my chagrin when they mentioned something about a brawl."

The Chinese woman gasped. Having forgotten the family governess was behind him, Buckley turned and scolded, "Au Sam, don't you have chores to perform this morning? We must leave the Chamberlains alone to their discussion." He urged the woman down the hall, toward the kitchen door. As the door swung open, a blur of gray skittered across the marbled floor. Meeker, the family cat, didn't slow down until she rounded the landing at the top of the carpeted staircase.

Chloe glanced at her husband and laughed nervously. "It was hardly a brawl. Look, could we discuss this later? I am extremely tired."

Cy's voice rose into its upper range. "And I'm not? I work hard all day, then return home to a night of terror, wondering if my wife will be found dead in some unseemly gutter, her throat slit!"

Chloe choked back her sudden urge to laugh.

He whipped about. "Please tell me, what is so funny? The part about my fears or your murdered body?"

"The part about slitting throats." She placed her hands gently on his arm. "Cy, I'm sorry. I didn't mean—I guess I'm so tired, I'm not myself."

Cy placed his arm around his wife's shoulders and drew her

close. "What if the tables were turned, and I went wandering through the slums of the city in the middle of the night while you were sitting at home, worrying?" He paused and searched her eyes. "Chloe, Chloe, Chloe, you will be the death of me yet."

Remorse swept over the woman. "Oh, Cy, you're right. Going down there alone was stupid of me. I admit it. And I am sorry."

He shook his head sadly. "I know you don't mean to, but you terrify me with the chances you take. What would I ever do without you?"

She gazed contritely at the black marble floor of the entryway. "You're right. I truly am sorry. I promise not to do it again."

She expected to hear him chortle at her empty promise. They both knew that when an emergency call came, Chloe would grab her medical case and go, without thinking, wherever needed. Instead of the expected response, Cy quietly said, "No. You probably won't."

She frowned at his ominous tone. "What do you mean?"

He cleared his throat. "They're calling me back east to run the head office in New York."

Chloe pulled away from him, her spine rigid. "What? Why? For how long?"

He stared at their reflection in the mirror—the image of San Francisco's refined, well-heeled establishment. "The President is forming an energy board to govern the use of oil and coal in case the country declares war on Germany, and Jenkins, the chairman of the board, has been asked to serve on it."

She scowled. "The President? President Wilson?"

"Precisely. As to how long, who knows? I suppose until the war in Europe ends."

"But that could be years, and besides, America isn't involved in the skirmish."

He arched his eyebrows but remained silent. Chloe studied her husband's face. "Do you know something the rest of us should know?"

Cy shrugged. Knowing she'd get no further information from him on that subject, Chloe shook her head and sputtered, "Don't they know you have a family here? I don't want you away from us that long."

Cy cleared his throat again. "I'm not planning to leave you and the children behind. The company will buy our home—for the next manager and his family. We'll sell—"

"Sell? Everything? What about my clinic?"

His hands brushed lightly over her shoulders. "I don't know what to say, except that the transfer is nonnegotiable."

Chloe pulled away from Cy, folding her hands defiantly across her chest. "My clinic. All the years I've put into the clinic—"

"You'd be closer to your family. You know how lonely your dad has been since your mother died. CeeCee is the only person who can comfort him in the same way you can. You'll both be there for him." Cy hurried on. "And my mother has been begging us to come east ever since she and Father retired to the family estate outside Baltimore."

Chloe whirled away from him. *Please, God, I don't want to go. I don't want to hear this!*

"Think of it. If we lived on the East Coast, Jamie could come home from medical school regularly, instead of only once a year."

A wisp of a smile flitted across Chloe's face. How she missed Jamie, the son of her first husband, James. He'd be finishing medical school soon and looking to set up his practice. She'd hoped he'd choose to do so in California. But lately, his letters spoke little of classwork and much of the war in Europe.

Cy traced his finger over the stitching on Chloe's gray gabardine suit jacket. "And what about CeeCee? If we move east, she could study violin at the Institute of Musical Art in New York or at the Boston Conservatory."

He cleared the sudden frog from his throat. "She's a fine musician with a brilliant future ahead of her. It would be selfish of us—"

Chloe dropped her head. *He's right. I know he's right. Oh, dear God, I know he's right. But to leave our home— the home we built together?* She glanced about the entryway. Sunlight streamed through the crystal teardrops of the chandelier, splaying into a rainbow on the marble floor.

Chloe ran her fingers across the mahogany Chippendale table and caressed the Ming porcelain bowl. "Leave California." Her words faded to a whisper.

"We can have the furniture crated and shipped east if you like." Cy stepped up behind her and caressed her shoulders gently. "I'll build you an even grander home on the Jersey shore. I know how much you love the sea."

"I don't need a grander home, Cy. You know that." She bit her lip. "It won't be the same. Nothing ever remains the same, does it?"

"I'm sorry, darling. I'm truly sorry."

She rested her head against his vest and gave a ragged sigh. Gently Cy turned her about to face him. He touched his lips to her forehead, coaxing the worry lines away. "We'll be together, love. That's what truly matters."

Swallowing the lump in her throat, Chloe whispered, "It will be good for Rusty to grow up near his grandparents as well."

"Come on." Cy coaxed her toward the staircase. "We can talk more this evening after I get home from the office. You'll be able to think more clearly after you've had a good sleep."

Above their heads, the muffled sound of running feet brought a smile to their faces. A bedroom door slammed. An instant later, a second door closed.

Cy chuckled. "Those scamps. They've been eavesdropping again. Oh well, they'll know about the move sooner or later."

Chloe nodded. "I know. I know. You're right. The move will be good for everyone—I guess."

Dear Emily

With my fingertips I traced the gold script engraved on the cover of the white leather notebook.

>Chloe Celeste Chamberlain
>San Francisco, California
>Nineteen hundred and seventeen

I allowed myself the luxury of a tiny grin. Pleasure over my latest discovery pushed my anger toward my mother temporarily into the background. *This one can't wait until tonight. I must tell Emily all about it—immediately.*

A little tug at the baby blue satin page marker caused the book to fall open on my lap. "February, day of Chinese new year, 1917." I removed the cap from my fountain pen and wrote:

Dear Emily, This morning I overheard my parents arguing. I looked up from my diary and grinned. *Mama says she and Daddy never argue, only discuss. Daddy's being transferred to the home office in New York. I can't believe it. My dreams are coming true. I'll be able to attend one of the music conservatories—that is, if I'm accepted.*

Meeker, my gray Persian cat, hopped up onto my bed and rubbed against my arm. "Hey, how'd you get in here?" Petting her long, silky fur, I stared absently into the early-morning shadows still lingering in my bedroom. The skirt on my white dimity graduation dress peered out from behind the partially open double doors of the mahogany chifforobe.

"*La jeune fille—très chic*," the dressmaker called it. I grimaced at the woman's phony French accent and at the dress's simple, little-girl style. *Mama's taste, not mine! Why can't I ever stand up to her, tell her when I don't like something? I don't know at whom to be more angry, Mama or me!* I eyed the dress with unveiled distaste. *It will be different when I go shopping on New York's Fifth Avenue. New York City's better shops won't carry such merchandise!*

New York! Boston! Sketches and photographs from my favorite magazines swirled through my imagination. To wear the latest creations of good taste and fashion while they're still in fashion! *In New York, I'll get to wear glamorous evening dresses and attend Aunt Drucilla's fabulous parties. Ashley and I will flit about Greenwich Village together, meeting oh so many famous artists, poets, and musicians. Art exhibits, concerts, the opera. Dashing young men in attendance.* My pulse raced. I could feel my color rise at the very thought.

Two days earlier I'd received a letter from my cousin Ashley, telling about her latest adventure shopping on Fifth Avenue in New York City and about a dashing and exciting boy named Chip. She'd met him while spending two weeks with Grandma McCall on Martha's Vineyard. I envied her. *In a few months, maybe I'll be able—*

Reality darkened my mood. *Mama will never allow me the freedom Aunt Drucilla grants her Ashley.* According to my mother, Ashley "doesn't have the sense of a pomegranate," but she is oh so much fun. I started daydreaming again. *With my smarts and her personality, we'll have the time of our lives.*

Placing my diary face down on my rumpled bed, I imagined a particularly handsome young man—no one I knew, of course—taking my hand, kissing my fingertips, then helping me to my feet.

With the grace of European royalty, I strolled across the room to my dressing table. Swirling my flannel nightgown as if it were an imported silk chiffon creation, I seated myself in front of the dressing table's large oval mirror.

I swept my auburn curls up off my neck, twisting first one direction, then the other. I imagined my curls gathered on top of my head and cascading down to my shoulders. A russet-haired

Empress Josephine. A jewel-studded tiara would be lovely. Or maybe a set of diamond combs. Perhaps a black seal cape. Or a glittering silk shawl.

I preened, lifting one shoulder and batting my eyelashes at my reflection. "Miss Chloe Celeste Chamberlain, the glamorous New York debutante, granddaughter of the Boston McCalls and a talented violinist in her own right, you know." I giggled and let my hair tumble down my back. *I'll go by Celeste, yes. And no one will call me CeeCee, ever again!* I wrinkled my nose and groaned. *Who are you trying to kid? Who can make a silk purse out of a pig's ear?*

I leaned forward and studied my complexion for a moment. Angel kisses, my foot! The freckles will have to go! Surely the *crème de la crème* of New York society uses a secret potion to bleach away such unsightly spots. Then a new, disturbing thought hit me. *Maybe people of the upper class don't get nasty little things like pimples or freckles! Ashley certainly doesn't—not one blemish.*

Narrowing my eyes, I tried to imagine what I'd look like if I were blond and blue-eyed and possessed a clear peaches-and-cream complexion like my cousin. *Tsk! It's hopeless.*

A sound in the hall near my parents' bedroom sent me flying to my bedroom door. I didn't want to miss overhearing any further information that my parents might yet discuss, especially about the move. I opened the door enough to peek out into the hall, undetected.

Glimpsing my little brother's red Indian-blanket bathrobe, I groaned and slammed my door. *Rusty!* I leaned against the closed door and surveyed my room—my massive four-poster brass bed with the thick down-filled mattress, my hand-carved chifforobe, the matching dressing table. *How much will I have to leave behind?*

Why am I so confused? First, I want to go; then, I want to stay. Go—stay—stay—go! Oh, I don't know what I want. Not that it will matter to anyone but me! My mood darkening, I wandered over to the bay window, pulled back one of the lace panels, and gazed down at the row of gray stone houses lining the street. *This is one thing I can't take with me.*

The alcove had always been my source of comfort. Here, in my little hideaway, I rocked in my armless rocker, hid from my little brother, cowered from irate parents, and stewed over slights, imagined and otherwise. Here, I became invisible. Here, I nursed my wounds. Here, I spun my dreams. On good days, when I sought the pleasure of solitude, or on bad days, when I vowed I'd run away and "everyone would be sorry," I could look as far to the left as possible, past the Mulligan place, past the Gramercy mansion, all the way to the bay.

I'll miss the bay. Wait a minute; Manhattan has a bay, doesn't it? I smiled and hugged myself. The grandfather clock at the top of the stairs gonged seven times. *I'd better hurry if I hope to practice before school.*

I glanced at the bed and my abandoned diary, which I called "Emily," after my favorite poet, Emily Dickinson. If she and I had been contemporaries, I know that we would have been confidantes of the soul. Mama gave me a book of her poems for my thirteenth birthday, the same year Uncle Joe and Aunt Beth gave me a diary. Since then, the birthday gift of a diary has become a ritual. Writing daily missives to someone called "diary" struck me as being supercilious. That's the word my Uncle Philip used at a family dinner last week to describe San Francisco's current mayor. *I should look that one up.*

I grabbed my dictionary off the bookshelves next to the window and turned to the *s*'s. *Let's see—super—super—supersci—* Disgusted, I threw the book down onto the rocker. *How, may I ask, can you find a word in the dictionary if you can't spell it?*

Horrified, I stopped short. *Didn't Mama say the same thing last week when she was writing a letter to my Grandma McCall? No, it can't be. People always say she and I look alike and act alike. Now we're thinking alike too?* I laughed in spite of my momentary discomfort.

The memory of Mama's drawn face when Daddy told her of the transfer to New York sobered me. I knew how important her clinic for the women of Chinatown was to her. Walking over to the rocker, I scooped up my pencil and diary, hopped onto the bed, and, with my back pressed against the heavy brass footboard for support, I resumed writing. Meeker lifted her head, meowed, licked my bare toes, then tucked her head on her paw and went back to sleep. Thoughts that my mouth would never let me speak flowed out onto the page. *A part of me feels sad for Mama. It will hurt her to leave her clinic. But, knowing Mama, she'll find another cause to support in no time.*

As the Bible says, "Ye have the poor always with you." And if there are poor, mistreated women in New York, sooner or later, Mama will find them and make their problems hers!

I clenched my teeth. *As you know, Mama is always so busy helping others. Sometimes I feel so proud of her and what she's doing. Other times, she makes me so mad. Last night, for that matter! I heard her leave the house in the middle of the night. She thought I was asleep. But I knew. I watched her go! And I couldn't sleep a wink until I heard Daddy come home a couple of hours later.*

I chewed on my pencil. Feelings of guilt and resentment rumbled inside me, resentment at Mama for leaving Rusty and me in the care of servants and guilt at feeling resentful. A voice inside me argued, *Calling Au Sam and Buckley servants is hardly fair. After ten years, they're practically part of the family.*

"But they're not my parents!" My words echoed through the silent house. I listened, hoping no one had heard my outburst.

It's not that I don't admire my mother for the way she helps people. Everyone talks about her dedication. Who knows how many women and babies she's saved over the years as a midwife? I guess I'd rather have her helping people than being like some of my friends' mothers. They flit about town, from shopping excursions to luncheons to afternoon teas to soirees. The only causes that interest them are the ones where their names or pictures will be in the newspaper.

So why am I angry? The tiny hairs on my arms stood up when I recalled my father's words, "Chloe, you could have been killed!"

What if Mama had died? What if those thugs had knifed her and tossed her body into the bay? What if— Fear and fury boiled inside me. *Last night wasn't the first time I fell asleep in the rocker beside the window, waiting for her to return from delivering someone's baby.* I punched a bed pillow with my fist and buried my face in my rumpled quilt to squelch the cry welling up in my throat. *Don't you care about anything besides your patients, Mama? Don't you care about us? Daddy, Rusty, and I need you too.*

I knew the answers to my questions even before I thought

them. I didn't really doubt her love. She would be horrified if she knew how I felt about her and her work at the clinic. That voice inside me screamed, *"So tell her. Let her know how you feel."*

I gave a wry smile. *Me? Mama's good little girl?* I was CeeCee, the quiet one, the one always hesitant to stir up trouble or cause the family worry or concern, the one who kept her measles secret until the school mistress sent her home with a fever of 102°. I pounded the pillow again with my fist. *Shouldn't mothers know these things? Shouldn't they see and know when their children need them? Sometimes, she makes me so mad!*

The single gong of the clock announcing the half-hour stirred me to action. *Practice! If I dress quickly, I can still practice for a half-hour before breakfast.* I sprang from the bed and threw off my flannel nightdress. It landed in a heap on the floor in front of the chifforobe. Scooping it up off the floor, I tossed it into the wardrobe. *I'll hang it up later—if Au Sam doesn't beat me to it.* Au Sam and Anna, our maid, have strict orders from Mama not to pick up after me. Anna obeys, but no one tells Au Sam what to do or not to do, not even Mama.

I reached for my carefully pressed navy blue gabardine skirt and white cotton waist, the uniform of the all-girl's school I attended. *Bless you, Au Sam. What would I ever do without you?* After quickly brushing my hair, I pulled the sides of my hair back and fastened them in place with a navy grosgrain ribbon; then I flew from my room and down the stairs to the parlor.

Drawing the double parlor doors closed behind me, I paused to savor the delicious sense of seclusion I experienced whenever I entered our somber, seldom-used parlor, with its drawn brocade draperies in muted tones of grape, lavender, rose, and gray.

The eyes of three generations of Chamberlains, McCalls, and Spencers stared down on me from the marble mantle over the tile fireplace. I rushed to the rosewood grand piano and opened the leather-covered violin case resting on the piano bench.

Lovingly, I lifted the fragile instrument from its midnight blue velvet cradle and checked each string for pitch. Once satisfied, I paused to wipe imaginary smudges from the instrument's dark, highly polished surface. For my eleventh birthday, Granddaddy Spencer, Mama's father, had purchased my first violin from the Sears Roebuck catalog for four dollars.

"I know it's not much," he told me, "but it should last you until you decide whether you want to continue violin lessons."

The image of Granddaddy with his red hair and infectious grin brought a smile to my face. Of my three grandfathers, Grandpa McCall, Grandfather Chamberlain, and Granddaddy Spencer, Granddaddy was my favorite. Not that I didn't love the other two. It's just that Granddaddy Spencer always took time for me. And he never called me CeeCee!

Last year, when Mama, Rusty, and I went back east to Shinglehouse for Grandma Spencer's funeral, Granddaddy asked me to play his favorite song, "Annie Laurie," over and over again. My grandmother's name was Annie.

When I wasn't playing his favorite song for him on the violin, he and I would take long walks across the grassy oil fields of northern Pennsylvania, where he used to work "checking the lines," as he called it. These were my favorite times. He'd tell me stories about my mother growing up and about how she had delivered my Aunt Dorothy. Although he never talked about the day Mama ran away from home, I knew the story well. I tried to imagine Granddaddy Spencer forcing her to marry a man she didn't love, just because she turned seventeen years old. I couldn't.

Now that I'm turning seventeen, I wonder if he'd try to marry me off too? Somehow, I doubted it. After rubbing the resin on my bow, I tucked the violin under my chin and drew the bow across the strings. The sweet, clear tones of "Annie Laurie" filled the darkened room, and I closed my eyes to better remember the smile of pleasure on Granddaddy's face. I strolled about the room, playing his song until my shin slammed against the mahogany tea table. An unearthly screech erupted from my violin in response to my pain. *Ouch!* I bent down and massaged the bruise.

If anyone heard that last note— Remembering a similar sound I made at my first music lesson when I was eleven, I grimaced. I giggled aloud when I remembered the look of horror on my violin teacher's face. *Poor Mr. Bohn.* I saluted my music stand with my bow. "Sorry, sir."

Mr. Bohn, a grave middle-aged man, obliged to give violin and piano lessons for his livelihood, played with the philharmonic.

At the sound of my violin's first nerve-grating notes, the poor man looked as though he'd accidentally bitten into an unripe persimmon. The man snatched the instrument from me, adjusted the pegs, and ran his bow across the strings. A sweet, melodic tone emerged. Satisfied that the problem was not with the instrument, he handed the violin back to me. Adjusting the small, gold-rimmed glasses that pinched the end of his nose, he swallowed hard. "Now, you try."

Obediently, I positioned the bow and drew it downward. A second dreadful cry escaped the tortured instrument. Mr. Bohn's face fell, along with his dreams of having discovered his very own child prodigy. The next few lessons reinforced his certainty that the violin, perhaps the entire field of music, would forever be out of my reach. Not wishing to take money under false pretense, he suggested to my parents that I quit taking the weekly lessons. But my mother assured him that, given time, I would, indeed, produce music. "Music runs in the family, Mr. Bohn."

A small, ironic smile flicked across his face. "Perhaps, in your daughter's case, it skipped a generation, Madam."

Daddy narrowed his eyes and pursed his lips. "I would suggest that we give her a little more time to learn. As encouragement for you, we could increase your weekly stipend by, say, fifty percent."

Mr. Bohn peered over his spectacles, one eyebrow lifted in surprise. "Fifty percent?"

My father nodded.

The man licked his lips. "Well, maybe I have been a trifle hasty in my evaluation of your daughter's musical ability."

Daddy grinned and extended his hand. "Then we have a deal? Say, six months?"

"We have a deal." Mother and I looked on as the two men shook hands to seal their agreement.

To Mr. Bohn's surprise and mine—and possibly even my father's—Mama's prediction proved right. In six months, I did improve—a lot. Then, the more I improved, the more interested I became in the violin, and the more I practiced. The more I practiced, the more interested Mr. Bohn grew in my future as a musician.

My violin became my life. Mama and Au Sam no longer needed

DEAR EMILY 33

to badger me to practice. By my thirteenth birthday, Mr. Bohn considered me his protégé. That year, he arranged for me to play last chair with the philharmonic for the Christmas concert. News reporters for the local papers picked up on the novelty of having so young a member in the orchestra, thus giving the organization free publicity. The concert master asked me back for the spring concert season. And the next fall, I was invited to become a permanent member.

At the beginning of my senior year, Mr. Bohn recommended I apply to one of the eastern schools of music. Three conservatories particularly interested me, two in New York City and one in Boston, where my Grandpa and Grandma McCall lived. My parents' enthusiasm, especially Mama's, didn't match mine. I knew she'd never let me go, that is, until this morning when Daddy announced our move.

On one hand, I was delighted. I might be able to continue my musical training at one of the best schools in the country. On the other hand, with the entire family moving east, I would still be living under my parents' watchful scrutiny.

I'll never be on my own. Daddy and Mama will be right there watching over me, every step of the way. If Mama has her way, I'll be a baby forever. Darling CeeCee. I didn't once consider that Daddy could be as smothering as she. And I didn't stop to think that my anger at my mother's overprotectiveness counteracted my earlier argument that she failed to give Rusty and me the attention I thought we lacked.

Angrily, I flipped through my stack of violin music. Bach, Brahms, Beethoven—no, not the German composers. Even though the United States was not yet involved in the war, American musicians were conscious of each composer's nationality.

Finding a composition by a French composer of the Romantic Era, I attacked the score with a vengeance. My strident notes hardly fit the composer's intended mood. *Sooner or later, you'll have to let go, Mama. I will break free. And no one will stop me! Not you, Mama. Not even Kaiser What's-his-name!*

Since my first concert with the philharmonic, I'd dreamed of one day touring the capitals of Europe as a concert violinist, not last chair nor third chair nor first, but as guest soloist. I would stun audiences from London to Petrograd with my talent, filling my days with adventure and my nights with music. Europe—huh! If the governments over there would ever stop squabbling, maybe.

My frustration distorted the next passage. The piece's delicate runs took on a decided militancy. *About war, Mama and I agree. War is so wasteful.* Why the Germans had to begin torpedoing passenger ships with Americans aboard, I couldn't understand. *This war could go on forever. I'll be too old to hold a bow, and my fingers will be too arthritic to play a tune before I can get to the concert stage. Why Jamie would want to enlist in the army makes no sense.*

One afternoon the previous fall, when I arrived home from school, I found my mother in a dither. I didn't learn the cause until Daddy came home for dinner. I'd just begged a shortbread cookie from Marta, the cook, when he arrived. Mama met him at the door with the news. "We got a letter from Jamie today."

Detecting the ring of trouble in her voice, I stopped on my way up the stairs to listen. My brother Jamie was, and always has been, my hero. He lives back east with my grandparents in Boston and was in his last year of medical school at Harvard.

My father handed his overcoat, hat, and umbrella to Buckley. "Thank you, Buckley."

"The evening paper, sir."

"Thank you." Daddy unfolded the paper to peruse the front page.

Mama's lips tightened. "Cyrus, I'm speaking to you."

Daddy looked up from his paper. "Oh? And how are his medical classes going?"

"Cyrus! Please put down the paper and listen to me."

My father folded the paper and kissed Mama on the cheek. "Sorry, dear. Now, tell me all about Jamie's letter."

"Cy, he wants to enlist in the Canadian Army, of all things. You have to stop him," she demanded, waving my brother's letter in my father's face. "You know people in the government. Stop him!"

Daddy patiently took the letter from her hand and studied it for a moment. "I know people in the U.S. government, yes, but not in the Canadian government."

My mother's hands flew into the air like startled pigeons. "What can we do? Let him enlist and get shot full of holes? What purpose would that serve?"

"None, my dear." Putting his arm around her, Daddy led my mother into the sun room. "It would seem to me that the best thing we can do right now is convince him to wait until after his graduation to enlist. A lot can happen between now and next spring." Mama placed her hand on her forehead and rubbed the creases from her brow. "Perhaps I should go back east myself and talk some sense into his head."

"Before you do that, dear, I suggest we wire a message to his grandparents to find out if they're apprised of the situation. In the meantime, you could write a letter, suggesting that Jamie wait until after he graduates before going ahead with his plans."

Mama took a deep sigh. "Cyrus, I hope you're right."

I watched my father place a gentle hand on Mama's shoulder. "In the meantime, try not to worry. It won't do you or Jamie any good. Having said that, you must remember that ultimately, Jamie will make up his own mind." He massaged her shoulder for a moment. "He's not a child any longer, Chloe. He's twenty-three years old, a man by any standards."

"I won't allow him to get himself blown up like his father did—and for so trivial a reason." My mother's hand shook. She reached into her pocket for a handkerchief.

Daddy blanched at my mother's words. "Chloe dear, I wouldn't class—"

She whirled about to face him. "I would. James died in his quest for gold. And war does nothing but line the pockets of greedy men with the same filthy stuff!"

Daddy put his arms around her and drew her close to him. "A sense of honor, not gold, drives Jamie to consider enlisting. And enlisting doesn't guarantee he'll get killed, or, as a trained physician, even see battlefield action."

Mama pulled away from him. "And your saying that doesn't guarantee he won't get killed, does it?"

I stumbled up to my room. *Jamie killed? No, that could never happen to my Jamie* . That night I knelt beside my bed to say my prayers. After asking God to bless my family, Meeker, Au Sam, and Buckley, I prayed, "And, please, dear God, don't let Jamie do something stupid like enlisting in the Canadian Army. Help him to remember how much I need him. Amen."

The first time he went east to the preparatory school in western Massachusetts, he kissed me and said, "CeeCee, don't be afraid. I'll only be gone for the school year; then we'll be together again. I'll always come back to you."

I never forgot his promise. Every September thereafter, as he boarded the eastbound train, I reminded him of his promise. And there, in the darkened parlor, I reminded him again. *You promised, Jamie. You promised.*

I lowered my violin. Somehow, I didn't feel much like practicing any longer. While Mama and my grandparents had managed to talk my brother out of enlisting before his graduation, they hadn't talked him out of enlisting. *Maybe now that we're moving early, I can succeed where everyone else has failed.*

After placing the instrument in its case, I lingered in the room's cool solitude a while longer until the sounds of the family stirring overhead jarred me out of my reverie.

I didn't see Mama and Daddy until that evening at the dinner table. Curiosity about the move bubbled up inside me, but one glance at the tension on my parents' faces warned me to be patient. Daddy waited until Anna, our maid, had served the dessert before he broached the subject. "This will come as no surprise to either of you, since you eavesdropped on your mother and me this morning." He peered meaningfully over his gold-rimmed glasses at Rusty, then at me. "We're moving to New York for a time—I don't know how long. The company's private railway car, the *Empress*, will be here for us the first of May."

"What about my graduation exercises?" I shrieked. "I can't miss my high-school graduation."

As I spoke, Mama's fork clattered against her Wedgwood china plate. "You didn't tell me we were leaving so soon, Cyrus."

His face reddened. He cleared his throat and continued. "For reasons I am not at liberty to mention, it can't be helped."

Rusty's eyes widened. "Does this mean we're going to war?"

"Eat your cobbler, son." Daddy glared at my brother.

Tears welled up in my eyes. "But my graduation. I'll have to miss my graduation."

Mama patted my hand and glanced toward Daddy. "Perhaps we should consider the possibility of your going on ahead of us. The children and I could come through a month later, after school is out."

New hope surged through me. I glanced eagerly at my father. He only shook his head. "That won't be possible, I'm afraid. The *Empress* won't be available again for some time."

"And why not, may I ask?" Mama insisted. "I suppose the company board members' lovely wives need to take a jaunt out into the countryside during the merry month of May."

"Chloe, your sarcasm doesn't become you." Daddy shoved his apple cobbler around on his plate with his fork.

"I'm sorry. You're right. But, please, help me understand the reason."

He cleared his throat and eyed her the length of the table. "I'm sorry, dear, but I'm not at liberty to tell you the reason right now."

Mama's mouth tightened into a grim line. I choked back a flood of tears. *It's hopeless. My life is ruined.*

My father reached over and patted my hand. "I'm sorry, CeeCee. It can't be helped." Taking a deep breath, he continued, "We'll stay in the cottage on Cape Cod until I can buy a suitable town house in Manhattan."

Mama's eyes filled with disbelief. "But, Cy, commuting from the Cape will be impossible."

"I know." Daddy nodded. "I'll rent a furnished flat in the city and commute to the Cape on weekends."

Rusty's face fell. "I thought we'd live in New Jersey."

"Your mother and I considered it." Daddy pursed his lips and tapped his fork gently on the edge of his plate. "But after discussing it with the home office, it seems that Manhattan will be a wiser move under the circumstances."

"And that settles it, I suppose?" Mama flung her napkin down on the table and pushed back her chair from the table. "If you will excuse me, please. I suddenly have indigestion." She stood up, her chin protruding defiantly. "Unless, of course, I need to check with the main office for permission."

Daddy reached toward Mama's departing figure. "Now, Chloe, don't go getting your Irish up."

Knowing how much Mama hated to have him refer to her roots, I snickered. He glared at me. "Finish your meal!"

I blinked back a new flood of tears. Daddy never shouted at me. He might scold, instruct, or warn, but he never, ever shouted. My lower lip quivered. "I'm not too hungry, either. May I please be excused?"

He hesitated, eyeing me like a general stripped of his command. Finally, he growled, "Why not? Go ahead!"

I pushed back my chair and fled the room, straight into Au Sam's arms. My former governess and trusted confidante grabbed my arm. "Missee?" She peered up into my face. She knew. I could tell she already knew. But in her face, I saw not a trace of worry.

"Come, Missee. Come to my room for ginger cookies and hot chocolate." Wrapping her arm about my waist, she led me down the hall to her room in the servants' wing.

Au Sam's room reflected the mystery of her culture, with the pungent aroma of jasmine incense permeating the air. I sat on the edge of her six-inch-high bed and marveled that the old woman would willingly choose to sleep on that unyielding surface.

When Au Sam first came to live with us, she had tried to sleep on what she called a Western bed. After two nights, she informed Mama that if she were to stay on, she'd need a decent bed. Daddy offered to go out and buy one immediately, but Au Sam refused.

"Let me borrow Buckley for the day, and if I could use that cotton batting stored in the attic—"

"Use whatever you like, Au Sam," Mama insisted. "We want you to be happy with us." That same day I remember watching Buckley construct the platform and four-legged structure that supported the mattress that Au Sam had hand-stitched herself.

Seems like she's been with us forever, I thought as I traced a finger around the large gold cabbage rose in the coverlet pattern.

Mama and Au Sam had met at Golden Gate Park following the earthquake of 1906. They became close friends while caring for the homeless Chinese people. After the quake, the city had established medical and food stations for the white victims but refused aid to Asians.

Mama appreciated the woman's indomitable spirit—spunk, Mama calls it. As the favored daughter of a warlord, Au Sam had been educated beyond her station as a woman. She could read, speak, and write four languages, including French and English. I think Mama liked the way Au Sam refused to kowtow, as she called it, to others, but carried herself with dignity and grace.

Having been kidnapped from her home when fourteen years old by a rival warlord, then sold to slave traders in Shanghai, Au Sam arrived in America, alone and penniless. A wealthy matron took pity on the girl and bought her to keep her from being purchased by the owner of one of the houses of prostitution on the wharf.

Au Sam had done the woman's laundry for thirty years. And as with so many others, the earthquake turned her world upside down. The home in which she worked burned to the ground in the fires that followed the quake. Au Sam never again found the woman for whom she had worked. Neighbors said the family had moved east immediately after the tragedy.

Au Sam volunteered to help Mama set up the new women's clinic in exchange for food and a place to stay. "Only until Cyrus and I return from our honeymoon," Mama told her. "I've watched how well you care for CeeCee. I'd really appreciate it if you'd consider being her nanny."

I couldn't imagine my life without Au Sam. Suddenly, a frightening thought struck me. *Will Au Sam move east with us? Or will she want to stay in San Francisco?* Tears welled up in my eyes. I wanted desperately to know but was terrified to ask. *I won't say goodbye to Au Sam, not for all the gossamer gowns east of the Mississippi River.*

Shilly-shally

Back and forth, back and forth, back and forth. I stared at the gold bob dangling from the gold chain our physics instructor swung back and forth in front of the class.

"Galileo sat in church one Sunday. Bored with the morning's sermon, the great scientist's gaze wandered about the cathedral, finally settling on one of the massive chandeliers—" The drone of Miss Sylvester's voice kept my mind focused on the pendulum in her hand.

"A breeze from an open window near the ceiling had set the chandelier in motion. Back and forth, back and forth, the chandelier swung. As the sermon dragged on, Galileo observed that the time it took for the chandelier to swing back and forth remained constant. His scientific curiosity was piqued. To check his theory, he timed the swings of the chandelier against his own heartbeat."

The round little teacher with the smiling eyes quizzed, "Ladies, what can you tell me about the discovery Galileo made that day? Miss Mumford?"

"That God has a purpose for boring preachers?" Bridget, the class clown, whispered. A ripple of laughter skittered across the room.

In spite of her outdated Gibson-girl fashions, Miss Sylvester exhibited a sharp mind and even sharper wit. While the teacher clicked her tongue and gave a disapproving shake of her head, we knew she appreciated Bridget's humor. "Miss MacAlder, we will have no sacrilege in my classroom."

"Yes, ma'am." Bridget bowed her head respectfully while the

girls around her hid their faces behind their textbooks.

"Now, Miss Mumford, what, beyond the usefulness of boring priests, did Galileo discover that Sunday morning?"

Ellie Mumford, the senior class's resident genius, unconsciously adjusted her glasses. "The pendulum theory?"

"Thank you, Miss Mumford. The great scientist went on to discover that it was the length of the tether and not the weight of the bob that determines the length of time it takes for the pendulum to swing back and forth. Examine your grandfather clocks at home, and you will see—"

Back and forth, back and forth. Morning to night, night to morning. My emotions had been like a pendulum ever since Daddy had made his grand announcement three weeks earlier. One moment I eagerly dreamed about the move to New York, and the next, I pushed the thought away, hoping that by ignoring it, the move could be prevented.

At home, no one talked about the impending move. Yet I could feel a tension in the house the moment I walked through the front door. I noticed that my father worked later than usual at the office and that Mama's eyes were often bloodshot from crying. Even Rusty moved through the house in silence. The routine of school and violin lessons and rehearsals with the philharmonic allowed me to suppress most of my anxieties—at least, until a morning at the end of February.

In the middle of Latin class, a knock sounded on the classroom door. The entire class looked at one another, then at the teacher. No one ever interrupted one of Miss Beedley's Latin lessons. An irritated frown crossed the diminutive woman's brow. Keeping time with her wooden pointer, she strode toward the door. "Keep reciting, ladies. *Amo, ames, amat.*" She opened the door. "Repeat, please. *Amo, ames*—oh, Miss Holling. May I help you?"

The headmistress towered over the Latin teacher. Without a word, she looked down her long nose at Miss Beedley, then scanned the faces of cringing girls until her gaze settled on me. "Miss Chamberlain, I need to see you in my office immediately."

At the mention of my name, I felt lightheaded. Tiny pinpoints of light danced before my eyes. *What? What have I done wrong?*

I arose from my seat, accompanied by a flutter of relieved

giggles from my classmates, the loudest laughter coming from my nemesis, Belinda Abbey.

The headmistress focused steel gray eyes on the source of the laughter. "That is quite enough, Miss Abbey, unless you desire to spend an hour of detention in my office this afternoon."

Belinda looked down at her desk and mumbled, "Yes, Miss Holling."

Instantly, the woman strode over to Belinda and rapped on the desk with her knuckles. Due to my own dubious plight, I struggled to suppress my glee. The wiry pouf of gray-brown curls perched on the headmistress's forehead bobbed in syncopation with the loosely pinned bun at the back of her neck. Miss Sylvester's physics lesson flashed across my mind.

"P-p-pft!" I chuckled.

Miss Holling and the entire class looked at me in surprise. Horrified, I managed to convert my laughter into a resounding cough. Clearing my throat, I apologized for the interruption. "Must have a case of the sniffles coming on." Out of the corner of my eye, I saw my best friend, Susanne, bury her head behind her Latin text.

A moment of uncertainty crossed Miss Holling's face. She paused, then returned her attention to the perspiring girl seated before her. "Look at me when you speak to me, young lady."

Belinda's head popped up, her eyes round and serious. Satisfied she'd intimidated the girl, Miss Holling continued. "Now, was that, yes, I desire an hour's detention, or, yes, I will stop laughing?"

"Yes, I will stop laughing, ma'am."

Miss Holling nodded her head emphatically. "Good! Now, Miss Chamberlain, to my office. And bring your books with you."

"Yes, Miss Holling." Straightening my back, I glared at Belinda. She ducked her head and grinned at Rebecca Sawyer, her deskmate.

When Miss Holling turned her back to leave, both girls made faces at me. As I followed Miss Holling into the hallway, I passed their desk and stuck out my tongue at them. Before they could respond, I stepped into the hall, and the door slammed closed behind me.

Miss Holling marched ahead of me toward her office. The determined click of her cubed heels and the softer tentative tap from my own black high-top shoes echoed down the tiled hallway.

Think, CeeCee, think! What did you do? Nothing came to my mind. Yet, I knew that it had to be something. Miss Holling never called a girl to her office except to administer discipline for an infraction of one of the school's "Old Hundred." That's what the students called the extensive list of rules at the Young Ladies' Academy of Arts and Sciences.

I hope she doesn't ask me about Margaret and Cora sneaking off to meet Cora's boyfriend when his ship docked last Thursday. I had nothing to do with that, unfortunately. I was on my way to a philharmonic rehearsal. I'd rather die than tattle on my friends. Well, maybe not die, exactly—

Miss Holling entered her office. "Come in, Miss Chamberlain. You don't have time to dawdle." The woman motioned toward the door. "Close the door, and have a seat."

As I turned to find a place to sit, I spied Au Sam sitting on the bench behind the door. My chest tightened, and my hands began to shake. *Something's wrong, terribly, terribly wrong.* In all the years I'd attended the girls' school, Au Sam had never visited the school, not even when I played the angel Gabriel in the seventh-grade Christmas pageant. "Au Sam, what are you doing here?"

The nanny looked down at her hands folded in her lap. From across the room, the headmistress called to me. "Miss Chamberlain, if I may have your attention, please."

I searched for answers in Au Sam's dark, inscrutable eyes. "What happened? What is wrong? Has someone been hurt?" *It has finally happened. Mama has been hurt at the clinic.* "Au Sam, is Mama all right?"

Miss Holling continued, "Miss Chamberlain, please! If you would listen—"

I eyed Au Sam's unchanging expression a second longer, then turned to face the headmistress.

"Thank you. That is much better. Your father sent this servant here with a message that you should collect any books and belongings that are yours and hurry home. Your driver is waiting outside, I believe."

My driver? I shot a glance at Au Sam, then back at Miss Holling. The headmistress adjusted a glass paperweight on her desk. "I understand you will not be coming back to the academy—even for graduation."

My mouth fell open. I glanced at Au Sam again. She looked away.

"Miss Chamberlain? Please! Do you know what this is all about?"

I shook my head. "I-I-I-uh-uh-uh-n-n-n-no."

The woman sighed. "Well, it's neither here nor there. But I do hope the academy did nothing to precipitate this action." She looked to me for verification.

I swallowed hard. "Oh no. My parents have been very satisfied with the school."

"I am certainly relieved to hear that. The Young Ladies' Academy of Arts and Sciences has maintained an excellent reputation over the years." The headmistress gave a self-satisfied little smile.

Not coming back? Tears filled my eyes. "Excuse me, Miss Holling, but before I leave, may I say goodbye to my friends and to Miss Duprey?"

I adored my French teacher, a cosmopolitan woman who'd lived in a garret on the Left Bank of the Seine. Miss Duprey wore the latest styles from Europe and plucked her eyebrows. I had no idea why she had left Paris or what brought her to San Francisco, but I longed to be like her one day, surrounded by a world of fine art, literature, and music, and a few doting beaus to squire me about the city.

By the look on Miss Holling's face, I knew her answer before I finished asking my question. I dropped my gaze to the faded red-and-blue Oriental carpet beneath my feet.

Miss Holling tightened her lips and shook her head. "We can't have you disrupting classes, now, can we? Also, Miss Chamberlain, your father said you must hurry right home."

The woman cleared her throat. "You have been a good student, Miss Chamberlain. I hate to see you go. While you were never the most brilliant student, your musical talents brought life to many student productions." Miss Holling leaned forward, her face filled with concern. "May I give you one piece of advice before you leave our hallowed halls?"

"Yes, Miss Holling."

"While here at the academy, you have demonstrated a propensity to follow your often unwise friends. Choose your friends more wisely, child, and you will go far." She straightened. "You are a talented young lady. You will marry well. Any man worth his salt will treasure such a wife."

"Yes, ma'am." I shuffled my feet, not knowing what she expected me to say next.

The headmistress walked around the desk and planted a vague dry kiss on my cheek. "You may be excused. Go with God, child."

"Thank you." Startled at the sudden display of affection, I ducked my head, then hurried from her office to collect my belongings. Au Sam struggled to keep up with me.

A propensity to follow unwise friends! Huh! A good wife! Huh! and treating Au Sam as an inferior creature. I sputtered all the way down the hall to the front door, bursting through the double oak doors onto the porch. Upon seeing me, Buckley hopped from my father's Pierce Arrow and opened the rear door. I stomped down the steps to the sidewalk. "Imagine the nerve of that woman calling you a servant!"

Au Sam hurried after me. "But I am a servant, Missee."

"Don't be ridiculous! You're not a servant. Annie and Marie and Lee Kwon, the gardener, and maybe even Marta, the cook—they're servants."

I slid onto the back seat, followed by Au Sam. "If I am not a servant, Missee, what am I?"

Buckley closed my door and climbed into the driver's seat. I searched my brain for the right word to describe the woman's position in our household. "You—you're family! Yes, that's it. You're family!"

Au Sam smiled sadly and patted my hand. "You're a sweet child, Missee—a sweet child."

Buckley revved the motor and threw the car into gear. The noise from the engine and the bouncing and lurching of the vehicle over San Francisco's cobblestone streets ended further discussion.

My concern over the family emergency that had snatched me from the classroom returned. I tried to sit back against the black leather seat, but I couldn't. Gray, dismal thoughts pummeled my mind. Clutching my book bag close, I pressed my forehead against the car window and stared out at my gray-on-gray world—the overcast sky, the four- and five-story office buildings, the businessmen in overcoats, hunched against the wind.

When the car pulled up in front of the house, I leapt from the car before Buckley even had time to shut off the motor. Throwing open the front door, I called, "Mama? Mama? What's happening? What's wrong?"

Stacked against one wall were Mama's favorite gilt-edged mirror and her set of San Francisco oil paintings she had bought and had framed. Marble tabletops stood bare, swept clean of the friendly clutter of porcelain knickknacks. The click of my heels on the marble entryway reverberated off the bare walls. I peered into the parlor and discovered similar disarray. "Mama? Mama?" No reply met my query. I ran up the stairs, two at a time, then peered into each bedroom. The entire house looked like spring cleaning had hit two months early. When I reached the door to my room, I paused with my hand on the knob, afraid of what I might find on the other side. Holding my breath, I opened the door and froze. Slowly, I scanned the room. My nightdress lay flung across the foot of my unmade bed. My quilt, dragging on the carpet, half hid my bedroom slippers. A tangle of hair ribbons protruded out of the top drawer of my dressing table. Relieved, I exhaled slowly. Except for the large steamer trunk sitting beside the chifforobe, the room looked exactly as I'd left it.

Mama, where's Mama? I've gotta find Mama! Whirling about, I slammed directly into my mother's chest. She'd been crying. "Mama! What is wrong? Did someone die? Miss Holling called me out of Latin class. She told me to bring all my belongings with me—"

Mama grasped both of my arms, then turned her face away for a moment. "Slow down, darling. I'll try to explain as best I can." Taking a deep breath, she led me back into my room. "Daddy called home from the office an hour ago with the news that he had received a telegram from the home office. They want your father back east as soon as possible. Fortunately, the *Empress* is being refurbished in Oakland, or we'd have to travel in a public Pullman."

A public Pullman? I shuddered at the thought. The public Pullmans, or sleepers, stacked travelers on shelves like everyday china. Velvet draperies separated one stranger from the next. On the unexpected trip east to Grandma Spencer's funeral, I had slept across from an old man who chewed tobacco and periodically spit on the floor. *Never again! I would travel in the comfort of the company Pullman or not at all!*

The *Empress*, the company railway car, came equipped with all the luxuries of a miniature mansion. In addition to the private sleeping rooms, a complete kitchen staff served all meals in the plush dining area. But my favorite luxury was the lounge, with its well-stocked library of current books and the observation deck. Daddy said that the only more comfortable way to travel would be on a luxury ocean liner, at least before war broke out in Europe. *Not that I'm likely to find out for myself anytime in the near future*—I thought—*not with the Kaiser's submarines sinking passenger ships!*

My mother's voice reciting the list of tasks to be completed before our departure drew me back to the problem at hand.

"So why? Why do we have to move so soon? I thought we weren't leaving until the beginning of May."

"CeeCee, you haven't heard a word I've said, have you?" Mama rubbed her forehead. "I really don't know the reason. But your father says tomorrow we must be on the afternoon eastbound out of Oakland."

"But, Mama, you promised that I could have a big farewell party and—"

"I'm sorry. This isn't my idea, I assure you." I could tell by the grim set of her mouth that she understood my frustration. "Please, I need your help, CeeCee. I need to tie up a few loose ends at the clinic today. After dropping me off, Buckley will fetch Rusty at school." Mama fidgeted with a pearl button on her sleeve. "Have Rusty sort through the toys he may want to discard, and you do the same with your things. Just pack what you'll need for the next few months. The staff will crate and ship everything else."

She turned to leave. "I'll be home around six. If I'm not back before Daddy gets home, tell him I contacted the family about the change of plans. They'll be here by eight for a farewell dinner."

The whole family? My stuffy Uncle Philip? My dumb cousins? Marvelous! My lower lip protruded defiantly. "Fine. Everything's just fine."

Mama's green eyes seemed to darken, and she swallowed hard. "Please, CeeCee, I really need your cooperation on this."

I shrugged and turned away. Seconds later, Mama's footsteps faded down the flight of stairs to the first floor. From the top of the stairs, I heard Marta stop her in the entryway to discuss the dinner menu while Mama put on her cape, hat, and gloves. "I'll be back as soon as possible, Marta. Please have Au Sam check on the children every now and then to be sure they're doing as they've been told."

"Yes, ma'am. Do you have any preference regarding tonight's dessert? I hardly have time to—"

"Don't worry about dessert. I'll have Buckley purchase two dozen almond pastries from the Swedish bakery on Fifth and California. I should see you around six, I hope."

"Yes, ma'am. Goodbye."

The front door closed. I ran to my bay window and watched Buckley help Mama into the Pierce Arrow. As he closed the door and climbed into the front seat, Mama waved and blew me a kiss. *How did she know I was watching from behind the lace curtains?* I returned the gesture.

I gazed at the automobile until it disappeared from view; then I slid down onto the floor in a defiant huddle. I knew I was acting like a five-year-old instead of a young lady of almost seventeen, but I didn't care. After chewing off my very best nail, I tried to smooth the rough edges on the upholstered rocker cushion beside me.

My diary fell off the chair onto the floor. I picked up the book and hugged it to me, tears of self-pity tumbling down my cheeks. My life was crumbling about me, and I could do nothing to stop it.

I don't know how long I cried. But the more I cried, the more frustrated I felt. I wanted to kick and scream and throw things against the walls. Somehow, knowing that only the servants would hear my kicking and screaming and that I had only my own personal possessions to throw and possibly damage, I resisted the urge. Instead, I grabbed my diary and scribbled furiously.

Dear Emily, Do parents realize how much they destroy their children's lives—or don't they really care? I know; I know. I was eager to move east this summer, but not now, not before I've said goodbye to my friends. I may never, ever see them again. New York City isn't around the next corner, you know.

And why the hurry? Well, one good thing, we won't have time to stop at all the little hole-in-the-wall towns where Mama used to live. I paused and remembered Aunt Gladys and Uncle Phineas. *I hope we have time to see the Putmans on our way through Denver.*

They aren't real family, but they are best friends with my parents. Whenever we visit them, Aunt Gladys spoils Rusty and me. On our last visit, she insisted on buying me three complete outfits. She dressed me from head to toe, much to Mama's chagrin. Chloe Celeste, you should be ashamed of yourself—looking for what you can get out of people. I squirmed uncomfortably. *That's not totally true, I really do like Aunt Gladys. And Uncle Phineas is so funny when he does those after-dinner shadow tricks on the dining-room wall.*

I laughed to myself, remembering the pompous-appearing retired banker, former chairman of the board, flapping his hands and squawking like a duck to make my little brother laugh. *It's still cold in Denver, so we'll be able to go ice-skating on the pond! Maybe moving earlier than we planned won't be so terrible after all.*

The front door opened and slammed shut. I heard my brother throw his school books on the hall table and stomp up the stairs. "CeeCee," he shouted as he reached my open bedroom door, "Buckley said that Mama said you're supposed to help me pack."

"You don't have to shout. I can hear you very well. And Mama didn't say I was to help you pack." I stopped my ears with my fingers. "She said I was to make sure you keep busy and don't dawdle. There's a difference, you know."

"Well, I don't want to go! I don't. I don't. I don't! Maybe if I don't pack, I won't have to go." He plopped down on the floor beside me.

I leaned my head back and massaged the back of my neck. "Don't be a dolt! If you don't pack, Marie and Anna will throw away all your precious junk! That's what will happen if you don't pack, smarty pants."

"My pants don't smart!" He wrinkled his nose. "Why are we leaving so soon?"

When I didn't answer immediately, he pulled himself up and peered out my window. "I guess it's not all bad. I didn't have to go to choir today and sing silly songs about the 'pretty little birdies' and 'daffa-down dillies.' And, ya know what else? I got out of doing an arithmetic assignment too—long division."

He hated long division. I grinned. "And I didn't have to take my Latin quiz either. Maybe this moving thing isn't all bad, huh?"

His face darkened into a pout. "I guess. Do you think Mrs. Parker will send my church-attendance pin to our new home?"

Mrs. Parker taught the children's lesson at church each week. For two years, Rusty had had a perfect attendance and a passel of Bible pins to prove it. Mama, Rusty, and I rode the ferryboat across the bay to attend church with my Uncle Joe and his family each week. After the meeting, we usually went home with Uncle Joe and Aunt Beth for dinner. Daddy attended with us whenever he was in town. But lately, he'd been gone a lot—something to do with the President's Energy Commission and the war in Europe.

I ruffled Rusty's strawberry blond hair. "Maybe you could write to her once we get settled back east."

My brother shoved my hand away. "Stop it. I'm not a baby!"

I laughed and ruffled his hair a second time. "You'll always be my baby brother."

Rusty lifted his arm to swat my hand away, then stopped. His eyes widened in horror. "What about Sundance? I won't be able to say goodbye to Sundance."

Named after a bank robber Rusty had read about in the newspapers, Rusty's palomino mare lived on Uncle Joe's ranch. My brother rode her on weekends and holidays. When Daddy had first mentioned the move to New York City and Rusty learned that a horse couldn't live in a brownstone town house, my brother cried. To make him feel better, Daddy had promised he could get a puppy.

The promise pacified the boy. But that was before the events of this morning, when the move was still months away. I looked at my brother and shook my head. *You are so gullible. We may never return to California to live.*

Rusty jumped to his feet. "Guess I better get packin', huh? Buckley said that Mama would pack my clothes. All I gotta worry about are my books and stuff. Shouldn't take me too long, I guess."

I groaned. *Too long? Only a month of Sundays, if you're lucky!* We called Rusty the pack rat—and for good reason. The weirdest, most disgusting things could be found in my brother's room—sticks, rocks, broken toys, shells with decaying creatures inside, the dead cocoons of moths and butterflies, half-eaten candy apples. Once when a putrid odor wafted into the hallway, Buckley uncovered a dead squirrel. The boy had planned to stuff it with cotton batting and mount it as a present for Daddy's birthday, but he had forgotten where he'd left it.

Whenever Rusty's chifforobe overflowed with his "treasures" and Mama threatened to get rid of the stuff, he would box it all and lug the stuff to the attic. I cast my eyes toward the ceiling. *Hm, I wonder who's gonna clean up that mess? Just so it isn't me.*

"Guess you'd better get busy. It may take you longer than you think. Mama told Marta that she's ordering some of those almond pastries you like."

Rusty's freckled face broke into a grin. With a sudden move, he slapped my wrist. "Gotcha last!" I swatted at the air.

"You missed." He laughed and ran from my room.

"You scamp!" I leapt to my feet and made a halfhearted attempt to chase him but stopped at my bedroom door. *I guess he's not so bad—for a kid brother, that is.* I walked over to the steamer trunk and opened it. *Where do I start?*

The day passed quickly. Sorting through my books alone took the rest of the morning. Later, as I closed the bottom drawer on my bureau, I heard Daddy's voice in the entryway. *He's never home this early.*

I glanced outside my window just in time to see the street lights blink on in front of the house. The clock in the hallway gonged five times. About me, my life and my room appeared to be in absolute confusion. Clothes covered every surface—clothes I wanted to take with me on the train, clothes to be shipped, and piles of clothes that no longer fit or that I hadn't liked in the first place, ready to give away to the church's mission relief or to the women at Mama's clinic. Many of her patients wore my size. Daddy ascended the stairs. "Chloe? CeeCee? Au Sam? Anybody home?"

Marta called out from the kitchen. "Mr. Chamberlain, is that you?"

Who do you think it is? Some wastrel off the street? Why do people ask stupid questions? I clicked my tongue and dropped a pair of shoes I no longer wore onto the giveaway pile. *They never fit right anyway.*

"I'm here, Daddy, in my room." I straightened and turned toward the shadow filling the doorway. Meeker, who'd been napping on the giveaway clothes pile, shot between Daddy's legs and out of the room.

"It's certainly dark enough in here. Let's put some light on the subject." Daddy stepped into my chaos, switched on my dressing-table lamp, and chuckled. "Now I see why you wanted it dark. What a mess! Come here and give your ol' dad a hug."

Linking my hands behind my back, I sashayed over to him and tipped my head to one side. "I don't know if I should, considering that this mess is your fault."

He laughed. "I apologize, Freckles, but it's not really my fault. Blame it on Mr. Rockefeller. Now do I get a hug?"

I threw myself in his extended arms. "Oh, Daddy, I'm so glad you're home. I was so afraid when Au Sam came to the school for me this morning that something terrible had happened to you or Mama. What did happen, Daddy?" All the questions I'd wanted to ask for so long tumbled out. "Why are we having to leave California so quickly? Will I get to graduate, or will I have to repeat my senior year? Will we live in the city? What school will I attend? Do you really think I'm good enough to get accepted at a school of music? Will we be able to spend a few days with Aunt Gladys in Denver? Do you think Mama will ever let me have a boyfriend? Cousin Ashley has one, you know—"

"Hey, one question at a time, CeeCee, my dear—one question at a time. Let's start with your last one and work backward. Mama and I decided to let you begin dating when you find your first gray hair or on your thirty-sixth birthday, whichever comes sooner." He slipped an arm about my shoulder, and together we walked toward Rusty's room. "Speaking of Mama, did she say when she'd be home?"

"She said she'd be here around six." Daddy had not answered even one of my questions, but at the moment, I didn't care.

"And the outlaws? Did she get through to them?"

I giggled. "Mama said they'd all be here by eight."

Daddy pulled his silver-plated watch from his vest pocket and flipped open the lid. "Eight?" He returned the watch to his pocket and rubbed his stomach. "I'm starving! Do you think Marta will let me have a crust of bread before then?"

"Oh, Daddy, you know Marta will do anything for you. She adores you."

He put a finger to his lips and glanced about furtively. "Sh, don't tell your mother."

I giggled. "You're such a tease, Daddy. Marta's as old as Grandma McCall. What about my other questions?"

"Let's go find your brother. I don't want to have to repeat myself any more than necessary." Daddy opened Rusty's bedroom door and flipped the light switch on the wall.

If I thought my room was bad— I gazed about the room, searching for my brother. "He was here, honest. I saw him."

Daddy peered around the end of the bed, then under it. "Rusty? Son, where are you?"

"Probably he was smothered when one of these mountains of garbage erupted on him."

My father eyed me over the top of his gold-rimmed glasses. "CeeCee, be kind. One man's trash is another's treasure."

"Daddy—" I swept my arm in a dramatic arc. "—this stuff is trash in any man's language!"

"Where could he have gone?" Daddy frowned and searched the area one more time.

I shrugged. "He might be in the attic. He's got a lot of stuff up there too, you know." I giggled. "Probably a few dead squirrels or an expired skunk or decaying possum."

He gave me a wry grin and left the room. I followed him up the narrow flight of stairs at the end of the hallway. One bare light bulb, draped with swirls of cobwebs, hung from the ceiling. "Rusty? Rusty," Daddy called.

My head cleared the landing, when suddenly I spotted what appeared to be my little brother in the corner by the storage chifforobe. "Over there. He's over there." I pointed toward the corner.

My father picked his way past the boxes to my brother. He looked down at my brother, then at me. "Sh, he's asleep. Poor little guy." Daddy bent down and brushed Rusty's disheveled curls off his forehead. "Son? Son, it's Daddy. Wake up, son."

My brother moaned and opened his eyes a crack. Then his eyes flew wide open. "Huh? Daddy? What are you doing here? Where's here? Where am I?"

Daddy laughed and helped my brother to his feet. "How long have you been sleeping, Rusty?"

"I dunno." Rusty rubbed the sleep from his eyes. "Ya know what?"

"What, son?"

My brother grimaced. "I hate moving!"

"Amen!" Simultaneously, my father and I responded, looked at one another, and laughed. The clock downstairs on the second floor gonged once on the half-hour. "Let's stop packing for the night, get cleaned up, and dress for dinner. Mama should be home from the clinic soon."

"I get the bathroom first." I whipped about and rushed for the stairs. At the base of the stairs, I paused and looked up at my dad coming down the stairs behind me. "You know, you never did answer my questions."

He chuckled. "No, I didn't, did I? I guess they'll have to wait until later. You'd better hurry if you expect to clean up first."

I grunted my displeasure and hurried toward the lavatory. Fifteen minutes later, smelling of lemon verbena, I opened the bathroom door.

Rusty ran past me and closed the door behind me. I heard him shout, "Eeuuww! What stinks in here? Do you have to use so much bubble bath?"

Downstairs, Buckley opened the front door, and I heard Mama's voice. "Hello? Anybody home?"

I peered over the railing enough to see my father greet Mama with his arms outstretched. "We're all here, waiting for you. How'd it go at the clinic?"

I tiptoed to my room and closed the door behind me. Leaning against the door, I smiled, shut my eyes to the room's disorder, and sighed contentedly. *Mama's home safely, the family's together again, and—for this evening, at least— all is well.*

Light Conversation

Uncle Joe Spencer, a six-foot two-inch mountain of muscle with brown hair and matching bushy mustache, leaned back from the table and sighed. "Remind me to tell Marta how much I enjoy her scalloped potatoes." He winked across the table at Aunt Beth. "I'm tempted to take her home to cook for us."

"And risk losing our Maria? I think not." Aunt Beth, as tiny as Uncle Joe is big, clicked her tongue. "It's the heavy cream in the sauce that you like. Imagine if you ate rich German cooking every day. You'd rip out your britches faster than I could let out the seams!"

Uncle Joe glanced at me and grinned. "Now, tell me, CeeCee dear, am I getting too big for my bitches?"

"I, uh, uh, I—" A sudden rush of heat scaled my neck, suffusing my face and ears with color. *The curse of the redhead!* I dabbed at my lips with my napkin to avoid making eye contact with my favorite uncle. He loved making me blush. It was only since my sixteenth birthday that I'd been allowed to sit at the adult table whenever we had dinner guests. Rusty and my cousins still ate at the children's table in the breakfast nook.

"She's speechless." He eyed Mama seated at the far end of the table. "But, then, I always did have that effect on the ladies, didn't I, little sister?"

Mama arched one eyebrow at him. Dimples appeared at the corners of her mouth. "The four-legged ones, at least."

Uncle Joe placed his hand over his heart. "Are you telling my impressionable niece here that I was once a hick from the sticks?"

At the opposite end of the table, Daddy snorted. "You still are."

"And I have the saddle sores to prove it." Joe chuckled.

Everyone seated around the dining table laughed, everyone except Uncle Phillip. Uncle Phillip, a high-priced San Francisco attorney, seldom laughed.

Seated on Mama's right, Daddy's brother, Uncle Phillip, shot a look of disdain across the table at his wife, Jenny. Aunt Jenny reddened and toyed with the buttered peas on her plate.

"Seriously," Mama broke the sudden silence, "Marta will be looking for a new position at the end of next month. If you hear of anyone needing a good cook—"

Uncle Phillip tapped his fork against the base of his water goblet. "I imagine that it will be difficult for her to find a position at this time, being German and all."

"That's ridiculous!" My mother glared at him.

His tone was condescending. "You'd be surprised at the strong anti-German sentiment I hear every day. Pardon me for saying so, big brother, but it's fortunate that she won't be working for you any longer, what with your connections to the President's Energy Commission. Could be considered subversive, considering the times in which we live."

"Phillip, you might have a point," my father admitted.

Mama's eyes flashed with indignation. "Cyrus Chamberlain! Marta is not an agent for the Kaiser—or for anyone else. Her loyalty is impeccable. The woman's as subversive as your German shepherd, Phillip!"

A series of polite chuckles circled the table. Uncle Phillip looked at Mama with disdain. Before Mama could continue, Daddy said, "I'd say the woman is quite dangerous. In fact, Chloe dear, you yourself have admitted that Marta's German chocolate cake is horribly decadent and subversive to your diet. Speaking of which, what's for dessert? Not German chocolate cake, I hope."

This time everyone laughed, even Uncle Phillip.

"Tsk! Cyrus, you are such a tease," Mama said.

Uncle Phillip toyed with his water goblet. "He never could be serious, Chloe. You knew that before you married him."

My mother turned toward Daddy. "Maybe that's what attracted me to him, his ability to see the lighter side of life."

When Mama caught my amazed stare, I blushed. She laughed and winked at Daddy.

Uncle Joe grew solemn. "Cyrus, you've never told us what prompted this, uh, pushing up your moving date by two months." He'd asked the question on everyone's mind. We all looked toward my father for an answer.

He removed his watch from his vest pocket and opened the lid, then closed it and returned it to his pocket. "If you all promise not to put in a call to the *New York Times* or the *San Francisco Examiner*, I believe it is safe to tell you what prompted the change of plan."

We laughed nervously and looked at one another.

My father lifted one hand. "I'm serious about keeping this in the family until tomorrow. Phillip? Joe?"

Uncle Joe laughed aloud. "Who am I going to tell? My stable hands or Molly, my riding horse?"

While the rest of us chuckled, Daddy's face remained unchanged. "Phillip?"

My uncle heaved a deep sigh. "Cyrus, really! Why the melodrama?"

"I need your word on this, Phillip."

My uncle clicked his tongue. "You have my word."

"As you know, President Wilson has organized a National Energy Commission should the United States be drawn into the war, and Jenkins, the chairman of the board, was chosen to serve on it. And, as you also know, the board asked me to run the head office during his absence."

"This is hardly news, big brother," Uncle Phillip sneered.

Daddy glanced at his brother, then across the length of the table to where Mama sat. "Tomorrow morning, President Wilson will be making public a telegram that will, in all likelihood, force the United States into the war." He paused to allow us to feel the impact of his words.

Mama, her hands gripping the arms of her dining chair, leaned forward. "He'll have the devil to pay, convincing the majority of Americans to fight someone else's war!"

My father responded, "I predict once America hears the contents of this telegram, the mood will change overnight."

Uncle Joe pounded his fist on the table, causing me and the sugar bowl to jump in response. "Whatever is in this mysterious telegram?"

Daddy ran his hand over his neatly trimmed beard. "It seems the British Admiralty intelligence intercepted a telegram being sent from Germany's foreign Minister, Arthur Zimmermann, to the German ambassador in Mexico. I don't have a copy to read to you verbatim, but I can summarize it for you.

"Apparently the German foreign minister instructed his ambassador to propose that, if the United States entered the war against Germany, Mexico should ally itself with Germany, which would help it regain its lost territories of Texas, New Mexico, and Arizona."

A stunned silence filled the room. Even Uncle Phillip had no biting quip.

"Now you can see why I'm being called back early and why I've been so secretive about the reasons."

"War!" My mother clutched her throat. "Jamie!"

Aunt Beth shook her head sadly. "Why? Why do a bunch of old men want to go to war, anyway?"

Uncle Joe spoke while staring into space. "Greed, pride, power. It always comes down to the same thing—young men spill their blood to line the pockets of greedy industrial magnates."

"Isn't that a trifle jaded, my dear man? I thought I was the cynic of the bunch," Phillip chortled.

"Well, whatever the reason," Daddy continued, "when the Kaiser comes hammering at our southern borders, we will be forced to stand and fight. And by the looks of it, my battleground will be in a Standard Oil boardroom."

"In the meantime, you, Chloe, must have been totally flabbergasted with the sudden changes. I admire you for hosting this dinner tonight on top of all your other responsibilities. We appreciate it." Aunt Beth glanced toward Uncle Joe, then toward Mama. "What are you doing about your servants on such short notice?"

Mama rang the bell beside her plate. "Most of the staff have family close by and don't want to leave California. We've invited Au Sam and Buckley to go with us." While she spoke, Anna appeared from the kitchen and cleared away the dinner plates and serving dishes.

Mama stomped her feet when Meeker sneaked though the open door into the dining room. "Meeker! Out of here! You know you don't belong in here." The cat darted back out of the dining room.

"Buckley has chosen to stay in California. While his only son died from consumption last year, he still has his four grandchildren in Sausalito. Fortunately, he's promised to see that all our belongings are crated and shipped to New York. However, Au Sam, she has no family but us."

Forgetting myself, I flung my hands in the air. "Oh, goodie!" Reddening again when all eyes focused on me, I did my best to explain. "I can't imagine saying goodbye to Au Sam."

Daddy came to my defense. "Au Sam has been with us since CeeCee was barely six years old, you know. She was here waiting to care for CeeCee when we returned from our wedding and honeymoon back east. As you know, when Rusty came along, she became his nanny."

My mother nodded in agreement. "Cyrus and I were delighted when Au Sam told us she was willing to go with us. Like Maria in your household, Beth, Au Sam's positively indispensable."

"And the clinic? Have you found someone to operate it until you find a buyer?" Uncle Joe asked.

Mama moistened her lips and cast a furtive glance at my father. "Uh—" Anna entered the room carrying dessert plates and clean silver. After the maid placed the last dessert plate on the table, she left the room.

Mama continued, "Wait until you see the luscious almond pastries I found at a new bakery on Fifth and California. One could gain five pounds simply licking the frosting off one's fingers."

Within seconds, Anna returned with two crystal serving platters stacked with pastries, placed one on each end of the table, and made a second trip with trays of fresh fruit and a variety of cheeses. The maid stood poised beside my mother, waiting to serve the guests.

"We can manage from here. Thank you, Anna." Mama smiled

up at the woman. Anna bobbed a curtsy and left. "Don't worry about etiquette; we're all family. Just help yourselves."

Aunt Beth leaned forward to study the dessert choices. "Chloe, about the clinic. Didn't you tell us that your assistant quit recently to have a baby? What are you going to do? I'd hate to see all your efforts to build up the women's clinic go for nothing."

I watched Mama cast another furtive glance—this one toward Aunt Jenny, then back at the dessert tray nearest her.

Uncle Phillip helped himself to an almond pastry. "From a financial standpoint, I am sure that the clinic has never paid for itself, and it never will."

My mother bristled. "Making money has never been a priority for me, Phillip."

"Obviously." My uncle looked at her with a condescending smile. "Forgive me for asking, but just what are the clinic's priorities, beyond sinking perfectly good money into a hopeless cause?"

Mama heaved a sigh. "Phillip, you and I have been arguing this issue for more than ten years now, and we will never see eye to eye on it."

"From what I see, these immigrants continue to populate the slums with illegitimate children, year after year, generation after generation. What good have you done?"

Mama's eyes filled with tears. "To be honest, Phillip, sometimes I've asked myself that same question. Yet, when I hold in my hands a slippery, wailing newborn, I remember why I'm there. And when I assist a terrified young girl of fifteen in delivering her first baby—a breech baby—and both mother and child live, I have no problem remembering why I'm there."

Uncle Phillip stabbed his fork into the pastry. "And next year the whore will have another squalling brat and another and another, until the woman dies from exhaustion at the ripe old age of thirty-two."

"Phillip!" Aunt Jenny gasped. "I can't believe you said such a thing. The child will bear more babies satisfying the lusts of irresponsible men!"

I stared at my aunt in amazement. So did everyone else at the table. Aunt Jenny seldom raised her voice to my uncle—or to anyone else, for that matter. Whenever Daddy read the Beatitudes about the meek inheriting the earth, I pictured Aunt Jenny as a wealthy landowner.

"Jenny Chamberlain, you are being positively obscene," Phillip sputtered, "and in front of your impressionable niece."

"Oh, Phillip. You can be so tiring. Do you think CeeCee is ignorant of the process of birth? She's been down at the clinic many times helping with the clerical work after school whenever Chloe finds herself short—" Aunt Jenny stopped and sent a look of horror toward my mother.

Across the table, Phillip narrowed his eyes. "Jenny, how would you—"

Mama quickly gestured toward the fruit tray. "Phillip, you haven't tried any of these mandarin oranges. They are positively delicious." Uncle Phillip grabbed Mama's wrist, stopping her hand midgesture. Everyone froze.

What is going on here? I glanced about the table at the drama unfolding. Uncle Joe and Aunt Beth looked as confused as I felt. Daddy flashed a searching gaze back and forth between my mother, Aunt Jenny, and Uncle Phillip, whose body was rigid, his jaw clenched.

In a low, threatening tone, my father growled, "Unhand my wife, Phillip."

Uncle Phillip released Mama's hand as if he'd touched a hot griddle, and both leaned back in their chairs. My uncle then glared at his wife through narrowed eyes.

Aunt Jenny took a couple of deep breaths. When my mother started to speak, my aunt shook her head. "No, Chloe. The time has come. He had to find out sooner or later."

"Find out? Find out what?" my uncle demanded.

Squaring her shoulders, Aunt Jenny rose slowly to her feet. "Phillip, I didn't intend to tell you this until we were alone tonight."

"Tell me what?"

"Once a week, for the last eight years, I've volunteered my time at the clinic." My aunt paused to let her news register. She took another deep breath. "I've become a pretty fair delivery nurse."

"Excellent, in fact," Mama mumbled.

Aunt Jenny grinned, then sobered. "After Andrew started school, I grew bored with the silly little garden parties and art benefit luncheons—"

My uncle hissed through his teeth, "Chloe, this is all your fault!"

"I beg your pardon?" My mother's eyebrows shot up toward her hairline.

"Oh no, it's not." My aunt lifted her chin defiantly. "I asked her to allow me to help."

"All this time you've been deceiving me."

While her voice remained soft and feminine, a frosty edge crept into her tone. "You would have known about my service at the clinic if you spent more time at home with Andrew and me."

"Of all the—" Uncle Phillip's face reddened. He sprang to his feet. "I thought we agreed that the clinic was no place for a lady."

My father slowly rose to his feet, joined immediately by Uncle Joe. But Aunt Jenny replied before any of the men could speak, facing off with her husband from across the linen-covered table. "You decreed, Phillip. I never agreed. You may not have noticed, but I am no longer the naive girl you married. At thirty-three, I cannot, in all honesty, giggle and flutter my eyelashes to gain the favor of the lord of the manor. I am a mature woman now, capable of making choices for myself."

"I'm hearing Chloe speaking—not you. This is your doing, Chloe Mae," Uncle Phillip snarled at my mother, then turned back toward his wife. "Jenny Chamberlain, next I'll be bailing you out of prison for marching with those insufferable suffragettes! I need to see you alone in the parlor. Now!" He banged his fist on the table, causing three of the mandarin oranges to tumble from the tray onto the table.

"I've thought about getting involved in the movement, but the clinic has kept me too busy." Aunt Jenny's eyes revealed a hint of humor. "However, there is more you need to know that involves the rest of the family. This afternoon, I was at Attorney Jenkins's office, purchasing the clinic from Chloe. It's all mine, mine! I've never owned anything in my entire life."

"Wha-wha-wha—" Uncle Phillip sputtered. His face reddened; his eyes flashed.

Aunt Jenny's face beamed with satisfaction, in spite of her husband's duress. "I've been saving my clothing allowance for over a year. I didn't need any new ruffles and frills. I know you don't approve, Phillip dear, and I would have preferred that this conversation took place elsewhere." Her eyes begged him to understand. "Please, I didn't do this to defy you. It has nothing to do with you, really. It's for me—it's something I want, something I need."

Uncle Phillip's furious gaze darted around the table at the stunned faces. "I-I-I won't stand for this. I'll break the contract! A man still has legal control in this country, in spite of the imbecilic women's-rights movement!" He paused, as if uncertain what to do next. Suddenly, his fury turned to horror. "You hired Oscar Jenkins as your lawyer? How could you humiliate me like this, Jenny? Oscar Jenkins? I'll be the laughingstock of the San Francisco courthouse."

Her face pale but determined, my aunt went on. "As you know, Oscar Jenkins is actively involved in legislation supporting equal rights. In fact, he was duly impressed. So, at this point, your peers consider you a wise and forward-thinking husband." Aunt Jenny moistened her lips. The corners of her lips curved upward slightly. "The only humiliation you would bring upon yourself would be choosing to go public by dissolving the contract."

"Are you trying to be impudent, woman?" He waited for his wife to answer. Instead, she returned his glare with a steady gaze.

"Get the boy. We are going home!" Uncle Phillip threw his napkin down on the table and stormed from the room. Stunned, we stared at one another until we heard the front door slam.

"Of all the—" Daddy tore out of the room after his brother, slamming the front door a second time.

Her defiance spent, large tears of humiliation spilled down Aunt Jenny's cheeks. My mother rushed to her, gathering her into her arms. Uncle Joe, Aunt Beth, and I sat by helplessly watching.

"My!" Aunt Beth pushed back her chair and swept around the table to Aunt Jenny's side. "I'm so sorry. I guess I asked the wrong question."

Aunt Jenny shook her head. "It's not your fault, Beth. I'm just sorry we wrecked your farewell dinner party, Chloe. I knew he'd be upset, but I thought I was ready for it."

Mama massaged my aunt's shoulders and neck. "Phillip is, and has always been, a stubborn man."

Aunt Jenny looked up into Mama's face. "But he's blaming you."

"Don't let that worry you. Phillip and I have been at loggerheads many times over the years and probably will be again." Mama walked Aunt Jenny toward the parlor.

Uncle Joe nodded at Aunt Beth. "Chloe, we'd better be going. It's getting late. We'll be at the station tomorrow to see you off."

Aunt Beth kissed Mama on the cheek, then kissed Aunt Jenny. "It will be all right. You'll see. Everything will be all right." Aunt Jenny nodded.

"Jed," my uncle called, "get your coat. We're leaving."

Like a shot, my eight-year-old cousin burst through the kitchen doors and ran to the front door, ready to leave with his parents. They left immediately.

At the parlor door, my mother paused. "CeeCee, please go to my room and get a handful of my linen handkerchiefs from my bureau for Aunt Jenny."

"Yes, Mama." Grateful for the escape, I ran up the stairs, grabbed the handkerchiefs, and hurried back downstairs to my aunt. When I entered the parlor, the two women were sitting on the sofa.

"I really think it would be wise to cancel the contract. There's bound to be someone—"

"No!" Aunt Jenny's usually gentle voice contained a ribbon of steel. "If I give in to his demands this time, I will forever be his chattel to order about at will. I gave it a lot of thought before I asked to buy the clinic. And as far as I'm concerned, nothing's changed. He reacted as I expected."

I handed the handkerchiefs to my aunt. She thanked me, unfolded the top one, and blew her nose. I backed away, uncertain what to do next. My impulse was to run and hide—I'd never seen adults scream at one another. Yet curiosity made me retreat to the love seat beside the piano.

"Oh, dear. Oh, dear." Mama shook her head vigorously. "I'm sorry, Jenny, but I don't agree with what you're doing. As important as the clinic is to me, I'd rather see the clinic closed forever than to cause trouble in your marriage. I just can't allow you to—"

"Allow? Allow?" Aunt Jenny jerked free of Mama's arms. "Why does everyone treat me like a helpless child? Phillip, now you, of all people? I am tired of it!" She leapt to her feet and paced to the opposite side of the parlor as she spoke. "Chloe, you don't know what it's like. Cy has always supported your causes. He's not only allowed, but encouraged, you to grow and use the gifts God gave you." She whipped about, her eyes alight with determination. "When I die, I want my life to matter beyond a stack of doilies I crocheted or pillowcases I embroidered!"

Mama stood up and smoothed the waist of her skirt with trembling hands. "I'm sorry. You're right. This is your decision. But, please, Jenny, please pray about it."

Behind me, the front door opened. I heard my father's footsteps approaching. He paused in the parlor doorway. "Jenny, I'm sorry. I tried to talk to Phillip. It doesn't seem to have done any good. He decided to take a drive to cool off. So I asked Buckley to drive you and Andrew home in the Pierce Arrow—when you're ready, of course. There's no hurry."

Aunt Jenny sniffed and threw my father a smile. "Thank you, Cy. I'm sorry about all of this tonight." She moved toward the parlor door like a woman twice her age. My father took Aunt Jenny's hand and led her into the hallway while Mama fetched her cloak.

Without a word, my fourteen-year-old cousin, Andrew, appeared from the kitchen. The tall, gangly boy took his mother's other arm. "I can take care of my mother from here, sir."

Daddy released Aunt Jenny to her son, walking them out to the waiting automobile. Mama ran up the stairs and into her bedroom. I turned in time to see my little brother step back into the shadows of the hallway. "Rusty? Come here." I held out my arms to him. He ran to me and buried his face in my blouse. "Come on; it's been a long day. Let's go upstairs and get ready for bed."

When we reached the landing, he looked up into my face. "Will we ever see Andrew and Uncle Phillip and Aunt Jenny again?"

"Of course, we will. We're family." I gave him a squeeze. "You know how you and I fight sometimes? We always make up, right? Well, it's the same way with Daddy and Uncle Phillip. You'll see."

Is it? I asked myself as I gazed into the dressing-table mirror and brushed the snarls out of my auburn curls. *Kids have to make up after a fight, but how about grown-ups? Granddaddy Spencer and Mama took a long time making up.*

If an earthquake had hit San Francisco the next day, no one in the Chamberlain household would have felt it through the incredible pandemonium. By the time we said goodbye to Marta and Anna, and Daddy had loaded the family and Au Sam in the Pierce Arrow, my feet ached and my head throbbed. Meeker protested being imprisoned in the bird cage I placed on the floor of the back seat, next to my violin case. I had no intention of allowing some thoughtless railroad worker to toss either about like unripe watermelons.

"I get the window. I get the window," Rusty shouted, breaking free from Marta's grasp. As he climbed into the car, he spotted Buckley sitting in the passenger seat of an open-bed truck loaded with our luggage. "Please, Daddy, may I ride with Buckley? I've never, ever ridden in a truck."

My father looked at Buckley. The aging butler nodded and smiled. "I would be honored to have Master Rusty ride in the cab with Grant and me."

Grant, a middle-aged man with a smoldering cigar protruding from his salt-and-pepper beard, waved toward Rusty. "Come on, kid. There's lots of room up here with old Bent and me." Relieved, I climbed in the automobile. All I wanted was to sink into the car's soft leather seat and close my eyes. I didn't care whether I ever saw our home on Clay Street again. I didn't care whether I ever saw the city of San Francisco again. I only wanted peace to close my eyes and rest.

My tranquillity lasted until we reached the ferryboat. Reluctantly, I climbed out of the car and walked onto the crowded boat. A damp, late-afternoon mist engulfed the boat, causing most of the passengers to find seats inside the cabin. Not wanting to be disturbed, I lugged Meeker and her cage to an empty wooden bench outside along the starboard wall. Placing the cage by my feet and the violin case on the bench, I sat down and leaned my head against the cold metal window frame. Meeker meowed one long protest, then curled into a despondent ball on the floor of the cage.

I took one last look at the shrouded city I'd called home for most of my life, closed my eyes, and swallowed the unwelcome lump in my throat. With any luck, people would think I was sleeping and leave me alone.

Ignoring other passengers milling about the area, I allowed the steady rhythm of the engines to lull me almost to sleep, until I heard familiar voices.

"I was sure Phillip would come to say goodbye."

"Perhaps he still will. They might have missed this ferry and will catch the next one. Or they could have decided to meet us at the depot in Oakland."

I opened my eyes a slit and saw a couple standing by the rail, staring as the San Francisco skyline vanished into the fog. The tall, middle-aged man had his arm about the waist of a gently rounded, well-dressed woman. In spite of the ferry's throbbing engine, I heard each word distinctly.

"There it goes." The woman waved a hand toward the horizon.

The man turned toward the woman. "Did I make a mistake moving you and the children so far from your home?"

While running her gloved hand along the side of his cheek and well-trimmed beard, the woman looked into his eyes. "Darling, you did what you had to do. I love you, Cyrus. I'd go to the ends of the earth with you."

Seemingly oblivious to me or the public surroundings, he kissed the tip of her nose. "Remember the first time we rode across the bay on a ferryboat? More than a decade ago, now."

She smiled softly and leaned against his gray wool overcoat, careful not to dislodge the confection of gray felt, feathers, and grosgrain ribbons on her head. "And who'd ever have known that memorable occasion would bring us such incredible happiness?"

They stood locked in one another's arms for some time. I closed my eyes and tried to understand the scene I'd witnessed. Instead of my parents, they seemed to be two strangers sharing their feelings of love, their fears, and their memories with one another.

I bit my lip to control a sudden rush of tears. Somehow, I'd never thought of my parents as lovers. I mean, I knew they loved each other, but somehow that was different from my schoolgirl dreams of romance based on episodes from favorite storybooks.

My father's voice broke into my reverie. "Do you think we'll ever return, I mean, to live?"

"I hope so, Cy. I truly hope so."

I held my breath as they shared a tender kiss, then arm in arm walked along the railing to the bow of the boat. My emotions of fear, hope, and sadness leapfrogged over one another, then back again. *They understand my feelings. They feel the same way.* I mulled over my disturbing discovery during the rest of the crossing to Oakland and throughout our teary goodbyes with Buckley, Uncle Joe, Aunt Beth, and my eight-year-old cousin, Jed.

Uncle Phillip and Aunt Jenny and Cousin Andrew never arrived. A number of times, I caught Daddy gazing over the heads of the people assembled on the crowded railway platform, searching. And I saw my mother watching him. The hurt she felt reflected in her eyes.

Let's go. Let's go. Let's go! Finally, the conductor called, "All aboard," and we climbed the steps into the private railway car at the end of the train.

I deposited Meeker's cage and the violin case in my compartment before joining the family on the brass-railed observation deck. We stood there waving until the depot disappeared from view.

One by one, the rest of my family slipped back inside the railway car. Before Mama left, she hugged me for a moment. "It's getting chilly out here. Better put on your jacket. The chef will be serving dinner in a little while."

When I didn't respond, she slipped her cape from her shoulders and onto mine. "Are you going to be all right?"

I nodded. She placed a gentle kiss on my cheek. "Everything's going to work out, CeeCee."

You don't know that. You can't promise me that. No one can. I felt a catch in my throat. Mama turned and stepped inside the lighted coach.

LIGHT CONVERSATION 71

If only I knew the future— If only— My thoughts shifted to the ever-changing scenery racing by me. The coastal hills began to flatten into the great Central Valley. *How would Emily describe this sight?*

What is going to happen to us, God? Do You know? Do You care? Is this move east part of Your plan for my life? Do You use presidents and kaisers to carry out Your plans? The last golden ray sank into the horizon, plunging the world I knew and loved into darkness. I shivered at the thought of the empty, frightening world beyond the distant Sierra Nevada.

From Little Girl to Lady

Hays, Kansas
March 9, 1917
Dear Emily,

    It's been eight days since we left California, and we haven't crossed the Mississippi River yet! What with Mama insisting we stop in Steamboat Springs, Hahn's Peak, and Columbine (I'll write about that part of the trip later, when I've had time to think through my jumbled emotions), and Daddy's three days of government business in Denver, Nellie Bly would never have broken Phileas Fogg's eighty-day around-the-world record if she had traveled with us!

    Three days ago, Daddy, Meeker, and the Empress left for Chicago (Meeker refuses to leave my stateroom), while Mama, Au Sam, Rusty, and I detoured on a public railway car to Hays, Kansas. Traveling aboard the cattle car they call a public Pullman convinced me, dear confidante, that lapping miles and making prairies aren't my forte. If you ever tried it, you'd agree. I giggled out loud at my reference to two of Emily's best-known poems.

    I turned my thoughts back to my journal entry. *I adore my Great Aunt Bea. She's one brave lady. Since she couldn't get away from her store today, Mama took Rusty, Au Sam, and me on a tour of the town and of the old fort that is now a teacher's college. Rusty loved it. I was much less enthused—and for good reason. Kansas is cold in March. They're still having winter!*

    Tomorrow, Aunt Bea is taking us out to the homestead where my mother and father lived the first few months of their marriage. And so, for tonight, dear friend, I bid you adieu.

Early the next morning, Aunt Bea, Mama, Rusty, and I piled into Aunt Bea's closed carriage and drove to the old homestead. (Aunt Bea hates automobiles and refuses to own one. She says, "I'll take a good-tempered horse any day over an oil-spitting, smoke-belching, nerve-jangling machine.")

Last season's prairie grass covered the spot where the house once stood. A broken windmill graced the top of the knoll near where the barn used to be. After Mama's first explosion of excitement at seeing the familiar surroundings, she disappeared into her own silent world. The four of us tramped across the uneven ground together. Aunt Bea and Mama told us a number of amusing anecdotes I'd never heard before. Before long, the biting winds drove Rusty and me back to the carriage to wrap up in the heavy carriage blankets. Aunt Bea soon joined us, allowing Mama time alone with her memories.

Farther down the road, Aunt Bea, Rusty, and I stayed in the buggy while Mama hiked an overgrown trail to an abandoned sod house. In the distance I could hear the mournful whistle of the afternoon train. Gazing across the prairie, I tried to picture Mama, her bonnet bouncing on the back of her neck, running along the fence line with my brother Jamie. Then I tried to imagine her thoughts.

What was it like being seventeen and stranded out here in this empty, forbidding land, caring for another woman's child? As she walked out there alone, did Mama imagine seeing James McCall, the mysterious man who gave me life, running toward her? If so, where does Cy fit into the picture?

In two months I'll be seventeen. Would I willingly push my dreams aside because of a sad little boy? My questions disturbed me—and I wasn't sure I liked my answers.

When Mama returned to the carriage, we headed back into town. On the way, new and disturbing questions continued. *Did Mama love my real father more than she loves Cy? Or does she love Daddy in a different way than she did my father, James? How does love work, anyway? Can a woman love more than one man in a lifetime without loving one man less than the other? Someday,* I vowed, *I'm going to have to ask her—someday.*

That night, I didn't write much to Emily. My thoughts were too heavy.

Hays, Kansas
March 14, 1917
Dear Emily,

Sometimes I don't like myself very much. I want to be like my mother. Everyone says she's kind and generous and thoughtful, and she is. But I'm so shallow and childish. It's like I'm stuck in the middle— too old to do kid things and too young to understand adults. Will I ever grow up?

I paused and remembered a night, a few weeks before the move, when Mama had wandered into my room while I was unbraiding my hair. I guess she felt lonely. Daddy was in Los Angeles, wrapping up his business. I remember how Mama picked up my hairbrush and began brushing my hair with long, even strokes. I liked the way it made me feel like a little girl again, protected and loved.

"CeeCee, the deep auburn color of your hair is so beautiful," she admitted. "I always wished mine were darker, like yours."

Surprised, I gazed up at her reflection in the mirror. She wore her naturally curly hair fastened at the back of her neck in one long braid, as she did every night as long as I could remember. "Oh no, yours is so fiery and alive. I always wished mine were bright like yours."

We laughed together. Then her smile softened; her eyes misted. "You are growing up so fast. I can hardly believe it."

Not fast enough for me!

"I still can't believe my little girl will graduate from secondary school in a few months. Before long, you'll fall in love with some strong young man, marry, and have babies of your own."

"That won't happen!" I shot her a devilish grin. "As long as you and Daddy keep me from meeting eligible young men."

She laughed gently. "Soon, honey, soon."

"But Aunt Drucilla lets Ashley go to parties and to date."

"That's true. But what your aunt and your cousin do has nothing to do with your decisions or mine, now, does it?"

We talked late into the night. She related memories from my

childhood, and I shared my dreams about playing my violin in the concert halls of London and Paris, Rome and Berlin. During a lull in our conversation, I asked her, "Do you ever wonder what it would have been like if you'd gone on to China like you dreamed of doing?"

"Once in a great while," she admitted. "But if it meant giving up you children or your father, I'd rather everything happened exactly as it happened. You know, God knows more about us than we do ourselves. And if we let Him, He'll lead us where we'll be the happiest."

"Hmmph! I wouldn't give up my dreams for a husband and kids. No siree!"

She laughed and brushed the hair off my neck. "Then why do you worry so much about dating?"

"Mother!" I groaned.

She squeezed my arm, then studied my face for a few seconds. "It's easy to say what we would or would not do before we're faced with the situation. But none of us really know what we'll do ahead of time. In my case, love made the difference."

A delicious shiver ran through me. My friends talked all the time about boys and romance and falling in love. I had so many unanswered questions. "How do you know when you're really in love? How do you know, this is it; this is the one? Does it hit you all of a sudden, like some of the popular songs say? Is that how it happened with you and Daddy?" I got up from the dressing table and leapt into the middle of my bed.

"You mean Cy?"

I nodded. "Or my real dad. It doesn't matter."

Mama perched herself on the foot of the bed. "No, it was a gradual thing with both of them. It took time. Grandma Spencer used to say, 'Marry in haste; repent at leisure.'"

"That doesn't sound too romantic, if you ask me."

"Maybe not, compared to the romance depicted in melodramas and in some of the novels your friends read. But it is the kind of romance that survives in real life." She drew her knees up to her chest, hiding her toes under her light blue nightgown. "With both James and Cyrus, we were friends first. Never forget, CeeCee, friends make the best lovers."

"Mother!" I couldn't believe she'd used the word *lover*, with all it implied. Suzanne, one of my friends at school, had found a book in her parents' library called *This Passion Called Love*. She smuggled it to school and shared it with the rest of us, leaving me stunned for days at what I read.

"What? Lover?" Mama threw her head back and laughed out loud. "CeeCee, my dear, there's nothing wrong with married love. Quite the contrary; God has a good thing going there. Trust me." She took my hands in hers as she continued, "During the next few years, you will meet a young man, probably a lot like your daddy, and you'll become friends. Over time, he will grow to be the most important person in your life. And somewhere along the way, you'll realize you can't imagine living your life without him. That's when you'll know you're in love—when his needs become more important to you than your needs, and vice-versa, of course. You see, God intended love between a man and a woman to be a delicate balance of giving and receiving."

Why Mama's words popped into my mind as I sat alone in Aunt Bea's guest bedroom, I didn't know. Maybe it was trying to imagine Mama without Daddy or that she was my age when she first fell in love. I closed my diary and turned off the small brass lamp. Padding to the bed in the darkness, I hopped under the covers.

The next morning Aunt Bea took Mama to visit the friends whom Mama hadn't seen since before I was born. And, of course, Rusty and I had to tag along. Bundled under heavy wool blankets in the back seat of the enclosed buggy, Rusty and I commiserated with one another over our fate. Aunt Bea drove the buggy over ice heaves and frozen wagon ruts at a speed guaranteed to loosen diseased teeth and realign popped vertebrae. The biting Kansas wind had no mercy on our thin California blood. *The temperatures must have dropped a good twenty degrees*, I decided, *since yesterday*.

My teeth chattered in spite of my burgundy wool tweed overcoat, the heaviest I owned. The leather in my matching boots and gloves couldn't keep my fingers from stiffening.

Aunt Bea leaned forward and gazed at the sky overhead and shouted, "Looks like the clouds are breaking. I'm so glad we're having good weather while you're here, Chloe."

"A-a-h," I wailed.

"Did you say something, darling?"

I shook my head. *Good weather? Deliver me, please, from their bad!*

Mama took a deep breath. "I smell spring in the air."

Spring?

Aunt Bea halted the carriage in front of a white farmhouse with a porch wrapped around three sides of the building. Before our feet touched the lowest tread of the porch steps, the front door burst open. From there, all went exactly as I had expected. Ladies I didn't know, with names I instantly forgot, swarmed us. My mother beamed with pride as total strangers engulfed me with kisses and hugs and embarrassing exclamations of delight.

"What a beauty! She looks just like you, Chloe."

"I bet the young men swarm around her like flies to honey."

"Your father, James, would have been so proud of you."

"Mark my word, those huge green eyes and all that gorgeous red hair spell trouble, Chloe Mae. You'd better keep a short leash on her until you marry her off."

I smiled until I thought that my lips might remain permanently stretched. Like a cresting wave at high tide, the women swept me into the overheated parlor. After the worst of the flurry had passed, our hostess, Mrs. Paget, a tall, commanding woman with dusty gray hair, weathered skin, and deep brown eyes, whispered in Rusty's ear. She handed him a cookie and took him to the front door. He afforded me one last pitying glance, then scooted out the front door.

Hey, that's not fair. Feeling frustrated and claustrophobic, I glanced over at Mama, hoping she would recognize my plight and help me escape too. She was too engulfed herself to notice my distress.

As I was about to give up hope, I felt a tap on my shoulder. Mrs. Paget stood behind me. "Here, let me take your wraps."

"Thank you." Reluctantly, I shed my coat, bonnet, and gloves. Her brown eyes held a glint of humor. "I'm sorry that we don't have any of our young ladies here today—school, you know."

"Oh, that's all right; thank you, anyway," I demurred.

She cast a bemused grin. "I understand, CeeCee, that you like music?"

I nodded. "Yes, ma'am."

"Your mother said she brought your violin along this afternoon."

"Yes, ma'am." I sighed. *And to every gathering between Kansas and Nob Hill.*

Mrs. Paget rested her hand on my shoulder. "If I help you escape, will you promise to play your violin for us at the end of my little luncheon?"

She'd read my thoughts. I cleared my throat. "Er, well, um—" I didn't know how to answer. "I, uh, guess, yes."

"Listen carefully; in the sitting room by the fireplace, there's a Victrola and a box of discs you might enjoy."

"Oh!" My face broke into a genuine smile. "Thank you." I glanced over at Mama, seated on the sofa, surrounded by her friends. "But Mama, perhaps I should—"

Mrs. Paget chuckled. "She won't even know you're gone."

"Are you sure?" I didn't try to hide my eagerness to escape.

"I'm very sure." She gave me a wink. "Help yourself to a couple cookies while you walk through the kitchen."

I thanked her, slipped out the door, and hurried across the hall. The large sitting room occupied a corner of the farmhouse's dining room and kitchen. In the middle of the room, a long trestle table groaned with food of every kind. I circled the table slowly, admiring the variety of potato salads, casseroles, fruit cobblers, fruit and cream pies, and plates of cookies. A cake, dripping with chocolate syrup and whipping cream and coated with walnuts, occupied a milk-glass pedestal at the far end of the display.

I helped myself to two peanut-butter cookies and one oatmeal-raisin cookie, then located the Victrola in the corner. As I selected an operetta and put it on the machine, I could hear the women's voices and occasionally my mother's laughter.

Closing my eyes, I let the music lift me from my surroundings and into a concert hall. *One day, one day—*

"Excuse me?"

My eyes flew open. The woman my mother called Minna smiled

down into my startled face. "I'm sorry if I frightened you. I guess you didn't hear me come into the kitchen a while back. I was wondering if you could do me a favor?"

I rustled to my feet. "Yes, ma'am, if I can."

"Would you mind going down to the barn to tell the children that it's time to eat?"

"I'll be glad to." I whirled about. "Do you know where Mrs. Paget put my coat?"

The old woman hobbled to the hall closet and back again, carrying my coat and bonnet. "Is this the one?"

"Yes, ma'am." She helped me into the coat and insisted on fastening the long line of buttons up the front while I tied the hat's grosgrain ribbon under my chin.

"Be sure to remind the children to come in through the kitchen door to the breakfast nook. They're sure to be covered with hay and straw. I have everything set up for them there."

I hurried out the front door onto the porch. The clear, brilliant sunlight blinded me. Overhead, I saw a V of birds flying north. The temperatures had risen; it must have been all of 40°.

Frozen mud crackled under my boots until I was within two yards of the barn door, where the mud had melted into muck. As daintily as possible, I lifted my skirts, stepping over and around the worst of the puddles. Once through the barn door, I could hear the squeals and laughter of children above my head.

The memory of playing in the hay at Uncle Joe's ranch swept over me. As I listened to the children for a few minutes, feelings of envy replaced my nostalgia, and a new temptation nibbled at me. I stiffened my resolve with more practical thoughts. *You're wearing your good taffeta skirt and your new dimity bodice. Be a lady, Chloe Celeste. Be a lady!*

I walked the length of the barn and climbed up the ladder until my head cleared the loft's wooden floor. "Hey, you guys, it's time to eat." I didn't have to repeat myself. Instantly, four boys and five girls of varying ages tumbled out of their hiding places and leapt off the loft into the pile of hay stacked below. "Use the kitchen door," I shouted, doubting seriously that they heard me. Even my brother didn't wait for me. I heard the barn door slam. *Good, they're all gone.*

FROM LITTLE GIRL TO LADY 81

I eyed the pile of hay on the barn floor beneath the loft. *Hmm. It would be such fun to jump— No, CeeCee, you can't. That's not the proper behavior for a lady.* I was four steps from the top of the ladder. All I had to do was complete the trip to the top and come down the simplest way possible. I looked around to find myself totally alone. *No one will know.*

Always, Uncle Joe warned us kids over and over again not to jump from the loft. "What if a pitchfork has been left under the hay? You could kill yourself."

Suddenly, I knew what I was going to do, taffeta skirt or not. I climbed to the top of the ladder, removed my coat and bonnet, and tossed them onto the hay below. As I watched them fall, I trembled with a delicious mixture of fear and excitement. I poised myself at the very edge of the loft and jumped. "Whee!" I squealed, landing with a bounce in the prickly hay. I rolled over and pitched the hay into the air, laughing until my sides hurt.

When I sat up, my carefully rolled hair tumbled free of its pins, which disappeared into the loose hay. My hands automatically flew to my head. *How am I going to get my hair to stay in place long enough to go back inside the house? Nice time to think about that obstacle! Oh, well, no sense crying over spilled milk, Mama always says. Might as well do it again.*

I jumped to my feet, scurried up the ladder, and did a backward free fall, my skirts flying into my face. I climbed the ladder and jumped a third time, then a fourth. As I stood up and brushed hay from my bodice, I realized I'd been gone a long time. *Just one more jump—*

I hiked my skirts up around my knees and scrambled up the ladder. At the edge of the loft, I adopted the diver's pose, rose onto my tiptoes, and extended my arms before me. *This one is going to be the best jump of all.*

As I drew my arms behind me to give me a thrust, I heard a man's voice from behind me shout, "Hey, what are you doing?"

"What the—" Startled, I turned in the direction of the voice in time to see a tall, dark-haired male, whom I suspected to be around the age of twenty or twenty-one, standing beside an open trapdoor at the rear of the loft.

"Lady, are you crazy?" He started toward me.

My hair! When I reached for my head, I upset my precarious balance.

"O-o-o-o—" Teetering on the edge, I spun my arms in backward circles trying to catch my fall. He lunged at me. In surprise, I stepped back and tumbled into open space. A split second after I landed, some hundred and eighty pounds landed on me, knocking me breathless and panicky. Gasping for air, I found myself staring into a pair of flashing brown eyes.

For an instant, neither of us moved. We just stared. I remember thinking, *How does he shave in that little cleft in his chin?* My next thought was, *I can't breathe! I can't breathe!*

"Get off me, you, you brute! What do you think you're doing?" I pushed against his chest with both hands and tried to wriggle free. I had heard horror stories from my friends at school about men who attacked young girls and had their way with them—and I had no intentions of allowing that to happen to me. Having gotten my breath, I started screaming, "Help! Somebody help me!"

"Hey, hey!" He grabbed my wrists and pinned them down. Inches from his face, I continued to scream.

"Stop yelling, woman!" He released my left hand and covered my mouth. Simultaneously, I bit his hand and raked my fingernails along the side of his face and resumed my screaming for help.

Howling in pain, my attacker rolled off me. Instantly, I leapt to my feet and grabbed for my coat, but before I reached it, he captured my wrist and pulled me back down beside him into the mound of hay.

"I'm not here to hurt you, Miss! Will you be quiet for a minute?" he shouted directly in my face. The impact of his words took me back for an instant. "Stop! Will you stop yelling? What in Sam Hill were you doing jumping from that hayloft?" He shouted. "Don't you know that you could have been killed?

Indignant, I continued to scream at him. "What was *I* doing? What were *you* doing, tackling me like a linebacker?" Suddenly, I thought of how ridiculous I must look, my hair filled with hay and flying in every direction, bits of hay sticking to my city-girl clothes. I chuckled.

"What? What's so funny? You think it's funny being stabbed by a pitchfork?"

"I-I-I—" While trying to explain, I dissolved into another bout of laughter.

"Will you please stop laughing? You're driving me crazy!" The man shook me by the shoulders, which made me laugh all the harder. I rolled into a ball, holding my aching sides. He scrambled onto all fours and stared at me as if I'd escaped from an insane asylum. "Did you hit your head on something? I'm going to get help."

He rose to leave and stepped over my legs. On a devilish whim, I lifted my foot enough to send him sprawling. The shocked look on his face as he lifted himself out of the hay told me I needed to be somewhere else, fast. I leapt to my feet, grabbed my coat and the ties on my bonnet, and raced down the barn's center corridor. I glanced over my shoulder in time to see a giant hand clamp down on my shoulder.

"Not so fast, Miss."

I wriggled to break free, but the more I wriggled, the more his iron grip tightened on my shoulder.

"I don't know who you are or what planet you hail from—" He glared down at me. "—but in these parts, tripping a man and sending him face down in the hay is a declaration of war!"

"Ouch, you're hurting me!" I wriggled and squirmed, determined to escape.

He released my shoulder, but not before he clamped his hand around one of my wrists. "You should have thought of that before." He hauled me in the direction of the door to the barnyard.

"Where are you taking me?" I wailed.

"To the pump. A good dousing will bring you back to your senses."

"No!" I dug in my heels and attempted to drop to the ground. My mulelike behavior caused little resistance. He didn't even break stride. "Please, please, no. Don't get me wet. I'll die of consumption."

He threw his head back and laughed. "You should have thought of that before." He stopped at the pump-house door and hefted me under his right arm by my waist. Kicking the door open with his boot, he stomped toward the well.

"You bully! You overgrown Neanderthal! You cretin!" I pummeled his kneecaps and kicked with all the force I had.

The more I fought, the more he laughed. "Pretty big words for such a little girl. Do you even know what you're calling me?"

"I am not a little girl! And, yes, I know what I'm saying, you brute!"

He laughed again. "Coulda fooled me."

When we reached the water pump, he plunked me in a sitting position on the wooden platform. Trapping both of my hands with his one hand, he grabbed the pump handle with his other and started pumping. The grim determination on his face told me he meant business. Any second, water would spew forth from the spout and drench me from head to toe.

Tears sprang up in my eyes. I shivered from cold air. "Do you always solve your problems with brute force? All brawn, no brains?"

"When necessary."

I was so cold my teeth started chattering. Without warning, a whimper escaped from me. I hated myself for showing weakness and tried to sniff back my first outpouring of tears. "Well, it's not necessary now. I apologize. I'm sorry."

He shot a look of surprise at me. "You *are* cold." He released my hands and removed his buckskin jacket. "Here, bundle up." He wrapped the still-warm jacket around my shoulders. I closed my eyes and sighed with pleasure. "It would keep you warmer if you slipped your arms into the sleeves." I obeyed. Then with stiff, frozen fingers, I tried to fasten the buttons.

"Here, let me help—" He started to brush aside my fingers, then trapped my hands between his. "You're fingers are like ice." I jerked free of his grasp. "I can do it myself!" I sounded like a petulant child.

He caught my hands and guided them to the jacket's sheepskin-lined pockets. When I started to remove them, he wagged a warning finger in my face. "Stay!"

"I am not a dog!" I again tried to remove my hands from the pockets. He again pushed them down.

"I said, stay!" He started with the bottom button. As he worked, he spoke in the quiet, subduing tone I'd heard my Uncle Joe use when dealing with skittish colts. "So, who are you? What's your name?"

"Chloe Celeste Chamberlain. I'm from California."

He looked up and grinned. "Oh, I remember you, or at least, I remember your mother. She used to live in these parts when I was a kid. I remember her." He lifted my long curls out from under the collar of his jacket and let them slowly tumble down my back. "Fiery red hair and a temper to match. I should have known."

I waited until he reached the top button. Then I pursed my lips and slowly lifted my eyes to met his. "And who might you be?"

He swallowed hard, dropping his gaze to my neck. "I can't fasten this pain-in-the-neck button."

"Don't worry about it. I'm feeling much warmer now. So, who are you? The Pagets' hired hand? Their son? Who?"

He cleared his throat. "Please, ma'am, let me introduce myself properly. My name is Shane Simons, son of Shane and Amy Simons. I'm working here on the Paget place so I can attend a university back east next fall."

I stuck out my hand. "It's nice to finally meet you, Shane Simons." He gave my hand a quick shake. "Which one? Which university are you planning to attend?"

Avoiding my gaze, he picked a piece of hay from my hair. "I'm in my sophomore year of engineering at the University of Virginia." For a moment, he forgot I was there. He stared out across the prairie. With a sweep of his arm, he revealed his dream. "I want to build bridges and roads that will span America. Someday, smooth, broad highways will link New York City with San Francisco, San Francisco with Los Angeles, and Los Angeles with Atlanta. I want to be a part of that."

"Well, if in the process of all this building, you find yourself in New York City, Mama would be pleased to have you visit, I'm sure."

He eyed me thoughtfully for a moment, then grinned. "Hmm, if I did come calling, say, in the next fifteen years or so, what might I find you doing?"

I grinned and breathed through my teeth. "If my dream comes

true, I may not even be there. After I finish my training at one of the East's finest music conservatories—I don't know which one yet, since I've not yet applied to any—I intend to dazzle the audiences in the concert halls of Europe." I ended my speech with a dramatic bow.

He applauded. "Do you sing? Play the piano?"

I shook my head. A strand of hay fell on my nose and tickled. "I play the violin." Suddenly a frightening thought hit. "Oh no, where's my coat? Where's my bonnet?" I spun toward the door. "I promised Mrs. Paget that I'd play for her guests when I returned from the barn."

Simultaneously, we spotted the burgundy coat lying in the mud between the well and the barn. My bonnet had landed in a mud puddle beside the barn door. "Oh no," I wailed. "My hat! My new coat!"

I gathered up my skirts and ran to the coat. He jogged along beside me at an easy gait. "What were you doing at the barn, anyway?"

He reached for the coat and held it up for my inspection. "Oh no, what will Mama say?"

"You didn't answer my question."

"Mrs. Paget asked me to call the children in to eat." I took the coat from his hands and tried to brush the mud away.

"Don't try to clean it until the mud dries. Most of it will brush off then." He turned to fetch my bonnet. When he returned, I groaned at the condition of my ostrich-plumed wonder.

"So how did you go from a simple task like that to jumping out of the hayloft?"

I felt the color creep up my neck to my hairline. I shrugged and cocked my head to one side. "I don't know. It just kinda happened."

"I'll just bet it did." He laughed and removed more pieces of hay from my hair.

"My hair!" My hands flew to the top of my head. "All of my hairpins are gone. I can't go into that house with my hair like this. You don't know where I'd find a brush or a comb, do you?"

"Yeah, in there." He nodded his head toward the tack room. "The ones we use on the horses' manes."

A curry brush? No! I glanced toward the house, then toward the tack-room door. Taking a deep breath, I set my jaw and demanded, "Lead me to the tack room."

By the time I returned to the farmhouse with my hair brushed and reasonably tamed, I knew my reputation must be in shambles. I felt the questioning glances of some of the women gathered about my mother. When she saw me, her eyebrows almost disappeared into her hairline. "Where have you been? I was ready to send Rusty to find you."

I held out my coat and bonnet and blushed nervously. "I met up with a mud puddle, and, uh, had to clean up a bit."

Minna Kline arched one brow and pursed her lips. "By the looks of the jacket, I'd say you also met up with Shane Simons."

My blush darkened. "Uh, yes, ma'am. He loaned me his coat until mine dried a bit."

Sensing my discomfort, the hostess interrupted. "Earlier, Chloe Celeste promised to demonstrate her skill on the violin for us today." She pushed me toward the kitchen. "If you ladies will make yourselves comfortable, we'll give her a few minutes to freshen up before playing."

I slipped into the kitchen and washed my hands. In a small mirror on the pantry door, I saw myself for the first time and groaned. I could only imagine what some of the ladies in the parlor were thinking. While Shane had pulled out the stalks of hay he noticed, he'd missed far too many. And my bodice and skirt, though free of hay, were rumpled.

After straightening up as best I could, I removed my violin from its case and returned to the parlor. My hands shook as I lifted the instrument to my chin and positioned the bow. Taking a moment, I paused and closed my eyes. Dr. Bohn's face sprang into my mind.

"Chloe Celeste, you are a professional—always, you are a professional!"

I drew the bow across the strings. My audience faded, and the music came to life. When I finished playing my favorite sonata, one of the women asked if I could play "Annie Laurie." I smiled and nodded. After playing that favorite, I broke into a lively version of "Put on Your Old Gray Bonnet," then changed tempo with "Coming Through the Rye." My audience applauded and cheered. I bowed first toward my hostess, then to the women immediately in front of me, and last toward the women seated in front of the parlor windows.

A movement outside one window caught my eye, sending unwanted color to my cheeks. I saw Shane Simons tip his cowboy hat toward me and leave. And so did half of the ladies in my audience.

Facing the Music

"Chloe Celeste Chamberlain!" My mother shook her head and paced to the other side of Aunt Bea's parlor, then back again. "Whatever possessed you to behave in such an unseemly manner today? I don't understand. One moment you're so mature and responsible, and the next—" She flung a hand into the air. "Imagine what those women think happened between you and that young man out there in the barn!"

I sank farther back on Aunt Bea's horsehair sofa, knowing I deserved her censure. How could I have let myself behave like that? I stared down at my hands folded in my lap, grateful that Aunt Bea sat in the wing chair throughout my mother's lecture without adding to my embarrassment by scolding me too.

Mama held up my muddied clothing, the coat in one hand, my bonnet in the other. "Totally ruined. And who knows about your reputation? You behaved like a hooligan. A hooligan!"

Aunt Bea cleared her throat. "I think I can get the coat and bonnet clean, Chloe, if you let me try."

My mother whirled about to face my aunt. "That's not the point, Bea. What? Why are you grinning?" Mama turned back to me slowly, a strange little smile quivering at the corners of her mouth. "CeeCee, in order to get all the chaff and dust out of your hair, you'll need to shampoo it—now."

"But, I—"

"Just go do as I say."

Nothing more was said about my transgression until that evening as I prepared for bed. I sat cross-legged in the middle of my bed, head bent forward, brushing my damp hair. *Seventy-eight, seventy-nine, eighty.* I paused when I heard a knock on my bedroom door. "Come in," I called, and resumed brushing.

Mama stepped into the room, her pale green satin robe belted loosely around her waist. "Hi, honey. You and I need to talk."

My stomach knotted. I'd been dreading this moment all evening. "I guess so."

She walked over to my bed and sat down on the edge. "CeeCee, I know it's difficult growing up. I sometimes forget what I was like at your age. Today, Aunt Bea reminded me." Her eyes held a inscrutable mixture of joy and sadness. "At times, it frustrates me when I see how much you and I are alike. What you did today, I can all too well see myself doing, even at my age. But that doesn't reduce the danger of such unwise behavior." She placed her hand on my knee.

"Mama," I argued, flipping my mop of hair back over my shoulder. "Have you ever heard of anyone dying from jumping out of a hayloft?"

"It's not the hayloft, dear. Not every male you'll meet will be as gentlemanly as your father or your brother Jamie or, so it seems, as this Shane Simons. Think about what could have happened if Shane had been a less honorable man."

I bristled at her lecturing tone. "I understand what you're saying. I am almost seventeen, you know."

She shook her head. "And still so incredibly young in so many ways."

"I know about the birds and the bees, Mother. When you were my age—" My lower lip protruded in defiance.

"The birds and the bees, yes, but—" Her probing eyes searched my face. "Oh, CeeCee, I want to protect you from all that's cruel and hateful. I've seen so many young girls come to my clinic, their lives in shambles as the result of foolish choices."

I jumped up in exasperation. "It wasn't planned, you know, our meeting in the barn. And it's not as if I'll ever see him again. You do believe me, don't you?"

Her eyes misted. "Of course, I believe you."

"What was I supposed to do, anyway? It all just happened."

She paused and hugged her knees. "I know how things just

happen. Do you remember the story of Joseph in the Bible?"

I nodded.

"What did Joseph do when he found himself in a compromising situation?"

"He ran."

"Exactly. A wise retreat can be a woman's best defense. If a situation doesn't feel right, it probably isn't."

I looked at her incredulously. "But Shane didn't do—"

"I know. And I'm glad. Unfortunately, rumors are next to impossible to refute. A woman's reputation means everything." She sighed. "Fortunately, we'll leave for Chicago tomorrow, before any gossip returns to bite you. Look, it's late. We'd better get some sleep." She took my hand and studied my fingers for a moment. "I didn't have the chance to tell you how proud I was of you today. Your violin never sounded sweeter."

She released my hand and strode to the door, her reluctance to leave evident. "I love you so much, CeeCee—more than you can possibly understand. Always remember that."

As the door closed behind her, I turned out the light and snuggled down under the covers, only to relive the day's strange events—over and over again. I finally fell asleep as a rooster began to crow from the chicken house beside the barn.

"CeeCee!"

I started awake at the sound of Rusty shouting my name in the hallway, followed by pounding on my bedroom door. "CeeCee! Wake up. Wake up, CeeCee."

Where am I? My eyes blurred as I gazed about the unfamiliar room. Spotting my wristwatch on the night stand, I rubbed my eyes, trying to focus. *What time is it, anyway? Six forty-five?" I'm going to wring that little toad's neck!*

The pounding continued. "CeeCee, Mama sent me to wake you up."

I staggered to the door and opened it. "This had better be important—or you'll be sorry!"

"It is, honest," Rusty hissed. His eyes sparkled with a sense of mystery. "That man's downstairs, wanting to see you."

"Huh? What man? Why are you whispering? You've already awakened the entire county."

Rusty whispered louder and pointed toward the landing. "That man's downstairs—"

"What man?" I yawned and scratched my head.

"That man you met yesterday, the one Mama scolded you about."

My eyes flew open. "Shane Simons? That man?"

Rusty's head bobbed enthusiastically. "Yup! That's the one."

"Oh no!" I whipped about, slamming the door behind me.

Rusty delivered the rest of the message through the closed door. "Mama says to come downstairs right away."

Before I could answer, my brother turned and ran back down the stairs. *What will I wear?* I dashed about the room in a frenzy—brushing my hair, hunting for lost shoes, trying on and discarding three different skirts and their coordinating bodices. Finally I settled on a gored navy gabardine skirt and white cotton sailor blouse.

Catching a glimpse of myself in a mirror—revealing frizzy hair and bloodshot eyes—I groaned and pinched my cheeks for color. At the top of the stairs, I counted to ten, then gracefully descended and made my way to the store, where my mother, Rusty, Aunt Bea, and Shane Simons waited.

"Well, well." Aunt Bea gestured toward me. "Here she is now. CeeCee, you have company this morning."

Shane stood with his eyes downcast, his wide-brimmed black cowboy hat in his hands. Finally, he looked at me with an embarrassed grin.

"Mr. Simons came by to speak with you." My mother smiled graciously. "He has shown an interest in touring Aunt Bea's garden beside the house. Perhaps you will do the honors, CeeCee."

I gulped and nodded.

"Here." Mama slipped her white knit shawl from her shoulders and draped it around mine. "There's a bite in the air. This should keep you warm enough for the short time you will be outside."

"Thank you," I mumbled, understanding her unspoken order.

Shane held the door open for me.

"Thank you," I whispered, and fled outside in the direction of Aunt Bea's garden. By the flush in his face as I passed, I knew Shane felt as uncomfortable as I.

When the door closed behind him, he called, running after me. "Hey, wait up. I came to talk with you, remember?"

I whirled about, the weight of my ankle-length skirt swooshing against my boots. "What are you doing here, anyway? Haven't you caused enough trouble for me for one lifetime?"

"I'm sorry. That's what I'm here to say. I'm sorry."

"Fine. You've said it. Now go." I hugged Mama's shawl tighter about me and turned my back to him.

"My mother gave me what for when I got home last night. I guess we did look a little suspicious, huh?"

My eyebrows shot upward as I turned back toward him. "Your mother scolded you too?"

He nodded.

"Good! You deserved it."

"I? I deserved it?" His face darkened. He shoved his thumbs into his belt and leaned forward.

"Well, it wasn't my fault you decided to throw yourself off the loft after me." I took a step backward.

"When I saw you lose your balance, I simply tried to catch you." He took a step forward.

I gave him a wry smile. "What about the flirting at the well? Are you sorry for that too?"

"Are you?" He inched closer.

"After all the trouble I got into with my mother?"

"Yeah, I know what you mean." He hesitated a moment before confiding, "Did you know that you have the cutest twitch on the right side of your mouth when you get nervous or angry?"

"Twitch? Next you'll be telling me I have a tick in my eye to match. Look, if you have said all you came to say, please leave."

He held my gaze for a moment, then looked down at the ground. "I'm sorry. This isn't going too well." Watching the toe of his boot make irregular circles in the soil, he continued, "My mother spoke with your mother about the possibility of my visiting New York sometime. It gets lonely at college, with no family around. Would you mind if I came to visit?"

"Why should I? I'm sure my parents will enjoy having you stop by."

His frown deepened. "I asked if you would mind—not your parents."

I rolled my eyes. "Of course not. You're of age. Do whatever you like."

"You make it sound like I'm tottering on the edge of the grave."

"I guess it's all in one's perspective." I gave him a saucy smile. "Now, I'm starving. Have you had breakfast yet? You're welcome to join us."

He rolled and unrolled his hat brim. "Thank you for asking. But I gotta get back to the Pagets' place. We're getting ready for spring planting."

He walked me toward the door of the hardware store. Beyond the corner of the building I could see the front bumper of a 1910 Model T Ford. "Is that yours?"

He shook his head and laughed. "It will be a long while before I buy one of those babies, I'm afraid. I have to get my engineering degree first. David, er, Mr. Paget let me borrow it this morning to come over to see you before you left, er, to apologize, that is."

We paused at the store door, where we said our formal goodbyes. I watched until the Model T disappeared over the first hill.

While I expected everyone to question me about Shane's surprise visit, no one did. I sensed that Rusty wanted to, but had been ordered to mind his own business. And Mama, well, she and I had too much to do to get packed and down to the train station before the eastbound roared into town.

A couple hours later, I made one last check of the room to be certain I hadn't left anything of value behind. I slipped "Emily" into my hand valise, grabbed my violin case, and hurried down to the waiting buggy. Walter, Aunt Bea's hired hand, had gone ahead to the station with our trunks. We wouldn't see them again until we connected with Daddy and the *Empress* in Chicago.

When I saw Mrs. Paget and Mrs. Simons waiting for us at the station, I groaned, my face flushing with color. *Oh no, there's no way I can escape talking with them.* They'd driven into town to say goodbye to Mama. Relief flooded through me when they each kissed me and treated me as if nothing had happened.

The biting wind forced us to wait inside the depot. While the women chatted, I wandered around the dusty waiting area. Even with my face pressed close to one of the soot-coated windows, I could see nothing. Moistening one of my handkerchiefs, I scrubbed one small circle of glass and peered out at the platform. A few hardy cowboys stood out there, coat collars turned up, hands jammed in their pockets, hats pressed low over their foreheads for protection.

I straightened and turned to find myself facing Mrs. Simons, Shane's mother. "CeeCee, I wanted to say goodbye to you." I inhaled sharply. Fortunately, she acted as if she didn't notice. "It's been a pleasure meeting you. You're so much like your mother was when she was your age. I thought the world of her, you know—and still do."

I mumbled an uneasy thank-you.

Gently, she continued. "You are a very talented and lovely young woman. I hope I am not being too personal by telling you that God has a purpose for your life."

"Yes, Mrs. Simons, er, I mean, no, Mrs. Simons."

She chuckled and gave me a squeeze. "I expect to hear great things about you. And any time you find yourself near Hays, Kansas, please stop by."

"Thank you, Mrs. Simons." I cast her a tentative smile.

Involuntarily, I sighed in relief when a distant train whistle announced the approach of the eastbound train. By the time we shared kisses all around, the giant locomotive had rolled into the station, with brakes squealing and cinders flying.

Passengers and well-wishers spilled out onto the platform, impatient to get underway. Goodbyes had been said. Promises of keeping in touch had been made. The time had come to leave.

The engineer and crew leapt down onto the platform, and local railway workers scurried in, out, and around the train, performing necessary tasks that would get us to Kansas City and Chicago. One by one the doors to the passenger cars opened, and black porters pulled down the steep steps. By each car's exit, a porter took his position, and redcaps with luggage carts waited to receive suitcases.

We waited to board until the first wave of passengers was on the train. Once inside the assigned car, I settled myself into a window seat. Au Sam chose the window seat across the aisle from me. For the first time since we had arrived in Kansas, I realized I had barely seen her.

I returned my attention to the waving people outside my window. Aunt Bea's broad smile didn't hide the sadness in her eyes. *What a fabulous lady, you are*, I thought. I waved and threw a kiss. She responded as the train began to pull slowly out of the station.

Two days and two nights later, we pulled into the Chicago station. Before our train came to a complete stop, I spotted the company's private railway car on a side railing.

I tapped my mother on the shoulder. "Mama, there it is. There's the *Empress*!" I threw open a window and leaned out as far as possible.

"Hey, lady," a workman beside the track shouted, "get your head back inside before you lose it."

I laughed and jerked back inside, banging my head on the window frame. "Ouch!"

Without glancing up from the valise she'd been packing, Mama said, "Be careful, darling. You could get hurt, you know."

Her remark made me feel like a twelve-year-old—and I didn't like the feeling. As I glowered and rubbed my sore head, I could hear Rusty snickering behind the brim of his hat.

I watched impatiently as we passed hundreds of freight cars from dozens of places. There were flatcars, open boxcars, cattle cars, and cars with ramps for transporting automobiles, as well as tank cars and coal cars—all waiting for their next assignment.

While Rusty and I gathered our belongings and prepared to disembark, Mama peered out the window, searching the platform for Daddy. The high color in her face and the sparkle in her eyes made her look more like an excited schoolgirl than a matron of thirty-seven.

Before the conductor lowered the steps to allow the passengers to disembark, my mother had maneuvered her way to the front of the line. I hid my smile from two irate businessmen who'd raced her to that coveted position and lost. *You poor men don't stand a chance against Mama when she sets her mind on something.*

Daddy was there to meet us and take us to the hotel, but not before I checked on Meeker. Meeker loved having free reign of the *Empress*. She'd made friends with the cook, which afforded her all kinds of scraps about which most cats can only dream.

Two days of sightseeing in Chicago while Daddy completed his business, two days traveling to Pennsylvania, the weekend in Shinglehouse with Granddaddy Spencer and numerous aunts, uncles, and cousins—then, we were finally within sight of New York City, the end of our journey.

I pressed my face to the window to watch as we passed row after row of tenement houses, linked by lines of flapping laundry. We passed store windows coated with soot; street vendors hawking their wares; carriages, automobiles, and horse-drawn wagons jostling one another for space on the narrow cobblestone streets.

Suddenly the *Empress* plunged into blackness, only to emerge seconds later in the train yard at Grand Central Station. With the *Empress* being the last car, we never needed to fight the crowds for a redcap; one was always waiting to manage our luggage. Seconds after our train eased to a stop, a black Packard Prestige rolled up beside the private railway car, followed by two Model T taxis. Rusty and I stared out the window as the uniformed driver of the Packard got out and opened the rear doors. A tall, slim woman, wearing furs, pearls, and cashmere, stepped out of the automobile followed by a gentleman dressed in a custom-tailored Harris tweed overcoat and matching hat.

"There they are, Daddy, Mama. There's Aunt Drucilla and Uncle Ian." Rusty bounced up and down on the velvet settee.

Where's Ashley? Why didn't Ashley come to the station? Disappointed, I slumped in the seat and folded my arms across my chest. All I'd thought about for weeks was the fun my cousin and I would have in New York City. *And now, she's not even here to greet me.*

The *Empress* staff, including the butler, the chef, the waiter, and the chambermaid, lined up at the door to say goodbye and wish us well. I suspect the tips for services rendered that my father had distributed in white business envelopes probably had more to do with their amiability than regret at seeing us leave.

Outside on the platform a porter dropped the steel stool in

place in front of the steep metal steps leading from our railway car, and a redcap was already rolling the first of our trunks to the waiting taxis.

Our butler performed one last service by opening the main door for us to disembark. Daddy exited first and helped Mama onto the platform; then the porter assisted Au Sam, Rusty, and me.

"Look at you." Aunt Drucilla hugged and kissed me. "You've grown into a beautiful young lady."

"Where's Ashley?" I asked.

"Ashley wanted to be here to welcome you, but she's still in school. What with her graduating in a few weeks, I thought it unwise for her to skip classes. She'll be at the house by the time we get there, though." Aunt Drucilla turned toward my mother. "The traffic is getting horrendous in this city. And it's always worse at this time of day, when everyone's getting off work. But tell me, how was your trip east? And how is dear Aunt Bea?"

From the moment Uncle Ian's Packard stopped in front of his brownstone town house and Ashley burst through the front doors, followed by Grandma and Grandpa McCall, she and I never stopped talking, except when compelled to by etiquette. During dinner, we endured listening to Drucilla tell the latest and not-so-late family gossip, to Grandma ranting about the increased threat the suffragette movement had on the government and the sanctity of marriage, to Uncle Ian and Daddy exchanging theories on the war in Europe. Finally, dessert was finished, and Aunt Drucilla suggested that the gentlemen retire to the study while the ladies join her in the sitting room.

"May we be excused, Mummie?" Ashley asked. "CeeCee here has had a long day. I'm sure she's exhausted."

Drucilla laughed. "Go ahead. You're excused. Don't stay awake all night, you hear?"

Before we could escape, Grandma McCall caught my arm, but directed her words toward my mother.

"I promised Ashley I'd take her and CeeCee shopping in Boston. The girls can ride up tomorrow with James E. and me. CeeCee could stay with us until you picked her up later when you come to open up the cottage."

Aunt Drucilla objected. "Ashley shouldn't miss school right now, Mother McCall."

"It's only for a couple days, Dru. You can all come up for the weekend. That way, you can bring Ashley home in time for school on Monday. Do let me spoil my girls a little."

Mama glanced over at Drucilla, then at Daddy. "As if CeeCee hasn't been spoiled enough since leaving home—as if we all haven't."

Ashley fell to her knees beside her mother's chair. "Oh, please, Mummie, please, please?"

Aunt Drucilla clicked her tongue. "I suppose it won't hurt if Ashley misses a couple days of school—if you let CeeCee go, that is."

Daddy's eyebrows narrowed in thought. "We would get to spend more time with Jamie before going up to the Cape."

Ah, I thought, *that should do it.*

My mother paused, eyeing Grandma McCall. "Julia, do you know what you are getting yourself into? Remember what happened last time the two of them went shopping together? I thought the manager would have apoplexy right there in the store when the girls sent that mannequin sprawling on the floor."

"Mama," I wailed, "that was years ago. We were only kids then."

"Yes." Mama eyed me knowingly. The memory of Shane brought a blush to my cheeks. "I know."

Knowing she'd won, my grandmother patted my hand. "Give Grandma a kiss, sweetheart. We are going to have a delightful time spending your grandpa's money." Grandpa McCall grunted while everyone else laughed.

After kissing each adult good night, Ashley and I dashed upstairs to her bedroom, after making a short detour into the kitchen for a handful of peanut-butter cookies and two mugs of hot chocolate.

When we reached Ashley's room, we found the bedding on her massive canopy bed turned down. She breezed into the room before me, turning on lamps as she went. "Make yourself comfortable."

I stood in the center of Ashley's room and gaped. At my feet, a

Persian rug done in blues, golds, and reds covered much of the pecan parquet floor. Royal blue velvet draperies framed the floor-to-ceiling windows covered with white lace panels. All the furniture was matching white-and-gold French Regency.

Ashley flung open the doors of the chifforobe. "I'm going to make myself comfortable. How about you?"

I spotted my trunk and valise next to Ashley's dressing table. Crystal perfume bottles, little jars of creams, and a collection of white porcelain containers covered the dressing table's mirrored top, along with a hand-painted music box. I gently wound the key, setting two porcelain lovers twirling in endless circles to the melody of the "Blue Danube Waltz." As the couple and the music slowed, Ashley came up behind me. "My father brought that back from Austria for my fifteenth birthday."

"It's beautiful," I whispered.

"Yeah, well." She sat down on the cushioned dressing-table seat and removed the pins from her hair. Her golden locks cascaded down around her shoulders. "I'm so sick of this hair. I can't do anything with it."

I wonder how many times I've said that? I smiled to myself as I unlocked my trunk and found my cambric nightdress and matching robe. "So, tell me all about that fabulous boyfriend of yours."

Ashley giggled. "Which one?"

"Which one? How many do you have?"

She shrugged, drawing her silver-backed hairbrush through her cornsilk curls. "It's according to where I am at the time. In Boston, there's Millard, a Harvard man, of course. At the Cape, it's Chipper and Rolph—they're best friends."

I thought of telling her about Shane, but reconsidered. *What could I say? That he threatened to douse me under the pump?* I removed the hairpins from the roll at the back of my neck and shook my hair free.

Ashley giggled and nibbled on her fingernail. "And, here in New York, it's Durwood and his delicious Pierce-Arrow. Next year, at college, who knows?" I bent down, dragging my tangled curls over my shoulder, and began brushing while my cousin prattled on about the men in her life. "Wellesley may be an all-girl school, but there are always weekends."

"Don't you get them mixed up sometimes? Aren't you afraid they'll find out about one another?"

"So what if they do?" My cousin whirled about and arched her eyebrow knowingly. "Oh, CeeCee, you naive darling. I adore Millard and his muscles, Chipper and his sense of humor, Rolph and, oh, I don't know." She pointed at me in the mirror and giggled. "Don't be too horrified, cousin dear. It's all in fun, you know. Oh, I forgot to show you my dress for the cotillion ball in May."

"Do the boys know it's a game with you?" I straightened and tossed my hair back over my shoulder.

She bounced to the chifforobe and withdrew a sleeveless gown of pale blue lace over matching silk. "Oh, pooh! Don't be such a party pooper."

I gasped, in spite of my irritation with her. Pearls and sequins outlined the pattern in the Austrian lace bodice that dipped down to her hips, where layers of silk chiffon swirled about her legs in varying lengths. "Isn't it a dream? Grandma promised that I can borrow the diamond tiara she wore for her debutante ball."

"It-it's beautiful."

"I'm glad you like it." She bobbed her head back and forth and giggled, then returned it to the chifforobe. "Mummie hopes to talk Aunt Chloe into letting you come out with me."

I chuckled to myself and leapt into the middle of the bed. "Somehow I doubt she'll succeed. My folks aren't too keen on such things, you know."

"Oh, pooh! You'd be such a hit with the fellas, what with all that luscious red hair. Together, we'd give them a case of the vapors." Closing the chifforobe doors, Ashley pursed her lips into a little-girl pout. "Forgive me, but your parents can be so stodgy sometimes. Even Boston bluebloods kick up their heels every now and then." She laughed and pirouetted across the room. "My knight in shining armor will see me descend the grand staircase and sweep me into his arms. And we will waltz the night away on the balcony, under a hundred million glittering stars." Whirling past me, she slammed into one of the canopy posts and staggered backward.

I burst into laughter. "And waltz right off the balcony into the sculptured boxwood bushes. Quite the midsummer night's dream."

Ashley laughed and pounced onto the bed. "Oh, CeeCee, where is your sense of romance?"

We laughed and talked until the first rays of sun burst over the East River.

Ostrich Feathers and Saffron Silk

The shiny black Packard eased between the gray stone lions guarding Grandma and Grandpa McCall's "modest estate," as my grandmother described the massive stone house. I drew back the Belgian-lace curtain in the guest room I'd been given.

My mother had inherited the seventeen-room cottage on Cape Cod from my father James, Grandma and Grandpa McCall's younger son, who had been killed in a mining accident when I was a baby. My parents had agreed to let me stay with my grandparents while they, Rusty, and Au Sam went to open up the place. I was tired of living out of a steamer trunk and had to admit that it would be nice to feel at home again, even if the arrangement was only for the summer.

Grandmother's chauffeur stepped out of the vehicle and polished the hood ornament with his sleeve before coming up the front steps to the double front doors.

I turned to examine my simple cream-colored chemise in the brass mirror. *At least the hem isn't edged with Mary Pickford ruffles. The last thing I want is to imitate America's film sweetheart—ruffles, ringlets, and all!*

I placed the white felt hat with the gray and yellow taffeta ribbons on my head. *Hmm—* I tipped the hat to one side and smiled at my reflection. Having styled my hair in waves around my face, then fastened the bulk of it in a roll at the back of my neck gave the illusion of having bobbed hair. I threw myself a provocative kiss. *Hardly a child anymore, Miss Chamberlain.*

Grandma's voice came from the foot of the stairs. "CeeCee,

Ashley, the car is here." I slipped into my matching wool cutaway jacket and buttoned the large bone button at the waist, then pulled on my white kid gloves. Grabbing my matching purse, I bustled from the room. At the top of the stairs, I paused, then descended with the grace of a European princess.

Out of breath, Ashley caught up with me on the third step. A blond ringlet popped out from under her misty blue felt hat. Her cobalt blue eyes flashed with irritation. "Oh, fiddlesticks!" She tucked the errant curl back under the edge of her hat. "How do you get your hair to remain in place? You have much more than I."

I leaned toward her and whispered behind my gloved hand. "I am wearing so many hairpins that I am sure to weigh an extra ten pounds."

Grandma stood at the foot of the stairs, her foot tapping out a message of impatience. Wrapped in a yellow wool plaid coat, she held one of the lapels in her hand and gazed down at her silver lapel watch. "We did agree to go shopping sometime today, did we not?"

"Oh, Grandmama, you are such a dear." Ashley skipped down the rest of the steps and kissed our grandmother on the cheek. "We have been so naughty to keep you waiting."

Forgetting my dignity and my two-inch heeled, criss-crossed strap slippers, I ran to join them at the foot of the stairs.

Ashley didn't wait for Lawrence, the McCall family butler, to open the door; she threw it open herself and rushed out onto the front portico. Her misty blue wool coat blew in the brisk springtime breeze. "Isn't this a fabulously marvelous, incredibly exciting day?"

"You've been reading the dictionary again, haven't you?" I teased. Everyone teased Ashley about her flighty behavior, but she didn't seem to care. "Oh, CeeCee, you're so funny! Reading the dictionary? Grandmama, isn't she a wit?"

Grandma tightened her lips and shook her head. "Ashley McCall, you are a silly goose."

Ashley laughed and skipped down the steps toward the waiting car. A strong breeze swept up the steps, cutting straight through my lightweight jacket. I shivered and wrapped my arms around my body. "I guess I'm still accustomed to California weather."

Grandma called to my cousin, "Ashley, is your yellow wool coat still in the upstairs closet?"

Ashley turned and frowned. Grandma prompted her memory. "You left it here after the midwinter luncheon at the club, remember? Would you mind if CeeCee wore it today? Her jacket will never do."

"No, I don't mind. Help yourself." Ashley climbed into the car.

I lifted a hand to protest. "I'll be all right, Grandma. I really don't look good in yellow."

"Get in the car, CeeCee; you'll catch your death out here." She rushed into the house and returned immediately with a wraparound yellow wool coat. She handed it to me and climbed in beside me. I cringed. *It's so, so yellow!* Folding it on my lap, I mumbled a thank-you. By the thrust of my grandmother's jaw, I knew, yellow or not, I would be wearing the borrowed coat, so I settled back against the plump leather seat. *Fortunately, it complements the ribbons on my hat.*

Within minutes, we arrived at the downtown shopping area. Grandma gave Fredrick instructions while Ashley and I climbed out onto the sidewalk, eager to begin our day of shopping with Grandma McCall.

In letters Ashley had warned me about Grandma McCall's shopping excursions. But no words could do justice to my grandmother's indefatigable energy. Shoes, dresses, hats, belts, hosiery—shop after shop after shop, we worked our way down one busy street and up another. I did appreciate not having to carry any packages, since she arranged with the shopkeepers to have the purchases delivered to the estate. S. S. Pierce, J. T. Sterns, and every other shopkeeper and clerk in the shops surrounding the Boston Common catered to their favorite customer. She knew them all by name.

After two hours of shopping, my adorable leather pumps seemed only half as adorable as they'd been when we left the estate. I glanced over at Ashley. The excitement in her eyes had long since faded. Her shoulders drooped, and stray blond curls bounced like springs from under the brim of her hat. I knew that

I probably didn't look any better. On the other hand, every hair, every feather, every tie, pleat, and button on Grandma remained stoically in place.

"Doesn't she ever get tired?" I hissed as I dropped onto a Chippendale settee in what must have been the eighth shoe store in a row that we'd visited. *How do you tell your grandmother that enough is enough, even when you and your cousin are the objects of her generosity?*

Ashley slumped down beside me. "Grandma McCall? Shopping invigorates her. My mother says she has more energy when she gets home from shopping than when she left."

"This morning, before my folks left for the Cape, my mother warned me not to tire poor Grandma today." I groaned and closed my eyes. "If only she knew!"

A tap on my shoulder awakened me with a start. Grandma stood behind us, adjusting her gloves. "Come on, ladies. Time's a wasting."

Reluctantly, Ashley and I rose to our feet and followed her out of the door. Outside, a cold wind swept across the Common, shaking the budding trees and nodding the jonquils that lined the sidewalks. Elderly men with gold-tipped canes touched the brims of their hats as they passed. At the edge of the park, two women in heavy coats sat feeding the scores of pigeons fluttering about their feet.

I turned to my grandmother. "Remember the time you and Grandpa brought me here to ride the swans?"

"You still remember that?"

"Oh yes," I assured her. "I remember the red-and-white scalloped awnings over the shops, the sidewalk cafe where Grandpa bought me an Italian ice, the tour of the State House. Oh yes, I remember every detail, even when Grandpa crashed the swan boat into the dock and the attendant scolded him."

"Grandpa? Someone scolded Grandpa?" Ashley asked incredulously. Grandma and I nodded and laughed. Ringing church bells broke through our reverie.

Grandma stopped abruptly and looked at her lapel watch. "Noon. Are you girls getting hungry?" Our heads bobbed at the mention of food.

"Me too." Grandma chuckled. "I know a little tearoom down past Faneuil Hall. You'll adore their pecan tea cakes and scones."

"Oh, that would be nice," Ashley and I answered simultaneously.

With renewed vigor, Grandma marched down the cobblestone street. "I instructed Fredrick to meet us there at one. From there, he'll take us to Cambridge, where you'll see the quaintest little boutiques. These shop girls are so talented with—"

Ashley and I stumbled after her, our bodies too exhausted to deal with any thought beyond keeping up with Grandma. We'd gone only a couple of blocks before I noticed the large number of women heading in the same direction. As they passed us, they waved and smiled.

How odd. I glanced down at the coat Grandma insisted I wear, then back at the hurrying women. *They're all wearing yellow.*

When we rounded the corner of the square in front of Faneuil Hall, we stared in amazement. I'd never seen so many people assembled in one place before, most of them women, and most wearing yellow. Many carried placards with sayings like STOP OPPRESSING ONE HALF OF HUMANITY—GIVE US THE RIGHT TO VOTE; WOMEN UNITED FOR EQUAL RIGHTS; and WE LOSE OUR SONS TO A WAR FOR WHICH WE CANNOT VOTE.

"Grandma," Ashley called, bumping into Grandma, who'd stopped without warning, "didn't you say the teahouse was on the other side of the square?"

"Unfortunately, yes!" Grandma clicked her tongue in disgust.

"What is going on?" I'd never seen anything like this before. Of course, I'd heard about the suffragette demonstrations in San Francisco and other major cities across the country. Once I had tried to talk my mother into attending. She had merely laughed and said that she already had a cause at the clinic and didn't need another.

Grandma's agitation was evident from her rail-rigid spine to the tight wrinkles around her pencil-thin lips. "Should be home, tending to the needs of their husbands instead of out stirring up trouble."

I looked at her, then at the mass of demonstrating females.

"Maybe we should find another place to eat."

She shot me a look of disdain. "Nonsense! I will not allow a few malcontents to thwart my dining arrangements!" Without warning, she plowed into the crowd. I stared as Ashley pushed her way past a motley group of curious businessmen and store clerks, standing on the outer fringe. Ashley grabbed Grandma's hand. "Come on, CeeCee."

Fear more than courage forced me into the shouting melee. No matter how hard I tried, I always seemed to be one body from grabbing Grandma's free hand. We wove our way through a throng of newspaper reporters, then into the crowd of milling women.

Grandmother was sputtering her fury at the inconvenience she was being forced to endure when a news photographer snapped her picture. "How dare you!" she shouted. "I am not one of these malcontented females!" I laughed at the look of astonishment on the photographer's face as Grandma delivered her barrage. "I would never consider attending one of these barbarous meetings! And you can print that!"

Ashley pressed on, dragging Grandma behind. Instead of angling toward the other side of the square, Ashley pressed toward the speakers' stand at the front door to Faneuil Hall. I tried to warn her, to suggest she angle more to her right, but she couldn't hear me. As we drew close to the front of the crowd, I overheard the women talking about the guest speaker.

"Mrs. Eastman has been in and out of prison more often than most felons," one woman confided to another. "What courage it must take to stand up against such persecution."

I'd heard of Crystal Eastman, one of the acknowledged national leaders of the National American Woman Suffrage Association. Recently she had attended huge rallies in Chicago, Washington, D.C., and New York.

I was surprised to see several men scattered throughout the crowd. Some held placards for the cause. Some, obviously uncomfortable, were there through their wives' arm twisting. And some stayed from what looked to be pure curiosity.

I thought of my father, probably more adamantly in favor of women's right to vote than Mama. At the dinner table at Aunt

Drucilla's house, Grandma and Aunt Drucilla had been decrying the suffragette movement.

Aunt Drucilla had waved her hand. "I don't understand why they want to vote so badly. What is the use? It seems foolish to me.

"Take the war issue. Women believe they should have a say on whether or not to send their sons to war."

"Well, personally," Grandma McCall looked down her nose at my mother, "I believe we already have a say through our husbands. Why, James E. wouldn't consider voting differently from what we discussed, would you, dear?"

"Of course not, darling." Grandpa gulped down a swig of water.

Cy leaned back in his chair. "Well, if women want the right to vote, they should have it. Immediately after the Civil War, we allowed Negro males who'd spent their entire lives in slavery to vote. And, what about the masses of illiterate immigrants arriving from countries ruled by dictators and demigods? They know little about democracy and even less about our Constitution, yet we grant them the vote."

"Yes, well—" Grandpa McCall admitted thoughtfully, "—it certainly is food for thought, isn't it? So what do you think about those Red Sox, Cyrus?" I smiled to myself at how smoothly Grandpa switched the topic of conversation.

By the time I grabbed Grandma's free hand, we were standing in the front row. Mrs. Eastman, dressed in an outfit that emphasized her wasp-waisted figure, stood in front of Faneuil Hall's main doors, before a grouping of megaphones. She gazed out over the sea of faces before her. Catching my eye, she smiled, which crinkled her freckled nose.

The tall, graceful woman looked very pleased with the turnout. "Ladies," she began. Immediately, her supporters gave her their attention. "Some of you ask, with our country on the verge of war, why continue the fight for voting rights? Isn't this the time to rally behind our men as we send them off to war?" She pointed at the red-brick building behind her. "We rally, today, in the awesome presence of history, where our grandfathers rallied to fight the great injustice of slavery poxing this great country of ours. We assemble today, where our great-grandfathers assembled to oppose England's attempt to overthrow our infant nation. We stand united on the spot where our great-great-grandfathers voted to boycott the use of English tea. They cried, 'Taxation without representation is tyranny!'"

A cry of support rose from the crowd.

"American women pay taxes, yet—as our forefathers were—are denied the right to vote. Hear the cry, today, from these stones on which you stand, 'Taxation without representation is tyranny!'"

Grandma McCall craned her neck toward me. "CeeCee, we must get out of here right away."

"Shh!" the women around her hissed.

Grandma tugged on Ashley's hand, but my cousin stood spellbound, listening to the speaker.

"Today, we, too, are soldiers at war, not in a war as bloody as the Revolution, but every bit as noble; not in a conflict of brother against brother, but one in which one-half of America's people are being oppressed. And like those soldiers of history, we are prepared to fight the battle until it is won."

The enthusiastic crowd cheered and surged closer, separating Ashley from Grandma.

"Ashley, come with us." My grandmother reached through the wall of people but failed to reach Ashley.

A man standing behind me cried, "Are you ready to dump tea in the harbor?"

The speaker smiled. "If necessary."

Cheers and applause erupted from the women.

Grandma turned around and tried to force her way back to my side, but the cheering women refused to give an inch. When the noise subsided, the speaker proceeded. "Since a year ago January's setback in the House of Representatives, much has happened. At that time, our adversaries celebrated our defeat with champagne and caviar. They thought that would be the end of us. They thought that they had disposed of us, and we would quietly return to our knitting. Well, looking out over your two thousand dedicated faces, I can tell you, ladies, they were wrong!"

This time, I cheered along with the two thousand voices around me.

Grandma McCall turned and snapped, "Chloe Celeste!"

The speaker continued. "Last year we had an election year. Many of those celebrated congressmen who voted against women's suffrage, who thought that by voting against women's rights, they could protect their jobs, found out they were wrong."

Again the audience cheered.

"We discovered how every representative from every state in the union voted. And at rallies like this one in cities across this great country, the wives of businessmen and the wives of farmers, the daughters of industrialists and the daughters of dray men, the sisters of merchants and the sisters of public officials, the mothers of store clerks and the mothers of bankers, marshaled their forces.

"While we could not vote, we made sure that our husbands, fathers, brothers, and sons could, and did. Our men voted many of those scoundrels out of office."

At the top of her voice, Mrs. Eastman shouted her closing words over the throng's thunderous applause.

"Since then, New York's lawmakers passed the right for women to vote on state's issues. Why not Massachusetts? Why not the nation?"

A sudden shrill of police whistles reverberated through the square. Women screamed as a large contingent of uniformed policemen charged through the crowd of demonstrators.

Frantic to escape, Grandma scanned the crowd for Ashley. "Ashley! Ashley!" she shouted.

A large woman, wearing what looked to be a squashed felt muskmelon on her head, grabbed my free hand and pulled me forward. "Come on! We must show support."

Frightened, I held onto Grandma's hand with all my strength, dragging her behind me to the circle of women's movement officers gathered around the speaker. All the while, Grandma continued to helplessly grasp at the air in the direction she'd last spotted my cousin.

When Grandma realized we were standing directly behind the suffragette speaker, panic flooded her face. She tugged on my hand. "CeeCee, come on. We've got to get out of here—fast!" I felt like a rag doll being stretched between two puppies, with my grandmother yanking me away from the speaker's lectern and the stranger holding me fast. At this point, the terrified demonstrators and angry policemen would never allow us to escape. "We're trapped, Grandma. We're trapped!" I shouted, but she couldn't hear me above the pandemonium.

Like Moses parting the Red Sea, the policemen, with billy clubs drawn, charged though the panicked crowd. Determined women, committed to the cause, closed ranks on each side of me and behind me, severing my hold on Grandma's wrist.

"Grandma!" Alarmed, I thrust my arm into the air and shouted, "Grandma! Grandma, don't leave me!" Strangers occupied the spot where she'd been standing. Even standing on my tiptoes, I couldn't see her anywhere. I searched the area for my cousin also, but to no avail.

The brass door handles of Faneuil Hall jabbed into my spine while hoards of women pressed in front of and beside me.

My breath came in short, frightened gasps. *I must get out of here. I can't breathe! I think I'm going to scream!* Feeling like a hare caught in a trap, I shoved the women in front of me, screaming, "Let me out of here. I've got to get out of here!"

When they failed to respond, a new burst of adrenaline surged through me, enabling me to yank my wrist free of my captor. Lowering my shoulder the way I'd seen Jamie do while playing football, I butted between two women and came face to face with a blue-uniformed policeman.

"Stay where you are, ma'am, and you won't get hurt," the young, clean-shaven policeman instructed. I craned my neck in all directions, only to find myself almost encircled by a wall of blue. The policemen, with nightsticks extended, moved in behind the speaker, surrounding us completely. My heart leapt to my throat. *Oh no. I'm going to jail. I can't believe this is happening to me. What will Daddy and Mama say?*

News reporters with pencils in hand formed a ring around the policemen. Camera flashes popped in our faces. I shaded my eyes.

"Who's in charge here?" the blustering officer heading the troop shouted as he tapped his nightstick threateningly in the palm of his left hand.

The main speaker batted her eyelashes. "Officer, since we poor women are too ignorant to vote," she simpered, "I don't think we ever got around to electing someone to be in charge." The women gathered about her snickered. I did too.

"You," the officer said, looking at the speaker. "Haven't we had trouble with you before? You're Mrs. Eastman, aren't you? Your husband is—"

"Yes, I am." The woman's hazel eyes deepened in color.

"You're going to have to come to the police station, Mrs. Eastman." He glanced at those of us cordoned in by his unit. "You're all under arrest."

The woman who'd gotten me into this mess shouted, "There are over two thousand women here. Do you plan to put us all in jail?"

The police officer shook his head. "No, the rest of the ladies can go home to their families. My orders are to arrest only those actively involved in the demonstration."

An expensively dressed woman wearing a hat with a wide, floppy brim topped with ostrich feathers and lace inched closer to the officer. The tip of an ostrich feather touched the end of the man's nose with each word the woman spoke. "But, sir, we were all active. Didn't you hear us shouting and applauding?"

He blew the feather aside before he answered. "Ma'am, you know what I mean—those of you standing up here on the steps in front of the crowd." Before he finished his response, the fine tendrils of the ostrich feather again brushed the end of his nose. He batted it away with his free hand, then stayed a sneeze with the side of his hand. The policemen on each side of him battled the urge to grin at their captain's discomfort.

"Let me see if I have this straight." The woman bobbed her head around playfully in front of the distressed policeman. "Then we are being arrested because we are standing on this step?" She lowered her head, causing the feather to flutter across his mouth and eyes. The man inhaled sharply, then sneezed. Then the woman handed him a monogrammed handkerchief. "God bless you, sir. You should take care. Sniffles can be dangerous."

After wiping his nose, he tried to hand the handkerchief back to her. "No, no, no. You keep it. You may need it again." She inched closer again. "Now, sir, help me understand what it is I and these other women have done wrong. About this step, suppose my sisters and I moved down to the sidewalk level?"

"Are you trying to make a mockery of the laws of our country?" the officer demanded, still fighting a losing battle with the persistent feather.

The woman grasped the cascade of ruffles at the throat of her bodice. "Oh, my dear captain, I would not consider making a mockery of the laws of our country. That's why I am asking you, upon what grounds are we being arrested?"

"I am arresting you for violating a city ordinance that prohibits an unlawful gathering." Trying to resume his dignity, the man tapped the nightstick against the palm of his other hand.

"Just a minute," Mrs. Eastman protested. "While the Constitution of the United States does not give us ladies the right to vote, it does give us the right to assemble peacefully. And that's what we're doing here today—assembling peacefully."

A look of mock horror swept across her face. She held her pose while newspaper photographers took advantage of the opportunity. When the last shutter clicked, she continued. "Are you trying to tell me that the officials of Boston have abrogated that right?"

The policeman's lips hardened into a thin line as he struggled to keep himself under control. "No, ma'am. But you are not assembling peacefully; you are inciting to riot. Now, if you ladies would come along with me, please."

I couldn't believe it. I, Chloe Celeste Chamberlain, was on my way to jail. However, before we took a step, Mrs. Eastman snapped, "No!" She arched one eyebrow and pursed her lips. "We would prefer not to do that."

"Ma'am, please don't make any unnecessary problems for yourself," the officer warned. "One way or another, you ladies are going to jail."

A woman on the far side of the speaker called out, "And how are you going to do that, sir? Beat us into submission?"

Horrified, I stared down at the nightstick in the hand of the policeman directly in front of me. My fear must have registered in my eyes, for the man shifted nervously.

The captain reattached the nightstick to his belt and nodded to his men to follow his example. "No, ma'am," he replied, folding his arms across his chest. "At least, I hope not."

A reporter shouted from behind the police line, "Are you saying that you would use force if necessary?"

Without turning in the direction of the inquiring reporter, the officer pleaded, "Please don't give us any trouble. I don't want to beat on a bunch of women." He swallowed hard. "But, ladies, I have my orders. I must take you down to the station."

Mrs. Eastman held out her arms toward the policeman. "Very well, cuff me and take me to jail."

The rest of the women followed her lead. I found myself lifting my hands as well.

"No, no, we don't need any handcuffs," the policeman assured her.

"Oh yes, you will," Mrs. Eastman insisted, her hands still extended and a triumphant smile forming at the corners of her mouth. "Cuff us, or you're going to have to beat us into submission."

"Mrs. Eastman, please. You know what it will look like if we men take you down to the city court in handcuffs," the captain complained.

"No, tell me. How will it look?" the speaker replied sweetly.

The news reporters pressed closer as the other policemen shifted restlessly. "What'll we do, Captain?" the policeman next to the captain asked.

The officer sighed in exasperation. "Cuff them."

Camera flashes exploded on all sides of us before the embarrassed policemen could push the photographers away.

The policeman standing in front of me clamped a set of handcuffs onto my wrists. "Sorry, ma'am. I hate doing this."

Around me, the other policemen were doing the same. Wide-eyed and frightened, I looked pleadingly into his eyes. "I only wanted to go shopping with my grandmother and my cousin, sir."

"I'm sorry. I have my orders." He shook his head slowly and grasped hold of my arm.

I looked into his face. "Please, be careful. I play the violin." The policeman averted his eyes.

With Mrs. Eastman leading the parade, the policemen escorted us through a line of reporters and photographers to the three waiting police wagons.

"Sing, ladies, sing!" the speaker urged as she climbed into the first wagon. The women closest to her joined in singing. Like a stone tossed into a tranquil pond, the song rippled out, until the square reverberated with "It's a Long Way to Tipperary." I learned later that this was the suffragette movement's rallying song.

The first paddy wagon filled before I reached the curb. I caught a glimpse of my grandmother, furiously jawing at the policeman who had her manacled. Momentarily forgetting my shackles, I tried to wave so she would see me before the policeman helped her into the second wagon.

The officer arresting me placed his hands about my waist and lifted me gently into the third wagon. Still unable to believe what was happening to me, I looked back at him to thank him. He returned a helpless shrug.

I found a seat on one of the two wooden benches lining the enclosed wagon. As others joined us, we were pressed closer and closer together. Again, the sensation of terror swept through me. *I'm going to faint! I can't breathe. I know I'm going to die!* While the women around me sang and cheered, I fought against the urge to claw my way free of the confining wagon.

Booked, Beleaguered, and Bailed Out

Swarms of people had surrounded the red-brick city courthouse by the time the police wagons arrived. Inside the building, the bedlam continued. Photographers and reporters covering the demonstration raced ahead of the policemen and prisoners to witness the booking process.

A policeman guided me to a battered wooden desk, where a uniformed officer sat with his feet propped up on the desktop, reading a crime magazine. "Here's one for you, O'Malley."

The man called O'Malley looked up from behind his magazine. "What's wrong with your writing hand, Conklin? This little lassie overpower you?" I had to concentrate to understand his heavy Irish brogue.

"Hey, I'm giving you the purtiest of the lot, youngest too. Besides, I brought in two others that need processing before Judge Myers arrives." Without looking my way, the officer gestured toward a wooden chair beside the desk. "Sit."

I obeyed immediately. I'd never been so terrified in my life. Even without looking in a mirror, I knew my face was pale.

The arresting officer eyed me suspiciously. "Are you going to faint on me, lady?" He placed a hand on my shoulder. Instinctively, I jerked away.

"Can I get you a glass of water or something?"

I bit my lower lip and shook my head.

The man straightened. "Sergeant O'Malley will take your statement, Miss Chamberlain."

Sergeant O'Malley sat up in his chair, yanked open the middle desk drawer, and removed a sheet of paper. "How did a winsome lass like you get mixed up with these daughters of a horseleech?"

Thinking he wanted an explanation, I leaned forward in the chair to explain. "Sir, I'm really not mixed up with the suffragettes. My being in that crowd was a terrible mistake. You see, my cousin Ashley, she's a scatterbrain— Maybe I should back up the story a little. My grandmother took Ashley and me shopping—"

The officer growled, "Just give me your name, Miss."

"Chloe Celeste Chamberlain. If you'll let me explain, I know you'll see that—"

"Address."

"Please, you must listen."

He looked up from the form he was filling out. "Don't tell me, young lady. Tell it to the judge. Now, where do you live?"

I squirmed in the straight-back chair. "That's a difficult question to answer right now."

He glared at me. "How difficult can it be to tell me the address of where you live?"

"Well, it's like this. My parents just moved east from San Francisco to New York, but my father hasn't found a house he wants to buy yet, so we're living here in Boston with my Grandmother and Grandfather McCall until the weekend, at least. Then we plan to go down to the cottage on Cape Cod, where we'll spend the summer. Of course, it's not really a cottage. I mean, how can a seventeen-room house be considered a cottage, right? Anyway, we'll stay until Daddy can find us a place in Manhattan—" I spat out my words with Gatling-gun speed, hoping to tell my entire story before his frustrations mounted further. "Oops, I already said that, didn't I?"

With his pen, the officer tapped out his irritation on the desktop. "Just answer my questions, Miss Chamberlain. Is that so difficult?"

"But, sir—" I unsuccessfully choked back a rush of tears. "—that's exactly what I'm trying to do."

"Don't cry! That's an order."

"Yes, sir." I bit my lip as hard as I could and swiped at the tears rolling down my cheeks. I slumped into my chair, wishing I could somehow become invisible, and tried to reply to the rest of his questions with one- or two-word answers. Finally the questions stopped. While he completed the form, I looked around the smoke-filled room, trying to locate my grandmother. Seeing that most of the women had already left the room by this time, I felt a new terror grow inside me. *What if I get thrown into a cell by myself or, worse yet, with a murderer or something? What if I have to face the judge alone? I'll die. I'll simply die! Please hurry, Sergeant O'Malley. Can't you please hurry?*

The officer finally lay down his pen and stood up. "Come, Miss Chamberlain. I'm going to let Judge Myers figure out this mess." He took me by the elbow and led me from the room into a long hallway.

Workers and curious onlookers shouted catcalls and jeers as Sergeant O'Malley escorted me down the narrow corridor. By the time he pushed open the swinging doors to the courtroom, I wasn't sure whether the jeers were directed against O'Malley or me.

All heads in the crowded courtroom turned to watch as the policeman marched me down to the front, taking me to the end of the line of arrested suffragettes.

"Stand still, and don't speak to anyone but the judge," O'Malley whispered, "and then only if he speaks to you."

When the officer stepped back, I leaned forward, hoping to spot my grandmother farther down the line. I felt a tap on the shoulder. O'Malley shook his head and wagged his finger in my face, but not before I counted twenty women all handcuffed and waiting to be arraigned.

The woman next to me whispered, "It's Judge Myers. That's good. I know for a fact that his wife is secretly a suffragette." Her encouragement didn't ease the panic I was trying to choke down. Soon the bailiff announced the arrival of Judge Myers, and the black-robed judge strode into the courtroom.

The judge took his place behind the bench, and the bailiff ordered the audience to be seated. Standing in stiff terror, I jumped when Judge Myers rapped his gavel to declare the court in session.

"Officer, why are these women handcuffed?" the gray-haired judge bellowed.

"Your Honor," the officer in charge answered, "they refused to come with us unless we handcuffed them."

Judge Myers lowered his spectacles and scanned each of our faces. By the time he reached mine, his frown had deepened. His gaze returned to Mrs. Eastman, who stood directly in front of him. "Is that true?"

"Yes, Your Honor. We are desperate criminals, you know. We want the vote." She paused while a teasing smile spread across her face. "How could any crime be more heinous than that?"

The judge released a long, ragged sigh. "Get the cuffs off these ladies at once!"

Two of the policemen started at opposite ends of the line and unlocked the handcuffs. I rubbed my bruised wrists, then dropped my hands to my sides. When I looked up, I found the judge studying our faces once more. His exasperated sigh could be heard throughout the courtroom.

"You know, Mrs. Eastman, and you too, Mrs. Beason, there are hardened felons serving lengthy prison terms who haven't appeared before my bench as often as the two of you. How many times does this make now, Mrs. Beason?"

"Seven, I believe, Your Honor."

"Seven." He shook his head. "And will it be seven more?"

"Seven times seven," the matron replied, "if that's what it takes."

"I assure you, Mrs. Beason, you are wasting your time appearing before me. I don't make the laws; I merely interpret them."

"And we break them," she said brightly, "and will continue to break them, because we consider them unjust."

The judge leaned forward. "Have you ever considered addressing your grievances by legal means?"

The woman thrust her hands dramatically into the air. "What legal means have we, Judge Myers? If we can't vote, we can't elect representatives to pass laws in our favor, nor can we defeat those against us." Mrs. Beason continued, much to the judge's chagrin. "Our only course of action is confrontation. And if that means a jail cell," she shrugged, "so be it."

Judge Myers turned to my grandmother, surprise registering

on his face. "Mrs. McCall, I am surprised to see you involved with this movement."

Grandma McCall stepped forward. "To tell you the truth, Harold, er, Judge, I wasn't involved until I witnessed the harassment these women suffer in order to fight for what they believe are their rights! The officials of this city are crude and overzealous. From now on, you will be seeing more of me, Your Honor, unless things change around here."

A cheer went up from the other women and from the audience. The shock on the judge's face mirrored mine. "Order! Order in this court. I will have order, or I'll hold every last person in contempt. And you, Mrs. McCall, will be the first charged!" The judge rapped the block with his gavel.

This is Grandma McCall? My grandmother? The woman who, only last night at the dinner table, said women should stick to their knitting and leave politics to the men?

Judge Myers worked the muscle in the side of his jaw for several seconds. "Ladies, if I release you on your own recognizance, will each of you promise not to do this again?"

I nodded and started to raise my hand when the woman next to me tugged at my sleeve. She gestured toward Mrs. Beason.

The matronly woman smiled up at the judge. "You know we can't make such a promise."

"I didn't think you would," the judge muttered. He picked up his gavel and slammed it down on a small block of polished wood. "Bail is set at two hundred fifty dollars apiece."

Mrs. Beason cleared her throat. "Sir, we have no money with us. We'll have to wait for someone to post our bail."

"Yes, I thought as much. Posting bail doesn't provide the newspapers with as much drama, does it?" He glowered over the rims of his glasses. "OK, ladies, most of you have been here before, so you know what to expect. Bailiff, take them to the holding cell."

The bailiff stepped up to the bench. "Yes, Your Honor." Turning to face us, he gestured toward the door at the side of the courtroom. "Ladies, please come with me."

"We know the way." Mrs. Beason marched to the door, which opened into the hall leading to the holding cells. Single file, heads held high, we marched into the glare of the news photographers' magnesium-powder pans exploding in our faces like lightning bolts. Clerks, policemen, and reporters jostled one another, each hoping to get a better view.

Down six steps and around the corner to the iron gate guarding the women's holding area. The women's matron, a strong, heavy-set woman met us at the entrance. The hard lines of her face softened into a smile when she saw Mrs. Beason.

"Well, hello, Maude," she greeted. "I heard you'd be staying with me for a bit. It's good to see you again. You too, Mrs. Eastman."

"Hello, Belinda," Mrs. Beason replied. "How is your daughter, Irene, getting along? Has she had that grandbaby yet?"

The prison matron hauled out a large ring of keys and inserted one into the metal lock. "Not for another month. But she's feeling fine, just fine, ma'am, thank you. How many came out for today's rally?"

"Oh, I'd say more than two thousand, wouldn't you, ladies?" Mrs. Beason answered, glancing at her colleagues for confirmation.

"Easily. Perhaps more," Mrs. Eastman agreed.

Belinda swung open the metal door. "I wish I could have been there. Keep up the good work." We filed into a brickwalled cell already inhabited by seven other women. I'd never before seen such hard and sullen faces as those of the women incarcerated with us. I rushed to my grandmother, who wrapped her arms around me and whispered, "I'm so sorry, CeeCee, for getting you into this mess. Whatever will your parents say when they find out?"

I shuddered when the cell door slammed shut. "I'm glad Ashley got away."

Grandma patted my hand. "I do hope she's safe. She can be such a fiddle-faddle sometimes."

"She's smarter than you think." I don't know why I felt compelled to defend her. After all, it was her fault we were in this predicament.

My grandmother pursed her lips. "And with nary a lick of sense!"

Before locking the door, the matron instructed the current occupants to move to the left side of the cell.

Mrs. Beason waved her hand toward the prisoners. "It's all right, Belinda. Stay right where you are. I'm sure there's room for us and our sisters."

"Sisters?" one of the suffragettes hissed.

Sisters? I looked first at the seven prisoners, dressed in drab gray prison uniforms, then at the larger group of privileged women dressed in fine wool suits or designer coats over matching dresses. The prisoners eyed us with envy, curiosity, and ill-concealed hostility. Ignoring the tension, Mrs. Beason walked across the cell and sat down next to one of the surly-looking women. Mrs. Eastman followed.

The suffragette with the floppy hat and droopy ostrich feather hissed as Mrs. Eastman passed. "What are you doing?"

Turning to the wealthy socialite, Mrs. Eastman confided, "I'd like to get acquainted with these women."

"Don't you think that might be dangerous? The diseases they might be carrying—"

A second well-dressed woman asked, "Wouldn't it be wise to stick to our own kind?"

"Our own kind?" Distaste filled Mrs. Eastman's face. "The last I knew, there were but two kinds—females and males. These are females, are they not?"

"Well, yes, I didn't say—"

"Doesn't that make them 'our' kind?"

"You know what I mean," the woman defended.

Mrs. Eastman turned away from her and approached the group of prisoners. "Hello, ladies."

A few of the prisoners snickered while the rest broke into guffaws. Mrs. Eastman sat down in an empty space between two of the prisoners. "Why are you laughing?"

"Ladies? You called us ladies." The woman spoke with a heavy brogue. "I ain't never been called a lady."

"What's a bunch of dolled-up gals like you doin' here, anyway? Slummin'?" a toothless prisoner next to the back wall asked.

Mrs. Beason leaned forward in order to face the questioning woman. "We're suffragettes."

"What in tarnation is a suffragette?"

The prisoner next to her clicked her tongue. "Don't you know nothin', gal? They's those women that goes 'round tryin' to get the men to let 'em vote."

The toothless prisoner squinted at Mrs. Eastman. "Aw, come on, now. Ya got to be funnin' me. Ya get yourself arrested for that?"

"I do." Mrs. Eastman grinned and pointed toward the rest of us, pressed in disgust against the opposite wall. "And so do they—as well as thousands of other women all across the nation."

"Why? Who gives a farthing about voting, n'aways?"

"You've asked a good question." Mrs. Beason frowned. "For one thing, men have the only say in the writing of the laws that govern our lives. We women don't, because we can't vote."

"Huh?" a girl, not much older than I, with dirty, stringy hair said. "I dun' get it."

"It's simple, really." Mrs. Beason raised her hand. "How many of you are in here for prostitution?"

Three prisoners raised their hands—a middle-aged woman with lifeless blond hair, painted eyebrows, and a ragged scar running from the corner of one eye to her chin; a dark-haired girl; and a woman with jet black hair and angry black eyes.

My grandmother gasped and mumbled something under her breath, as if trying to shield me from contamination. Mrs. Beason continued. "Were any of the men who took part in the act with you arrested?"

The prisoners snickered.

"What do you think?" the oldest of the prostitutes snorted. "They don't arrest johns when they haul in a hooker."

"Why not?"

" 'Cause they don't."

"But why not?" Mrs. Beason asked.

I leaned forward. I didn't want to miss her reply. "Because men write the laws. And they write them for men." She strode to the center of the cell. "Did you know that in some cities, a woman can be arrested for bike riding on a city street? In the city of St. Louis, a woman, no matter how old she is, can't spend the night alone in a hotel room without the written permission of her husband or father."

I glanced at my grandmother. "Did you know that?"

She shook her head.

Mrs. Beason paced back and forth in front of her audience, pointing her finger at the women she passed. "It is against the law in twenty-two states for a woman to own property or to open her own bank account, unless a male member of her family signs with her."

"And you think you can change all that?" The toothless prisoner wrinkled her face in disbelief.

Mrs. Beason walked toward the cell bars. "We want to try. But I can promise you one thing." She stopped at the bars and whirled about to face us. "Nothing will change if we do not get the vote."

I whispered in Grandma McCall's ear, "I never knew there were places where women couldn't own property, did you? Doesn't Mama own the cottage?"

My grandmother nodded. "Only because James, your father, gave it to her in his will, and your grandfather and Uncle Ian drew up the deed for her."

I struggled to understand all I'd heard. I thought of my gentle father, of my Uncle Ian, and of my three grandfathers. *Would any of them vote for such ridiculous laws against women?* After the farewell dinner in San Francisco, I could see my Uncle Phillip doing so—but the others? I couldn't imagine it.

The prison matron called Mrs. Eastman's name, then five other ladies' names. "Your husbands have posted your bail." Before leaving, the suffragette leaders shook hands with each of us, then with the prisoners.

Less than five minutes later, the prison matron returned. "Mrs. Julia McCall and Miss Chloe Celeste Chamberlain? You're free to go. Your bail has also been paid." Like Mrs. Eastman, we shook hands with each of the remaining suffragettes and with the prisoners. When I took the youngest prostitute's hand and looked into her sad eyes, my breath caught in my throat. *This girl can't be more than fourteen years old, at the most!*

Grandma and I emerged from the courthouse to the waiting Packard town car. Fredrick held open the rear door and tipped his chauffeur's cap. "Ma'am."

Grandma grunted. We climbed inside the car, where Ashley and Grandpa McCall sat. Grandpa gave Grandma a hug and a kiss. "Are you both all right? I've been worried sick ever since Fredrick came to my office with the news of your arrest."

"We are both quite well, thank you." Grandma's razorsharp tone didn't fit the civility of her words.

"I'm certainly glad to hear that." Grandpa shook his head in an attempt to hide a smile. Finally, he gave up and laughed out loud. "So tell me, Julia, how does it feel to be—"

"Don't say another word, James E. Not one word!" She wagged her gloved finger under his mustache.

"Of course not, my dear. I wouldn't think of it." He grinned and lifted his hands defensively. "Seriously, though, it was due to dear Ashley's quick thinking that we could come to your aid so quickly."

Grandma bristled. "And how did dear Ashley's quick thinking rescue us from our vile incarceration?"

"Oh, that was easy." Ashley missed the edge in Grandma's voice. "When I lost you in the crowd, I went to the tearoom and waited for Fredrick." As she spoke, her blond ringlets bounced in a self-satisfied cadence. "Remember? You said he would pick us up at one, and he did—me, anyway. The police had already taken you and CeeCee to jail."

"Lost us in the crowd," Grandma muttered through clenched teeth.

Wide-eyed with innocence, Ashley bubbled with excitement. "I hope you won't mind, Grandma. While I waited, I got hungry, and I ordered a cup of hot chocolate and some of those yummy scones. When I explained to the maitrè d' all that had happened, he told me not to worry, that you were a good customer and could pay him later."

Grandmother sucked in her breath sharply. "Hungry? My dear Ashley, we wouldn't want you to be hungry, would we?"

Grandma's sarcasm flew past Ashley like a butterfly on a summer afternoon. "Oh, Grandma, I knew you'd understand."

Oh, Ashley, you are so—I don't believe it. I stared out the car window so my grandparents couldn't see me struggling not to laugh. *Madder than a wet hen—that's how I'd describe Grandma*

McCall. I'd never seen her so angry. Even Judge Myers hadn't infuriated her to this extent. A growl from my stomach broke the tension of the moment.

"Now, that's hungry, Ashley." Grandma pointed at my stomach. "CeeCee and I have been hassled and handcuffed, threatened and thwarted, badgered and brow-beaten all afternoon. And on top of all this, we've had not one morsel of food since breakfast!" Grandma's eyes flashed as her attack on Ashley continued. "And do you know why we were forced to endure these indignities, Ashley dear?"

Ashley shook her head, her eyes brimming with tears.

"Because, you, darling Ashley, dragged us into the fray in the first place."

My cousin's lower lip quivered. "B-b-b-bu-but, Grandma, I-I-I didn't kn-kn-know the police would arrest you."

"If you'd obeyed me, if you'd listened to me, none of this would have happened."

Ashley cowered under Grandma's virulent attack. I felt sorry for my cousin in spite of all I'd been through that day. *It's not that Ashley tries to be fatuous*, I told myself. *She can't seem to help herself.*

The tips of Grandpa's mustache twitched as he patted his wife's arm. "Now, now, Julia, the child had no way of knowing that the demonstration would turn into a riot."

Grandma jerked toward him, her nose less than an inch from his. "It was hardly a riot, James E.; it was police harassment, plain and simple."

"Thank God we got through it unharmed," I added cheerfully.

"Thank God? God had nothing to do with it. It took good old Yankee grit and gumption!" Grandma clicked her tongue. "Do you know before whom we were arraigned? Harold Myers, of all people!"

Grandpa's eyes twinkled as he stroked his mustache.

"Laugh, you—you grizzly old buffoon!" My grandmother folded her arms in a sulk. "We will never be able to socialize with him and Esther again. I've never been so humiliated in my life!"

"You should have heard Grandma in the courtroom, Grandpa."

I wanted her to know how proud I was of her. "She really told him—"

Grandma shot me a withering stare. Grandpa's eyebrows almost disappeared into his hairline. "Oh, really?"

I wavered whether or not to continue. "—what she thought of—" My words faded into a whisper, and I leaned farther into the town car's black leather seat.

Grandpa chuckled. "Just what thoughts did your grandmother share with the venerable Judge Myers?"

I bit my lip and cast a pleading glance at my cousin. She stared down at her hands, refusing to come to my rescue.

Grandpa winked at me and patted Grandma's hand. "Never mind, now. Perhaps we should talk about your adventure later, after we've taken the edge off everyone's, er, hunger. The important thing is that you're both unharmed."

Grandma's response was to grunt and turn toward the window. Grandpa pursed his lips. "It looks like we're in for a heavy frost tonight."

Ashley's eyes lighted up. "Really? After such a warm afternoon?"

Grandpa and I stared at my cousin in amazement, but she continued on, without notice. "Do you know I actually perspired while waiting for Fredrick? And I was wearing my spring coat too."

Grandpa cleared his throat and closed his eyes, and I dipped my head to conceal my grin.

When we reached the estate, the cook had dinner ready for us. No one spoke of the events of the afternoon. For that matter, no one spoke of anything. We ate in total silence.

Unfortunately, for me, after a few bites, exhaustion overpowered my hunger. I excused myself, took a quick sponge bath, and fell into bed. I didn't have the energy to write in my diary.

I hadn't been asleep long when I heard loud voices downstairs. Mama and Daddy had returned from the Cape. I didn't need to hear their words to know the topic of their conversation. I yawned and put a pillow over my head. *No more today. I can't take anymore today.*

I heard Mama's knock on the door and her gentle call. "CeeCee?

CeeCee, are you awake?" I chose to ignore both.

The next morning I staggered downstairs to Grandma's music room, hoping to get in an hour of violin practice before the rest of the family came down for breakfast. But that was not to be.

My father met me at the foot of the stairs. Thrusting the morning newspaper into my hands, he demanded, "Have you seen this?"

"No, sir." I stared in stunned disbelief at a photograph on the front page. There I was, my hair disheveled, my hat askew, being led in handcuffs to the paddy wagon. The headline read, "Twenty Women Arrested for Rioting at Faneuil Hall." The caption underneath the photograph read, "San Francisco schoolgirl, Chloe Celeste Chamberlain, protests ill treatment of women in Boston. More on page 7."

"Why would they choose to print my picture? With all the famous suffragettes at the demonstration, why pick on me?"

"Oh, don't worry. You weren't the only one. Your grandmother didn't escape, either. Look at page 7." There was an edge in my father's voice as he drew me into the McCall library. "Of all times for a thing like this to happen, while I'm involved with such sensitive negotiations for the government."

I turned to page 7 and forgot my own discomfort. The photographer had caught my grandmother shouting and waving an angry fist in the arresting policeman's face. "Julia McCall, the wife of a prominent Boston business tycoon, was one of the twenty women arrested today."

I laughed in spite of myself. "Grandma's going to throw a tizzy."

"And that's only the beginning." He glanced over my shoulder at the photographs of yesterday's events. "Wait until your mother sees it."

"We, uh, could destroy the paper," I suggested. "That way, neither of them will have to get upset over something they can't do—"

Midsentence, I noticed that my father looked past me and paled. Instantly, I understood why.

"About what does Mama not need to get upset?"

I whirled about to find my mother standing directly behind me.

Her eyes stared straight into mine. I gulped. "Good morning, Mama. Ooh, I love that dress you're wearing. Is it new?" I closed the newspaper and rolled it in my hands.

Without lowering her gaze, my mother gently slipped the paper from my grasp. "What in here do you not want me to see, darling?"

I cast a desperate glance toward my father. "I-I-I-uh, well, oh—"

Still staring into my eyes, she unrolled the paper, then looked down at the front-page photograph. *Escape!* I skirted her and dashed for the open doors.

"Chloe Celeste Chamberlain, stay right where you are."

I dropped my head. "I'm sorry. It wasn't my fault, honest. It wasn't anyone's fault, really. We got swept along with the crowd. Two thousand women, Mama, that's a lot of—"

Still reading the article, she interrupted. "Why is it that whenever Ashley McCall is around, you end up in trouble, and she escapes? I still remember the time you two went down to the beach at Grandma McCall's place at Martha's Vineyard, and Ashley dared you to run the waves. You could have lost your—" Mama turned to page 7. "—l-i-f-e!"

Daddy and I studied my mother's face when she turned to page 7 and saw the picture of my grandmother. First, the corners of her lips twitched, followed almost immediately by a delicate snort. I couldn't believe it. *Mama's laughing! She thinks it's funny*. Her chuckles deepened into laughter until tears rolled from her cheeks. "Oh, my, Cyrus. This is hilarious."

Miffed with her reaction, my father tugged on his vest. "I surely don't see anything humorous in this. Have you lost your sense of propriety?"

Mama dropped into one of the blue brocade occasional chairs by the library's floor-to-ceiling windows. "I am sorry, Cyrus. I can't help it. This is very funny."

My father scowled, his eyebrows meeting over the bridge of his nose. "CeeCee, would you please excuse us? Your mother and I have something to discuss."

Grateful for the escape, I rushed into the hallway, but not before I heard my father say, "Chloe, there is nothing funny about this entire situation. You know that the President is depending on—"

"Cyrus Chamberlain, where's your sense of humor? You're usually the one who sees the comical side of life—and this is comical. You are being unnecessarily paranoid."

I closed the double doors and leaned my forehead against them. Grandpa McCall stepped out of the door of the sun room, where the family ate their breakfasts. "CeeCee, have you seen my morning paper? Lawrence said he left it in my chair at the table. I've looked all over for it, but it's nowhere to be found."

"Um, yes, sir." I studied the pattern in the Oriental carpet beneath my feet.

"Well, where is it? Speak up, child."

"I believe my father has it in the library," I mumbled, then hurriedly continued, "Excuse me, Grandpa. I'm starved. What's for breakfast?"

"Pancakes, I believe. You say he's in here? Alone?"

I shook my head. "No, sir, my mother's with him."

"Oh, hmmph!" He grunted as he walked back to the sun room. "I did so want to read my morning newspaper."

What happened next, I have no idea. I didn't hang around to find out. I sneaked into the kitchen, made myself a scrambled-egg sandwich, grabbed a glass of orange juice and two sweet rolls, and ran upstairs to my room, where I could eat in peace.

Later, I learned that Rusty ate in the kitchen with the household staff, and poor Ashley got caught in the morning's maelstrom. I stayed out of sight most of the morning. By lunchtime, the adults in the house had come to a tacit agreement to quit discussing the indiscretions of the day before.

After lunch, Daddy took me to the New England Conservatory of Music for an interview with the school chancellor, Dr. Leopold Vandergarth. I sensed an uneasiness in my father from the moment we left the house, but I was too absorbed with the prospect of having an interview to question him.

After a tour of the campus, we entered the chancellor's office. There, I was directed to a straight-back chair across the desk from the chancellor. My father sat in a similar chair beside the heavy oak door. While Dr. Vandergarth organized the papers on his desk, I gazed about the book-lined office.

The man asked me several questions regarding the music I was currently doing and my musical and personal ambitions. I twisted and untwisted my linen handkerchief, answering the questions as best I could. *And I thought I was nervous yesterday during the questioning at police headquarters.*

The chancellor peered down his aristocratic nose at the three letters of recommendation I had provided. "While I'm sure your Dr. Bohn is an excellent musician, to the eastern music establishment, the man is an unknown quantity. I'm sure that you can understand our position. In addition, we have found, over the years, that female students seldom make the grade, so to speak. They either drop out to marry or find our program too rigorous for their delicate constitutions."

My face reddened, not from embarrassment but from anger. I felt the strangest urge to defend, not only myself, but all the women who had attended the school and failed. To my dismay, my words came out in barely more than a whisper. "Sir, I—"

Daddy, a muscle in his cheek twitching from irritation, interrupted. "Dr. Vandergarth, my daughter is a dedicated student and an exceptional musician. If treated fairly, she will one day bring honor to your establishment."

The chancellor gave us both a condescending smile. "Mr. Chamberlain, it is understandable for a loving father to feel—"

"Sir," my father interrupted a second time, "I don't think you understand. Her violin professor compiled a list of excellent schools of music here in the East. My daughter is only considering applying to your school—considering." He stood up and tapped his hat against his trouser leg. "Of course, finances will not be a problem, regardless of the school she chooses."

At the mention of money, Dr. Vandergarth cleared his throat and studied the appointment calendar in front of him. "I believe we could schedule her audition for next Thursday at ten o'clock. She should choose to play three numbers by memory that reflect her level of competence on the violin."

Neither of us said much during the drive back to Grandma and Grandpa's house. Daddy stopped the car outside the massive wrought-iron gates. Instead of immediately opening the gates, he paused. "You haven't said how you liked the school. Do you think you could be happy there? Living here with your grandparents?"

I shrugged and ran my fingernail along the upholstery piping. "I-I'm not sure."

He nodded. "I understand." We didn't speak again until we pulled up in font of the house and he turned off the engine. "Would you like to tour the New York Conservatory of Music and perhaps The Institute of Musical Art before you decide?"

"Oh yes." I sighed with relief. He'd read my mind.

"Good." His eyes sparkled with happiness. "Your mother will be pleased. Oh, did I tell you? Jamie will be here for dinner tonight."

"Really? Great." It had been seven months since my older brother had returned east to complete his last year in medical school. Jamie was my buddy, my protector, my hero.

"He had a major examination today. That's why he couldn't come to see you earlier." Daddy opened his door and climbed out, then came around to my side of the car and opened the door. "Mama and I stopped by his dormitory yesterday on the way back from the Cape. What with all the excitement around here last night and this morning, I forgot to tell you."

He helped me from the car, took my arm, and escorted me up the steps to the front door. I held my head high. I felt like a real lady walking by his side, though I had the most uncontrollable urge to skip like a child half my age.

Lawrence met us in the foyer. Behind him stood a blue-uniformed messenger boy holding a sealed envelope for my father. "I was instructed to wait for your reply, sir. I must return with acknowledgment that you did receive it."

The butler helped me with my coat while Daddy opened the envelope. My father's face paled as he silently read the message. "No, oh no!" He lifted his gaze from the yellow sheet of paper to the messenger's face. "Excuse me. I'll write my reply immediately. Please wait right here."

Daddy strode into Grandpa's library and closed the door. I wondered whether the messenger knew the content of the note.

Before my father returned, my mother swept out of the sun room into the hallway with Grandma McCall close behind.

"CeeCee, you're back." Mama gave me quick hug. "Where's your father? I thought I heard his voice. How did the interview go? Who is this young man?"

Lawrence replied, "He delivered a message for Mr. Cyrus, ma'am."

My mother looked at me. "Where is Daddy?"

"In the library, writing a reply." I gestured toward the closed doors.

Mama frowned, crossed to the closed doors, and knocked gently. "Cyrus? May I come in?" She opened the doors and slipped inside, closing the doors behind her.

"Cyrus is certainly being quite secretive, isn't he?" Grandma clicked her tongue, displaying her disapproval. "Come, CeeCee." She pulled me toward the sun room. "Come in here and tell me all about your interview. It will be such fun having another female living in the house."

Wrought with curiosity, I sent a glance over my shoulder toward the closed doors, then allowed her to lead me into the sun room.

Trouble Comes in Bunches

The petal pink satin dress shimmered in the dim lamplight. Carefully, I fastened each of the tiny mother-of-pearl buttons. "There, that's the last one. Now do me."

Ashley studied herself in the mirror. Soft blond curls, held in place with a matching satin ribbon, splayed out playfully in every direction. "Do you really like this dress? Are you sure this style flatters me?" She patted the dress's square neckline. "Maybe I should change into my blue tulle."

Still dressed in my chemise, I crossed my arms and tapped my stockinged toe impatiently. *You look fabulous—and you know it!* I fumed.

"Would it help you to decide if I refused to unbutton or button another dress for you this evening?" I asked. I didn't tell her that Jamie was bringing two medical-school buddies along. If she knew that, I'd starve to death while buttoning and unbuttoning her dresses all night long.

She giggled. "I suppose I deserve that, after the last three frocks I've discarded. But, you really don't think it exposes too much, um, flesh?"

I didn't answer her immediately. I didn't dare. The fact that her body had curved in all the right places by the time she turned thirteen and my body still resembled Rusty's gnawed at me. Once, I complained to Mama about the problem. She laughed and told me I was a late bloomer. *Late bloomer! The rate I'm going, I'm going to miss the entire growing season. I won't even qualify as the last rose of summer.*

Irked, I walked to the bed, where my French-heeled, cream-colored pumps and the spring green dimity dress lay, an outfit Grandma McCall had bought for me on our fateful shopping trip. "It's fine. Besides, tonight is just a family dinner."

"I guess you're right." She gazed into the mirror while I slipped the green dress over my hair.

I'd considered piling my hair on my head until Ashley burst into my room with her hair similarly styled. So, instead, I fell back on my old schoolgirl style. I caught the sides of my hair at the crown of my head, allowing the curls to cascade down my back. To look more festive, I added a spring green taffeta bow that matched the ribbon at the waist of the dress.

The dress slid over my slight figure with ease. *Slight, humph! More like gaunt.*

"CeeCee, you're so lucky." Ashley stepped up behind me and began buttoning the fabric-covered buttons. "You have such a petite little figure. Wait, I'll tie your sash in a bow." I nursed my jealousy while she secured the wide taffeta ribbon in place. "There, now, don't you look lovely. That green looks almost delicious enough to eat."

I laughed away my irritation. "Well, let's hope the cook fixes plenty of food or, who knows, we could all be embarrassed."

Ashley clicked her tongue. "CeeCee, you say the most outrageous things sometimes." Peering into the dressing-table mirror, she moistened her finger and ran it over each of her eyebrows and pinched her cheeks to add a blush to an already perfect complexion.

Catching my reflection over her shoulder, I wound a wisp of a curl around my finger and pressed it against one cheek, then did the same with a curl on the other side of my face. *CeeCee, you still look like a ten-year-old playing dress-up in your mama's clothes while Ashley looks like a princess from a fairy tale.*

The front-door chime sounded. "Oh, Jamie's here." I squealed and whirled about. "Where are my shoes? They were right here a minute ago."

"On the bed, you simpleton. There's no rush, you know. Mama says it's more dramatic for a woman to wait five minutes and make a grand entrance."

Hopping from one foot to the other, I slipped into my shoes on my way out the bedroom door. I could hear my brother's voice coming from the foyer at the bottom of the stairs. "So where's the most beautiful little sister in the whole world?"

"Here I am." Laughing, I skipped down the first four stairs to meet him. Jamie stood at the foot of the staircase, his arms outstretched to greet me.

"Wait! Stop!" Jamie shouted in a stage whisper. "Don't you dare come down here looking like that." Surprised, I steadied myself with one hand on the shiny English oak banister. Color flamed in my face.

"How dare you show up here in Beantown looking so grown up and beautiful!" Slowly, he ascended the stairs. When he reached me, he kissed the back of my hand. "You are too lovely for words, little sister." He slipped my hand into the crook of his arm and escorted me down the rest of the flight of stairs. "If I'd known how gorgeous you'd become, I never would have brought these dunderheads around to meet you."

Blushing, I playfully slapped his arm. "You're in the house less than five minutes, and you're already kissing the Blarney Stone. Now, be a dear, and introduce me to your friends."

Jamie introduced his roommates, Galen Bronwyn and Hershel Green. The two men were as different as sunlight and shadow. From Galen's slicked-down, sandy brown hair to his navy wool blazer and white flannel trousers to the tips of his white buckskin shoes, he looked like he stepped off the pages of *Vogue* magazine. His hazel eyes danced with humor.

"This must be my lucky night, Miss Chamberlain."

"Remember, fellows, she's my little sister! I don't take that lightly." An edge had entered Jamie's voice.

"Never will I let that thought escape my thinking." Galen arched an eyebrow and bowed graciously.

Jamie frowned and turned toward me. "Watch out for this guy. He's a ladies' man, and he's not to be trusted."

"Ah—" Galen dramatically clutched his chest and moaned. "You, dear friend, have injured me to the quick."

Jamie drew the dark, silent Hershel into the circle. Hershel's deep brown eyes warily searched mine for an instant before a small, tentative smile spread across his face.

"Now, Hershel, here," Jamie explained, "spends his time studying instead of hanging out at Mac Alister's Pub with the dollies."

I looked up at my brother. "Dollies?"

He reddened. "Hershel most likely will graduate next term at the top of his class, and he'll make a terrific physician."

"And I, Jay?" Galen interrupted. "What kind of physician do you predict me to be?"

Jamie laughed and thumped his friend on the back. "A rich one, my friend."

"Jamie!" Mama glided down the stairs on my father's arm. Her light blue, ankle-length chiffon dress floated about her body in a diaphanous swirl. Jamie's two friends stared in surprise.

"This is your mother?" Galen croaked. Jamie just glowered at him.

Just then, my grandparents and Ashley's parents arrived.

After introductions were made, Grandpa suggested we retire to the library for drinks. "I must warn you, we run an alcohol-free establishment here. Knowing that, what would you like to drink?"

Galen grinned. "What else is there?"

Aunt Drucilla sidled over to me and whispered, "Where is Ashley?"

I shrugged my shoulders. "I thought she was right behind me."

"Mummie?" Ashley's voice from the top of the stairs caused us all to look her way. I glanced over at Jamie's two friends. They stared, agog, at the golden-haired confection swathed in petal pink satin floating down the stairs toward them.

Whatever impact I might have had on Jamie's friends instantly evaporated. *Talk about grand entrances! This woman could give the queen lessons.* One flirty glance, and Ashley reduced the smooth-tongued Galen to a quivering mass of marmalade.

Lawrence's timely announcement that dinner was ready ended Ashley's magical moment. Before Jamie could introduce her to his friends, Galen had recovered enough to introduce himself and to offer to escort her to the dining room. An unbidden sigh escaped my lips.

I felt a firm hand on my elbow. "May I have the honor of escorting you to the table, Miss CeeCee?"

I glanced over my shoulder into Hershel's warm brown eyes. Instantly, I knew he'd read my thoughts. I blushed and lowered my gaze. "That would be nice. Thank you."

Grandma and Grandpa McCall played the perfect Back Bay hostess and host. The conversations at the dinner table flowed as smoothly as did the strawberry mousse and chocolate butter creams following the main course. Galen's sparkling wit and herculean effort to impress Ashley would have kept even a roomful of undertakers laughing, especially his anecdotes about Jamie and his first year in med school.

The stories continued around the table, each person taking a turn. Grandma delighted everyone with her version of the arrest.

"Excuse me, Grandma, but you left out the best part of the story."

Grandma's eyebrows knitted together in thought. "No, no, I don't think so."

I grinned. "What about when you told Judge Myers about the policemen harassing innocent women and how he'd be seeing more of you if the harassment continued?" I turned to my audience. "When everyone cheered, the judge threatened to charge us all with contempt of court."

"CeeCee," Grandma hissed. "You make it sound worse than it really was. Harold would never have—" Grandma gulped and grinned sheepishly at her husband.

"You didn't tell me that part of the story. Here's to my spunky sweetheart." Grandpa saluted her with his water glass. "Seriously, though, our judicial friend has been know to carry out such threats, my dear. He's tough on criminals."

"James E.," Grandma sputtered. "Chloe Celeste and I were hardly criminals."

The clock in the hallway gonged nine times. Daddy checked it against his pocket watch. "It's getting late." He eyed my mother, who studied the tea-rose-and-bluebell pattern on Grandma's bone china.

He stood up. "I have an unfortunate announcement to make. I received a memo from our main offices, calling me back to New York tonight. This evening at eight-thirty, President Wilson appeared before the joint session of Congress and asked them to declare war on Germany."

"Yeah!" Jamie and Galen jumped up from their seats and cheered.

"It's about time!" Jamie said. "After all the submarine attacks on passenger and merchant ships and all the Americans who have died, it's about time."

"Here, here!" Galen raised his glass. "Now, I can enlist as an Amer—"

Mama interrupted, "Why do you wish to go to war?"

Galen looked at her in surprise. "Why, this is the greatest adventure there is. I would be greatly disappointed if I missed the opportunity to participate. Besides, there will be little fighting once the Yanks get there."

"If I were young enough—" Uncle Ian toyed with his water goblet. "—I'd enlist. What an opportunity to see the world! Can you imagine being in Paris for the victory parade?"

"Parades? See the world? Adventure?" Mama shook her head in disbelief. "Ian, you surprise me. Have any of you would-be heroes ever seen the effect real bullets have on human flesh?" Her voice raised with her blood pressure. "This is no game of cowboys and Indians on the prairie. The rifles are real. The cannons blow holes in people. The shrapnel rips off limbs and gouges out eye sockets."

"Chloe!" My father's sotto voce warning urged a change of topic.

"Must you be so graphic?" Aunt Drucilla covered her lips with her napkin.

"That's the reason I'm going, Mother—to care for our wounded soldiers," Jamie defended.

"Don't worry, Mrs. Chamberlain." Galen leaned back in his chair, the image of self-confidence. "If we should ever find ourselves in actual combat, which I doubt, a good soldier knows to stay in his trench and let the bullets fly over his head."

Hershel, who'd been silent most of the meal, spoke up. "From what I've read about trench warfare, I'm glad that my poor vision disqualifies me for military service."

Galen scowled at his friend. "Are you saying you don't want to go to war?"

Deep concern filled Hershel's face. "I didn't say that. Personally, I wish no one ever had to go to war. And I know I'll feel guilty having to stay home while my friends go to defend me."

"You talk so freely of patriotism and honor. Where's the honor in this skirmish?" Mama grunted. "Why should Americans die because some archduke went to Sarajevo, where he wasn't wanted, and got himself shot by a radical young student? It's a family feud between a greedy king, an arrogant crown prince, and a rapacious emperor!"

"She's right!" The crystal goblets rattled against the bone china when Grandma pounded a fist on the table. "It's not our war."

Stunned by her outburst, everyone looked nervously at one another until Grandpa McCall said, "It *is* our war, Julia. When the Kaiser's submarines killed Americans aboard passenger liners, it became our war, like it or not. Call it patriotism, call it foolishness, but if I were fifty years younger, I, too, would serve my country."

"It is an honor to serve and to die for one's country," Hershel began, his voice low, but determined. "But I have no country."

"What?" Jamie stared at his friend.

"It's true. I'm Jewish. Why should a Jew die for any country but his own?" Hershel shrugged at the stunned faces around the table. "By his own, I don't mean Germany, the United States, England, or Austria. I mean a Jewish home state."

Grandma choked on a butter cream, and Mama leapt to her aid. And I stared in open amazement at Jamie's dark-haired friend. *I've never before met a Jew.*

I remembered hearing a street orator in San Francisco shout, "Jews are behind all of America's problems. If we go to war, it will be to feed the pocketbooks of Jewish merchants. No matter who wins or loses, Jews are the ones who ultimately profit from the war and the suffering." Whenever he used the word *Jew*, he spat it out as if the word were the vilest of profanity. "Jews are a pestilence worse than the Black Death of olden times!"

An elderly gentleman, his hair white beneath a gray felt bowler, stepped from the back of the little group of people lingering near the speaker. "We've heard enough of your speeches. This is a God-fearing country. And God is displeased with your hatred of His children."

"God? Angry?" The orator shook his fist in the face of the old man. "God cursed the Jews to darkness when they killed His Son, Jesus!"

In reply, the gentleman shook his bone-handled cane. "Enough, you disgusting worm of a man. It is people like you, people sick with malice and vengeance, who bring on the wars and the suffering in this world."

The orator's eyes narrowed. "You're one of 'em, aren't you?" You're a Jew!"

"No, sir, I am not." The old man straightened his spine and lifted his chin. "I'm more Anglo-Saxon than you'll ever be. But if I were, I'd wear my Jewishness with pride."

Having heard more than enough, I had hurried on down the street. I felt dirty and contaminated from listening to the man's poisonous hatred. For weeks, I couldn't get the orator's hate-contorted face or his malevolent message out of my mind. Hershel's statement brought it all back to me.

"Wherever I go, I'm identified as a Jew first and as an American second. The only way I could get accepted at Harvard Medical School was to anglicize my name and drop the second syllable. My grades, my abilities, my test scores meant nothing as long as *baum* was part of my name." Hershel dotted his lips with his napkin and noted my grandmother's flushed and agitated face.

"And, now, I can see, Mrs. McCall, that I am no longer welcome at your table." He stood up and shoved his chair back in place. "Please excuse me. And thank you for a delicious dinner. You've been a gracious hostess."

In stunned silence, we watched Hershel walk from the dining room. We could hear him ask Lawrence for his overcoat.

"Stop him," I hissed. "Someone go stop him!" When no one moved, I leapt to my feet and rushed toward the foyer.

"CeeCee, come back here," Mama ordered, barely above a whisper. "It's not your place—"

I didn't hear the rest; I didn't need to. I skidded to a stop just inside the foyer. Lawrence stood with his hand on the doorknob while Hershel put on his gloves.

"Hershel?" Suddenly I felt shy, very shy. I sauntered toward him, unable to think of anything to say. I held out my hands to him. "I'm glad you were here tonight. And I'm glad I met you. I don't know what to say about—" I gestured toward the dining room.

He smiled, his large brown eyes filled with pain. "CeeCee, you are a lovely young woman, with a gentle heart. I'm glad I met you too."

My indignation surged within me. "I can't believe they just let you walk away from—"

"Don't be too hard on your family. They're good people," he interrupted.

"Bu-bu-bu-but—how can you say that?"

He place a gloved finger over my sputtering lips. "We all have our prejudices, even you and me. And most of them rise out of ignorance." He took my hands in his and raised them to his lips. Tenderly, he placed a kiss on the back of each one.

Holding Hershel's hat in one hand, Lawrence opened the door with the other. The early-spring breeze sent a chill through me. "Will you ever come back with Jamie? Will I ever see you again?" My words came out in a broken whisper.

"Probably not." He held my hands a second longer before releasing them. Then he turned, took his hat from Lawrence, and tipped it toward me. "Chloe Celeste Chamberlain, if I had a kid sister, I'd want her to be just like you."

I stood in the open door, watching Hershel stride into the darkness. The wrought-iron gate at the end of the driveway squeaked twice as it opened, then closed. In my heart, I felt a profound sadness that was new to me.

"CeeCee—" Mama placed her hands gently on my shoulders. "Come on inside." Too disheartened to disobey, I turned to find my family watching.

"How long have you been standing there?"

"Long enough to be ashamed of ourselves." Jamie threw his arms around me. "Have I ever told you how much I love having you for my sister?" He swallowed hard. "I've never been so proud of you as I am at this very moment. You are one special young lady."

Emotion swept over me. With all that had happened during the last few days, I was too tired for anger or joy. "Please." I looked at my parents, then at my grandparents. "May I be excused?"

"Of course, sweetheart." Mama led me up the stairs to my room.

As I passed Daddy, he kissed my cheek and gave me a hug. "See you next weekend, Freckles."

The next day, when I came down to breakfast, I read the morning's headlines.

"April 3, 1917. PRESIDENT WILSON CALLS FOR DECLARATION OF WAR. Washington, April 2, at 8:30 p.m. President Woodrow Wilson appeared . . ." It was all there, just as my father had predicted. "Wilson asked Congress to declare war on the German Empire and promises full cooperation with the foes of Germany. The President declared 'that the world must be made safe for democracy.' Wilson's message was met by thunderous applause."

I finished reading the article as Mama entered the sun room. Without a word, I handed her the newspaper. She read the headline and moaned. "I guess I was still hoping."

"Will Jamie enlist?"

She placed her hand over her mouth and grasped the closest chair.

"Mama, are you all right?"

Ignoring my question, she held onto the chair for several seconds.

"Should I call Grandma? Do you need help? Are you sick?"

My mother shook her head. "I-I-I'm fine. CeeCee, go wake up your brother. I want to leave as soon as possible for the Cape."

"Are you going to drive Daddy's new Packard?" I gaped at her. "I know you know how to drive, but this automobile is much more comp—"

"Stop asking questions, and do as I say!"

"Yes, ma'am." I darted from the room and up the stairs, taking them two at a time. I understood her need to leave, to escape, to run as far and as fast as possible. It had been my first reaction too.

A strange exhilaration flooded through me. I had tender

memories of lazy summer days at the cottage by the sea. By the time I burst into Rusty's bedroom, I could almost hear the squawking sea gulls and the pounding surf.

Within the hour, Mama, Rusty, and I, much to my grandparents' disapproval, climbed into the front seat of Daddy's touring car and drove down the driveway and through the wrought-iron gates. Lawrence had loaded as much luggage as possible in the trunk. The rest filled the rear seat from floor to ceiling. What did not fit, we left behind. *Free! We're free!*

We made two stops before heading south to the Cape, one at the conservatory to cancel my audition and the other at Jamie's dormitory in Harvard. It took us half an hour to track him down at the library, where he was hunched over a stack of leather-bound books. When he saw us, he hurried to meet us. "What are you doing here?"

Mama explained as best she could. "I need time to reestablish my roots, even if only for the summer, to feel at home again somewhere."

Jamie avoided Mama's gaze. "I understand," he responded softly, gazing at the oiled hardwood floor.

Jamie walked us out to the automobile. It was the first time he'd seen Daddy's new purchase. Running his hand along the door of the car, he exclaimed, "Wow! This is some buggy! Does Daddy know you're driving this thing?"

Mama planted her hands on her hips in frustration. "Why does everyone ask me that? Of course, he knows. Why do you think he left it in Boston? To gather dust?"

"Mama's a good driver," Rusty defended. He should have stopped there. "For a woman, that is."

"Huh!" Mama playfully cuffed him. "You may walk to Cape Cod, young man!"

Rusty laughed and ran around to the other side of the car. "I get the window."

"Oh no, you don't!" I shouted. I gave Jamie a quick kiss and dashed around the car to defend my territory. Being older and stronger has its advantages. As I climbed in after him, I wondered, *How much longer will I be able to strong-arm him?*

When Mama got settled in the driver's seat, Jamie leaned

inside the open window.

"You will come down to the cottage this weekend, won't you? I promise I won't nag you about the war."

"Of course, I will. I'll be down every chance I get."

Mama squinted up at him. "Will we need to meet you at the depot?"

"Naw. Hershel said I could borrow his motorcycle any time." The clock in the tower gonged ten. "Gotta go. I've got to be in the lecture hall in five minutes." He kissed Mama, then stepped away from the car. The Packard engine purred as Mama slipped it into gear. Rusty and I waved goodbye to Jamie as Mama eased the luxury touring car into the midday traffic.

As we rode through a tangle of narrow streets, I stared, fascinated by Boston's red-brick tenement houses, where lines of laundry linked each building to the next. Excitement bubbled up inside me when we finally headed south toward the Cape.

It was a long ride, over bumpy and badly rutted roads. To Rusty and me, it seemed we stopped in every tiny burg and hamlet for fuel. "I don't want to run out," Mama said with each stop.

When we crossed the Cape Cod Canal, I allowed myself to believe that the trip to the cottage, called Bide-a-wee, would soon be over. I'd never lived there for any length of time, yet I felt as if I were coming home.

On a map, Cape Cod appears to be nothing more than an insignificant peninsula, shaped like a man's arm, jutting out from Massachusetts forty-five miles east and twenty-five miles north. But upon visiting Cape Cod, you lose your heart. The world changes on the eastern side of the bridge. Weather-beaten cottages, jetties, fishing boats in the sparkling bays, emerald green marshes, salt ponds, blinding-white sand dunes, jagged cliffs, piney woods, and the surf—always the sound of the roaring surf. Yet, for all the beauty I saw, I couldn't wait to get to Bide-a-wee.

An artist had built and named the gray-shingled cottage on the northeastern side of the Cape as a summer place, where he and his friends could go to escape the heat of New York City. Taking advantage of the ocean view, he designed a porch and balcony to run the full length of the front of the two-story house.

Less than a year later, the man died, leaving no heirs. That's when my father, James McCall, had bought the entire estate, from the pulley clothesline and bag of clothespins by the kitchen door to the furniture and bedding in each of the seven bedrooms on the second floor.

One summer, when we came east to spend time with Jamie, we spent a week at Bide-a-wee. Otherwise, no one had lived there since before I was born. I could only imagine how much work it had taken for Au Sam to whip the place into shape in little more than a week.

By the time Mama stopped the car behind the cottage, I could sit still no longer. I hopped out of the car and ran toward the gray-shingled house. "Au Sam! Au Sam, we're here!"

The screen door to the kitchen flew open, and my precious Au Sam rushed toward me. "Missee, you've come home."

A big yellow creature bounded out of the bushes beyond the lawn.

"What is that?" I cried in horror.

Rusty shouted and threw his arms around the beast. "My dog. Daddy kept his promise. My dog!" The golden retriever lunged at Rusty, knocking him off his feet. They rolled on the grass, the boy laughing and the dog drooling. Then as Rusty leapt to his feet, the dog bounded out of his reach.

"Here—" My brother looked at Mama, then at Au Sam. "What's his name?"

"He doesn't have a name. I guess you'll have to name him." Mama hauled a valise from the back seat.

"Hmm, I think—I'll—call—him—Sundance. Yeah, Sundance!"

"Rusty, you can't name the dog that."

Rusty's lips tightened into a pout. "Yes, I can. Yes, I can! It's my dog."

I clicked my tongue. "That's the name of the horse you left at Uncle Joe's place."

"I know. So?"

"Why?"

"I like it."

Au Sam slapped her thigh and laughed. "Good name, good name. Besides, this dog's a real bandit. He'll snatch a freshly baked pie right off the windowsill."

Jamie clapped his hands and called, "Here, Sundance."

Instantly, the dog bounded to him. "See? He already knows his name."

Mama handed me two valises. "Here, make yourself useful." Returning to the car for more luggage, she asked, "How is Meeker adjusting to the dog?"

Au Sam rushed to help Mama. "At first, she'd sit on the back porch railing and spit every time the dog came near the house. But the other night, when she didn't know I was watching, I saw her rub up against him and nuzzle him."

I started toward the house. "Where is she?"

"She could be anywhere." Au Sam caught up with me, her arms loaded with additional suitcases. "She loves it here. She's turning into a real mouser. I do wish she'd stop leaving her spoils on the back porch for me to see."

"Eeuuww!" I imagined myself stepping on a dead mouse some morning. I shuddered and followed Au Sam into the house. We dropped the luggage in the front hallway and hurried back for more, but not before I inhaled the aroma of corn chowder wafting from the kitchen.

Later that night, after everyone else had gone to bed, I wandered out the French doors in my bedroom onto the second-story veranda overlooking the ocean and inhaled the clean, fresh aroma of the sea. The wind whistled up from the beach, tossing my tangled curls about my shoulders. I sat down cross-legged in a rattan chaise lounge and watched the moonlight shimmer on the water.

An atmosphere of peace surrounded me. Meeker hopped up on the chaise and rubbed against my leg, purring, coaxing me to give her my attention. I picked her up and placed her on my lap, idly stroking her soft gray fur.

The local people say that the sound of the surf is the song of the Cape. I closed my eyes and allowed the ocean's melody to wash away all thoughts of trouble, war, and hate from my mind. Burying my face in Meeker's soft, round tummy, I whispered, "We're home, Meeker. We're finally home."

Diary, Dear Diary

Dear Emily, I awoke before dawn this morning. While falling asleep last night, I realized that in a little over a month I will turn seventeen. On the seventeenth of May in the year of nineteen hundred and seventeen, Chloe Celeste McCall Chamberlain will be seventeen! Isn't that totally amazing? I wonder if I'll feel any older than I do now. Probably not. I don't feel much older than I did when I was twelve, for that matter.

According to my Granddaddy Spencer, a girl is officially a woman on her seventeenth birthday. What did that make my grandma when he married her, I wonder. Mama says Grandma Spencer had three babies by my age.

Three babies! Can you imagine such a thing? Not me. I have too much to do, too much to see before I get saddled with a husband and babies. On her seventeenth birthday, my mother was already acting as Mama to Jamie, my half-brother. By her eighteenth birthday, she'd married my father.

Yikes! I don't even have a boyfriend. And if Mama has her way, I won't until I'm twenty-six and too long in the tooth to attract anything but the gravest of male specimens.

A series of staccato barks beneath my bedroom window startled me. *That dumb dog! He'll awaken the entire family!* I glanced up from the puddle of light illuminating my notebook page and rubbed my eyes. The rest of my bedroom still lingered in the shadows, except for one sliver of light seeping between the French doors and streaking across the foot of my unmade bed.

Another round of barks, and I flew across the room and threw open the French doors. Leaning over the railing, I searched the shadows for the beast, but saw nothing. *Probably rousted a rabbit or gopher from its burrow!* "Sundance! Be quiet! Sundance?"

The world outside my window lay swathed in a gauzy film of morning fog. To the north, I could see light from the kitchen below spilling out onto the lawn. My eyes misted. *Faithful Au Sam. Up before dawn, preparing breakfast for us.*

I thought of how much I'd missed the tiny Chinese woman during our trip east and the stay in Boston. I knew that Au Sam had hated the long ride from California. But during the excitement of the move, I had failed to notice the woman's almost invisible comings and goings. When Mama and Daddy brought her down to the Cape, she insisted on staying. "Meeker and I will stay here and get things organized while you visit with your family." It was agreed that until we moved into our New York brownstone and a new household staff could be hired, Au Sam would make the kitchen her domain.

I ambled back to the oak lady's secretary and picked up my pen once more.

I promised to write more about my visit to Colorado. Here goes—

Since I visited the mine where my real father, James Edward McCall, died, certain questions have haunted me. I had heard the story of the cave-in dozens of times during my childhood, but it was just a story until I stared down into the yawning cavern of darkness that became his tomb.

Emily, what was it like for him down there alone? Did he die instantly or linger in the blackness, afraid and alone? Will I ever know? Mama says that one day, at the resurrection, I'll be able to ask him those questions myself. And, I guess I believe that—sort of.

I mean, if God loves us enough to come back to this earth for us, why didn't He love my father enough to save him in the first place? Once I talked with my friend, Susanne, about life and death and God and things. She said she believed in a Being, as the Designer of all living things, but, like dress and automobile designers, once He completed His creation, God moved on to His next project.

I don't know what to think—I guess I'm still confused. I closed my diary and capped my pen. *These aren't the thoughts I want to think on this glorious day—my first day on the Cape.*

I sauntered out onto the balcony once more. Leaning with both elbows on the railing, I stared out over the Atlantic and watched as the Cape awakened in stages, a sullen red-streaked sky with banks of threatening clouds building in the northeast.

The biting morning wind whipped my blue-and-white checked flannel nightdress about my ankles. *So this is the beautiful Cape Cod sunrise I've heard so much about.*

"I love it!" I shouted to the wind. Flinging my arms into the air, I pirouetted back into my bedroom. "This is going to be a fabulous day. An absolutely fabulous day! Good weather or foul." I pulled on my brown suede knickers and the Irish cable-knit sweater Grandma McCall had bought for me during her most recent trip abroad.

As I passed the mirror over my dressing table, I laughed at my unkempt appearance. *If I go out onto the beach like this, I'll scare the clams out of the sand. And I don't even eat clams!* After unbraiding my night braid, I grabbed my tortoise-shell hairbrush and brushed vigorously until satiny ripples cascaded down my back. Daddy once called my hair liquid copper.

Not wanting to take additional time, I pulled my hair into a horse tail at the nape of my neck, wrapped a yellow ribbon around the tail, and tied the ends into a bow. Before leaving my room, I made a halfhearted attempt to straighten my bed and put away my nightdress. I grabbed my woolen stockings and my boots on the way out the bedroom door.

In the hallway, the aroma of cinnamon-nut muffins baking in the oven below accosted me. I inhaled deeply. *Maybe a small detour to the kitchen before braving the wind would be a good idea.* Silently, I hurried down the carpeted stairs, past the rosewood grandfather clock in the hall, through the dining room, and into the kitchen, banging the swinging door against the butler's pantry.

"A-i-e-e!" Au Sam, who'd been leaning over a large mixing bowl, straightened and covered her heart with a flour-coated hand. "Oh, Missee! You'll be the death of me yet."

I chuckled and sniffed about the enormous kitchen, with its massive wooden sink and huge cast-iron range—Au Sam's new kitchen. I knew without asking that the kitchen had been the first room settled. Au Sam would have insisted upon it. On the shelves she'd placed the scrubbed cast-iron pots and pans and her rice bowls, nesting in one another. Beneath the rice bowls, she had two rows of neatly aligned jars and bottles containing her tea canisters and Mama's herb collection. Alongside the herbs, Au Sam stored her favorite copper kettle. The empty brass hook beside the pantry door would later hold one of her red-and-yellow calico aprons—she loved red-and-yellow calico.

I pulled her apron ties and peered over her shoulder into the bowl. "M-m-m, lemon cake batter. My favorite." While the woman struggled to retie her apron, I swiped my finger through the mixture, slurped the thick batter into my mouth, and sprang out of her reach.

In mock anger, she grabbed a wooden spoon and flailed it in the air in front of me. "Missee! You leave Au Sam's kitchen, or she won't finish baking your favorite cake."

"Ha, ha, you can't get me." I darted to the other side of the table. To emphasize the advantage of my youth and agility, I took another swipe at the cake batter before dashing out the back door.

Behind me, I heard her high voice warning, "Put on your shoes before you catch your death of cold, you little tomboy. And be careful of the changing tides."

I leapt off the porch and looked around for Sundance. I much preferred finding him before he found me. After the way he had leapt on me the evening before, I wanted to avoid his large puppy prints on my sweater. I called to him, but he didn't respond.

"Humph! A great watchdog you've proven to be!" I shouted in the wind.

Oblivious to the weather, I cavorted in exaggerated circles on the lawn, the roar of the ocean drowning out my laughter. Cawing gulls circled overhead, enticing me toward the surf. I charged through the stretch of tall grass between the yard and the sand dunes, then ran across the sand dunes and down onto the deserted beach. The earliest of summer visitors were still weeks away.

I kicked a spray of sand into the air, uncovering broken shells and tiny bits of driftwood, carved and polished by the sea. Spying a delicate pink-and-white shell farther down the beach, I ran to it and crouched to extract it from the sand.

A rogue wave took advantage of my inattention, enveloping my toes and the back of my knickers in icy water. I squealed and dashed for safety, dragging my woolen stockings in the surf as I ran. *Aw, who cares?* I tossed my boots and soggy hose onto a rock and threw myself down in a patch of dry, cool sand. *This feels so good.*

I recalled my recent experience in the Kansas hay mound and laughed. *If Shane Simons could see me now!* I stared at the patterns of light and dark in the eastern sky. A cloud bank from the northeast moved south, overpowering the early-morning rays of sun, plunging the Cape and everything on it into a vat of dismal gray.

Defiant, I leapt to my feet and shook my fist at the sky. "I don't care what you do; it's still a fabulously beautiful day. Do you hear me? A fabulously beautiful day!" Laughing, I scooped up handfuls of sand and tossed them high into the air. The wind accepted my challenge and whipped the yellow hair ribbon into the surf, tumbling my mass of hair over my shoulder, into my face, eyes, and mouth. I sputtered and clawed at the sudden curtain obstructing my view.

That's when I first saw the boy, a lone, lean figure, standing atop a sand dune toward the south. He was laughing at me. A rush of heat flooded my face, from the neck of my sweater to the tips of my ears. My hands flew to my cheeks. *Oh no, where had he come from?*

With as much dignity as I could muster walking barefoot in the deep sand, I stomped over to the rock where I'd abandoned my boots and stockings. In my haste to retrieve my boots, I knocked one into a shallow tidal pool on the other side of the rock. *How do I get myself into these predicaments? Au Sam is right—I am a tomboy.*

I groaned and scrambled over the rock to retrieve it, only to come face to grinning face with the source of my embarrassment. The boy held one of my boots and one limp stocking in his hands.

"Lose something? Here, take them." The dark-haired boy close to my own age thrust my clothing toward me.

When I reached for the boot, he yanked it away.

"Take it," he teased, dangling the boot tantalizingly close to my face.

My hand shot out toward the object. Again, he anticipated my move and snatched the boot out of reach.

"Come on, you can do better than that."

I glowered at my antagonist, then at the boot. Focusing my attention on the boot, I tensed my muscles and lunged the way I'd seen Jamie tackle a football.

My momentum unbalanced my startled adversary, tumbling him backward into the sand. With my arms tightly wrapped around the boot, I sailed over the boy's head. In my mind, I could hear Jamie yelling, "Tuck and roll. Tuck and roll."

Tuck and roll? What's that? As I landed face down in a mound of yielding sand, I remembered the meaning of "tuck and roll." Spitting sand and brushing away stray hair, I scrambled to my feet and resisted the urge to respond to my opponent's laughter. I grabbed the other boot, wrapped what dignity I could muster about myself, and stalked from the beach.

At the crest of the first sand dune, the boy caught up to me. "Hey, are you mad at me? Don't go away angry. I'm sorry. What's your name?"

My nose shot up into the air. *As if I'd—* Slowly, I turned my head and studied him as I would snail slime, bread mold, or any other noxious substance. The boy's gray eyes and wide grin tugged at my resolve. But what dissolved it was the stray brown curl dangling over his left eyebrow and the matching set of dimples edging the corners of his mouth.

"Hey, come on. I was just funnin' ya. Where's your sense of humor?" He circled me, pleading, coaxing. "My name's Thaddeus Adams—Thad for short. My pop runs the local grocery store."

"Humph!" I lifted my nose an inch higher and narrowed my eyes into my Meeker gaze. Daddy named my leave-me-alone-if-you-know-what's-good-for-you look after the way Meeker looks when she doesn't want to be bothered. I kept walking until the roof of the house appeared over the top of the next sand dune.

"Hey, you're the girl who just moved into the old McCall place, aren't you? Spooky house, huh? My buddies and I used to say it was haunted. Is it? Haunted, I mean?"

"Haunted! What nonsense!" I clicked my tongue and kept walking. "No. Of course, it's not haunted."

"I heard that the local police boarded it up after the owner murdered his wife with a meat cleaver in the parlor."

I swung about to face him. "Indeed! My grandfather boarded it up after my real father died in a mining accident in Colorado. Later, when my mother remarried and my stepfather was transferred to— Why am I telling you this?" I swung around and headed toward the house. "It's none of your business!" I'd taken three steps when he leapt in front of me, blocking my path.

Intending to go around him, I stepped off into the waist-high grass that billowed on each side of the narrow pathway. He grabbed my arm. "No. Don't! You're barefooted. Don't you know about the venomous Massachusetts razortail snake?"

Snake? I hopped back onto the pathway, my eyes darting from side to side, searching and hoping not to find.

He glanced down at my bare ankles. "Being barefoot and all, before you knew what happened, a swarm of those reptiles could lacerate your legs with their razor-sharp tails. Ooh! I'd hate to think of the bloody consequences!"

I imagined thousands of snakes with inch-long fangs and serrated-edged tails, poised, ready to attack. Hearing rustling in the grass to the right of the pathway, I froze. My hands shook with fear as I pointed at a long, slender creature less than a foot away. Thad put his finger to his lips, then carefully parted the grass and lunged at the unsuspecting object.

"No, no," I whispered. "Leave it alone! Just leave it alone! Stomp; maybe it will go away."

But he didn't listen. He attacked the beast, throwing himself on top of it before it could escape and writhing with it in the grass for several seconds. I gasped as the boy leapt to his feet and thrust the creature in my face. "Here!"

Without stopping to look, I dashed, screaming, toward the beach. Thad ran after me, laughing and shouting for me to stop. One look at the yard-long stick in his hand, and I was ready to grab it and break it over his head. And I would have—except the grass to my right moved, and Sundance broke through the thicket. On the prowl for excitement, the dog mistook the raised stick as a challenge and bounded to my defense. The golden retriever raced past me and pounced on the startled boy, sending him sprawling onto the footpath.

I burst into laughter. Sundance, my gentle knight, stood atop the stunned boy, grinning and drooling over his conquest. Unable to stop laughing, I fell to my knees and continued to laugh until I was breathless.

"Call him off," the boy choked. "Call the monster off!"

Still enjoying the pleasure of unexpected retribution, I managed to gasp, "Sundance is as gentle as a lamb."

When Thad lifted his head to glare at me, Sundance slurped his tongue from the boy's chin to his hairline.

"I don't care. Just get him off me."

"Come on, Sundance. You're a good boy." The dog trotted over to me and slurped my face as well. I scratched him behind the ears. "Good doggie. What a good doggie!"

Sundance growled when Thaddeus scrambled to his feet and brushed at his clothes. "You should keep that mangy mutt on a leash, you know. He's gonna hurt somebody, someday."

When Sundance growled again, I patted his head. "Yeah, I know. He'll lick 'em to death."

"Hey, what's your name? I told you mine."

"Chloe Celeste, CeeCee for short."

"Are you here for the summer?"

I nodded. "Probably. Do you walk along the beach often?"

"Every morning, before school."

As we talked, Sundance decided I was in no danger, which turned Thad into a potential playmate. The dog picked up the coveted stick with his teeth, carried it over to the boy, and dropped it at his feet.

"He wants to play fetch," I said to Thaddeus.

"Are you crazy? He's likely to take off my hand!"

"Come on, Sundance. Thaddeus doesn't feel much like playing right now. He can't help it if he has no sense of humor." Laughing, I bounded up the grassy slope toward the house. When I reached the porch, I paused to see if Thaddeus was still there, but only the gulls remained—the gulls, the grass, the sand, and the retreating surf.

I opened the screen door and remembered I had left my boots somewhere in the tall grass. I stood with my hands on my hips, trying to decide what to do next. The tale of the razor-tailed snakes convinced me that I needed help. *Rusty! Little brothers are good for some things.*

I bounded into the breakfast room and skidded to a stop. I hadn't seen the room in daylight since Mama and Au Sam had redecorated it. The wide-plank hardwood floors gleamed with a new coat of wax. Crisp white-cotton curtains, tied back with white eyelet lace, framed each of the six windows looking out onto the porch. The yellow-checked wallpaper and the white rattan chairs with the their red-purple-and-pink-flowered seat cushions gave the room an open, sunny feeling—even on this, the grayest of mornings.

Four white-framed arrangements of pressed, dried flowers hung above a chest of drawers, painted medium blue. American-made Blue Willow china decorated the shelves in a white breakfront. The table had been set with a pink linen tablecloth and napkins and the same blue-on-white china.

In the center of the table, Au Sam had arranged red, yellow, and purple tulips in a blue ceramic pitcher. Yes, I definitely liked what I saw. *You know,* I mused, gazing about the room a second time, *I wouldn't mind living here year round.*

My stomach growled, reminding me of the cinnamon-nut muffins. *Maybe if I—* Hands clasped behind my back, I ambled out to the kitchen. "Au Sam, is my brother awake yet?"

"No one's come downstairs yet this morning except you. What do you want with him?" Au Sam eyed me suspiciously. If Au Sam protected anyone more than me, it was Rusty. And I really can't blame her for being suspicious. Rusty and I antagonized one another incessantly. Mama called us beloved enemies. I suspect she was right.

"I think I'll practice a while before breakfast. When Rusty comes downstairs, tell him I need to see him, OK?" Helping myself to one of the muffins, I breezed through the sun room toward the parlor, where I'd left my violin and music case.

"Missee, where have you been?" The woman hounded my heels.

"I heard shouting down by the water. What happened to your

hair and your ribbon?"

Oh no! I'd forgotten the condition of my hair. I tried to run my fingers through it like a comb, but the tangles were too numerous.

"Did you lose your boots in the tide? And your stockings?"

"M-m-m, this muffin melts in my mouth. You are the greatest cook, Au Sam." To divert her attention, I sniffed the air. "Is something burning? Something's burning in the kitchen."

"The cake!" She gathered her skirts and flew to the kitchen.

I chuckled to myself and skipped across the hallway into the book-lined combination sitting room and study that Mama called our parlor. No renovations had been made yet on the musty parlor, where every square inch of two entire walls was covered with built-in bookcases, which were filled with books of every kind. Even the window and fireplace walls had books stacked in front of them. When I saw the room during our tour the evening before, I had begged Mama to let me help her decorate the room. It didn't take much convincing on my part.

Now I stared at the leather-bound treasures on those shelves. *I can hardly wait.* I wandered over to the two upholstered sofas that faced each other and three armchairs clustered around the fireplace. *These are hopeless. They'll need to be replaced, or at least recovered.* I ran my hand along the edge of the antique trestle table under the windows that stretched the entire length of one wall. *A good coat of wax should shine this up in no time. Same goes for those drop-leaf tables by the door.*

I set a carved walnut rocker in motion and eyed the scratches and nicks on a natural wicker chaise. *It will come alive under a new coat of varnish.* The fact that we'd never refinished furniture before didn't present a problem to me or my mother. *How difficult can it be?*

A mound of ancient sea chests, dough chests, and carpenter chests stacked in the back corner of the room begged to be restored to their earlier beauty. I opened one of the larger sea chests and found a tin Paul Revere lantern and a Bristol glass oil lamp, as well as two pewter bowls and a brass cuspidor separated by old quilts. *This is better than Christmas morning.*

Thad's and my second encounter went much better than our

first. I don't know how long I'd been sitting on a large rock overlooking the incoming tide, when I spotted him walking toward me, a sketch pad tucked under one arm.

He waved and called to me. "Do you know you can be trapped on this rock at high tide?" He climbed up and sat down beside me. "See." He pointed at the eddy of water forming behind the rock. "A friend of mine had to sit out the tide, right on this spot. It seems he fell asleep and awoke to find himself surrounded by deep water."

I gave him a sidelong look. "Oh yes, I believe you, like I believe your story about those razor-tailed snakes."

He reddened and grinned, his eyes shining with deviltry. "Yeah, about those snakes—"

"Don't worry, I didn't believe you for a moment."

He threw his head back and laughed.

"What is so funny?"

"You should have seen the look of terror on your face when I told you about the snakes."

"And you should have seen the terror on your face when Sundance pounced on you."

Upon hearing his name, Sundance bounded up the beach. "Come here, boy," I called. "He really is quite harmless, you know."

"Touché." He pointed to the advancing tide. "This time, you can see for yourself. Either we jump from this rock in the next few minutes, or we'll have to go wading."

Reluctantly, I acceded to his advice and allowed him to help me down before the next big wave crashed against the rock.

"Race you to that big log over there," he shouted.

"You're on." I tore up the beach for higher ground. Pushing myself as hard as possible, I reached the driftwood seconds behind him. Together, we watched the sun fill the crystal-blue sky.

"Is it always so beautiful here?" I asked.

"The weather on the Cape changes more often than a woman changes her mind." Ignoring my glare, he continued, "You can be sitting by an open fire when suddenly the wind will change direction, and you have to throw open the windows in order to breathe."

As we sat there, we talked about our dreams and about life on the Cape. But when Thad mentioned the war, I was ready to go back to the house. "I'd rather not talk about the war."

"Why?"

I shrugged. "I just don't want to."

The next day, as Mama and I prepared to go to the depot to meet Daddy's train, I took one last look at our efforts. The room glistened from floorboards to ceiling. A fire danced in the massive stone fireplace, recently cleaned by Barney, the local chimney sweep. I had stained and polished one of the largest of the sea trunks and positioned it between the sofas. A bouquet of budding tree branches in a copper kettle provided the finishing touch.

I gazed at the room with satisfaction. My nails were chipped, my hands stained, and my muscles ached. Never in my life had I worked so hard and felt so rewarded. While the room was hardly San Francisco chic or Boston Back Bay splendor, it charmed me. *I hope Daddy likes it too.* I crossed my fingers, then ran to the waiting car.

We arrived in Woods Hole an hour before Daddy's train was due. Mama parked the Packard in front of the general store. "I need to pick up a few groceries before meeting Daddy at the depot."

A bell tinkled over our heads as we entered the cluttered little shop. From behind the counter, a tall, gaunt man with a white mustache and bushy sideburns stood up. "Good afternoon, ladies. May I help you?"

Mama walked to the counter and handed him her list. I wandered over to a stack of newspapers sitting on a chair beside the potbellied stove. The headlines leapt up at me. "Congress Declares War on Germany."

My heart caught in my throat. *No, it can't be. This isn't supposed to happen! No!* Somehow, I'd convinced myself that by pushing the war from my mind, I could make it go away forever. Shuddering, I thought of Jamie and Galen, and possibly Shane Simons, and remembered how Mama described the horrors of war.

"Oh, dear God." I squeezed my eyes shut. "Can't You do anything to make it go away? Please, God, You can do anything, right? You're om-omnipotent—yes, that's the word—omnipotent, aren't You? Please!" I felt a hand touch my shoulder.

"CeeCee, are you ready to go?" My mother leaned over my shoulder. "I called to you, but you didn't hear— Oh, no, it's really happened." She reached around me and picked up the Boston newspaper. "This will change our lives." Her voice broke as she turned back toward the counter, taking the newspaper with her. In a daze, I heard her speaking to the clerk as she paid for her purchases.

We walked out of the shop into the sunlight and climbed into the car. Rusty, who'd been looking in the store windows farther down the street, saw us and came racing back to the car.

"Did you hear, Mama? Did you hear? We're gonna beat the daylights out of the old Kaiser. Yes, we are!" Rusty climbed into the back seat. "Do you think the war will last long enough for me to go?"

Mama shook her head sadly. "I certainly hope not, son."

"Aw!" He groaned and leaned back in the seat. "That's not fair! President Wilson says it's the war to end all wars. I'll never get to fight."

Mama glanced over her shoulder at my brother. "One can only hope, son."

Days of Innocence

Daddy was leaning against the depot's porch railing, reading the afternoon paper when we arrived. After a round of kisses and hugs, Mama relinquished the driver's seat to him. Except for the initial small talk, a pall hung over our conversation on the ride back to Bide-a-wee, as if by unspoken agreement we would avoid talking about the war during our short time together.

Minutes after we returned to Bide-a-wee, Jamie roared up to the house on the motorcycle he'd borrowed from Hershel. Rusty and I dashed out of the house to meet him, both of us begging to ride on the noisy contraption.

"Tomorrow morning, I promise." Jamie scooped Rusty onto his shoulders. "Both of you will get a chance to ride."

At dinner Daddy announced that he had a surprise for us in the trunk of the car. Mama shepherded Rusty, Au Sam, and me into the parlor while he and Jamie went for the surprise.

They set the bulky wooden crate in the middle of the parlor floor. "This should keep you company during the week while we're gone," Daddy said as he ripped open the crate.

"A Victrola!" I squealed. Although my violin instructor preferred I play the classics from the Romantic Era, I loved learning different kinds of music. Impatiently, I watched as the men assembled the instrument. At last, Daddy straightened.

"CeeCee, can you carry in the box of discs from the trunk of the car while Jamie attaches the crank?"

"Sure, Daddy." I leapt to my feet and raced to the Packard. The leather-bound box was much heavier than I imagined, but I managed to lug it inside the house and set it on the trestle table. "Oh, look, *The Mikado*! And *The Pirates of Penzance!*

Rusty reached over my shoulder. "Here's an album of Enrico Caruso."

"Here, let me do it!" I took the set of records from his hands. "You're going to break something."

"No, I won't!" My brother snatched an album from my hands. "And another, Mama, by Jan Kubelík."

Rusty and I took turns during the rest of the evening, cranking up the Victrola and choosing the music. At one point, I sank back against a stack of pillows and gazed about the softly lighted room. Au Sam rocked by the fireplace, mending the heels on Rusty's woolen stockings. Mama relaxed at one end of the sofa, with Daddy's head in her lap, running her fingers through his graying hair. Jamie sat at the trestle table studying for an upcoming test, in spite of hearing Gilbert and Sullivan's "Three Little Maids From School" five times in a row. In the middle of the floor, Rusty searched through the box of discs for his next musical choice with one hand and gobbled popcorn with the other.

I never want to forget this moment. This is what family is all about. Often since leaving California, I had wondered if we'd ever all be together again. I sighed contentedly.

The next day, before the rest of the family awakened, I slipped out of the house and down to the water with Sundance at my heels. High tide from a storm at sea had strewn seaweed and seafoam on the shore during the night, then had abandoned it to the daylight. My face stung from the nippy breeze. As I walked, I did a series of cartwheels and handstands on the firm, wet sand. Sundance barked his applause.

We'd almost completed our walk when Thad appeared over the crest of the next sand dune. He waved and jogged down to meet me.

"Hi. You're late this morning, sleepyhead."

"Yeah, I guess. Pop and I had a tiff last night. Guess I didn't sleep too well." He shortened his long strides to match mine.

"I know how that is." I folded my hands behind my back and walked in silence for a while. "Want to talk about it?"

Thad picked up a stick of driftwood and tossed it into the surf,

Sundance in pursuit. "I'm going to enlist as soon as school's out."

"Oh?" *This war! Don't people know how to talk about anything else? I hate it. I truly hate it.*

"My pop says I should wait to be drafted, but I don't agree." Sundance returned with the stick and dropped it at Thad's feet. Now used to the friendly dog, Thad picked up the stick and threw it back into the surf. The dog bounded after it. "What do you think?"

"Think? Do you really want to know what I think?" I stopped and shook my finger in his face. "I think you men are a bunch of bloodthirsty Mongols, aching for a fight. That's what I think."

He looked at me and shook his head, his voice oozing with condescension. "And you women don't understand the importance of honor, of defending one's country against aggressors like the Kaiser."

"You're right. I don't understand." I threw my hands up into the air. "I never will understand. Will I see you again before you go?" I turned and started back toward Bide-a-wee.

"Oh, sure. It will take awhile." He again fell into step beside me. "Probably not until after graduation in June."

I rolled my eyes heavenward. "Good. I'm glad you haven't abandoned all your senses. And what about your art?"

He glanced down at the sketch pad under his arm. "It will have to wait."

When Thad had first shown me his sketches of seascapes, he talked about going to art school in Boston in the fall. He was good, very good. To most people, one sea gull looks pretty much like the next, but Thad's pencil could capture the personality of individual birds. He'd also promised to sketch a picture of Sundance and me. *Oh, well, that will never happen now*, I mused.

Thad and I walked the rest of the way in silence, afraid we might break the uneasy truce we'd established. We parted, promising to meet again the next day.

I trudged up the bank toward the house, preoccupied with thoughts of our conversation. As I drew closer, I spotted Jamie standing on the balcony outside his room at the opposite end of the house from mine. He waved. And I returned his wave.

"Stay there," Jamie shouted. "I'm coming down."

I nodded and bounded up the steps and onto the porch. *Oh no, did he see Thad? Of course, he did. From up there, Jamie couldn't have missed him.* I hadn't mentioned Thad to anyone, because I didn't know exactly how to explain him.

Making my way over to one of the wicker rockers, I slumped down into the chair. *What am I going to say? Thad is hardly a boyfriend. I'm not even sure we're friends, exactly. Sometimes I don't like him at all.*

Jamie burst through the door onto the porch. "Good morning, Cricket." Over the years, Jamie had had a number of nicknames for me, and Cricket was his latest. I didn't mind. In fact, I kind of liked the special bond his nicknames implied. "You're certainly up early. I don't remember your being fond of mornings. What's happened?"

"It's Cape Cod. Did you hear the surf last night? Woke me out of a sound sleep. Must have been a big one out at sea."

"Yeah. It sounded like a steam engine coming through my bedroom walls. Is it always like that out here?"

I tucked my legs up to my chin and wrapped my arms about my knees. "No, one night last week the tide sounded like soft thunder in the distance. I could even hear the peepers in that bunch of wild apple trees over there." I pointed to the heavily wooded area north of the house.

"Apple trees. Are you sure?" He leaned over the porch railing in the direction I had pointed.

"Yeah, and a couple of pear trees too. If you push through the thicket, you'll find an old stone fence that must have marked the edge of an orchard at one time. From the kitchen window, you can see one of the pears blossoming."

Jamie sat down in the rocker beside me. "I never thought I'd like it here much. I came down every once in a while to check on the place for the folks. To me, it was a Sunday drive, a place to go—"

We rocked for five minutes to the squeaks from our rockers and the incessant calls of the gulls swooping overhead.

"Jamie?" I stared straight ahead at the horizon. "Do you really have to enlist?"

"Yeah, Cricket, I do."

Abruptly, I stopped rocking and slowly rose to my feet. "That's what they all say!" I walked down the steps onto the grass.

"They?" I heard Jamie follow me. "They, like in the boy on the beach?"

I blinked back my angry tears. "He said I couldn't understand how he feels. I guess he's right. I don't understand."

Jamie came up behind me and rested his arm on my shoulder. "You really care for this boy?"

I whirled about in surprise. "No. Of course not. I just met Thaddeus last week. It's not Thad; it's the whole frustrating nightmare." I buried my face in my hands. "If Mama's right and you die—" My words caught in my throat. "Oh, Jamie! I don't know what I'd do without you."

My brother tilted my face up toward his. "CeeCee, honey, remember the first time I was getting ready to leave for Boston, and you were convinced I would never, ever return?"

I nodded.

"Do you remember how I promised I'd be back, that I'd always be there for you?"

I swiped at my tears with the back of my hand. "That's a promise you can't make this time, can you?"

"You're right." He drew me into his arms. "We're both too old for those kinds of promises now, aren't we?"

"So lie to me." I buried my face in his scratchy wool sweater.

"No, I won't do that." Gently he eased me away from him and gazed into my eyes. "But I will promise you that nothing short of death will keep me from coming home to you, little Cricket." He reached into his pocket and handed me a handkerchief. "If for no other reason than to discover the identity of your mysterious stranger."

I blushed and choked back my tears.

"Hey, you two, getting hungry for breakfast?" We turned to find Mama standing in the doorway.

"Like a bear waking from hibernation," Jamie called. "We'll be right in, Mama." Turning back to me, he asked, "Are you going to be OK?"

"I guess." I handed back his handkerchief. "I'd better go dress for breakfast."

As I climbed the porch steps, Jamie called, "When do I get to meet Thaddeus?"

I sent my brother a coy smile. "When you come up next weekend—maybe."

"At dawn?"

I laughed. "At dawn."

"It's a date." Jamie strolled across the lawn toward the beach while I ran into the house to get ready for breakfast.

By the time I buttoned my white cotton pleated skirt and red sailor top, brushed my hair, and fastened it back into a bow, I could hear the family assembling in the sun room. I slid my white-stockinged feet into my patent-leather slippers and skipped down the stairs.

"Ah, there you are." Daddy looked up from the financial section of the morning paper. Tradition in the McCall family allowed the newspaper to be read at Sunday breakfast. "How's my girl this morning?"

I skidded to a stop by my father's chair. "Morning, Daddy. Isn't it a beautiful day?" I kissed the small balding spot developing on the top of his head and took my place at the table. Jamie didn't look up from the sports page. "Beautiful? Looked overcast to me."

"Perspective is everything, dear brother." I adjusted the napkin on my lap and filled my bowl with hot oatmeal. The steam from the hot cereal spiraled into my face as I poured on the maple syrup. "May I please have the society section?"

"Society section?" Jamie chortled. "Do I hear echoes of dear, sweet Cousin Ashley here? How too, too divine." He mimicked Ashley's fluttery hand motions.

I stuck out my tongue at him, and Rusty giggled.

Mama tastefully dabbed at her lips with a napkin to hide her grin. "Now, Jamie, be kind to your sister. And, as for you, Chloe Celeste, we'll have no unladylike crudities at the table."

"Yes, Mama." I glanced toward Rusty. He wrinkled his nose at me. I returned the gesture.

"CeeCee, I mean it."

I hung my head, feigning remorse. "Yes, Mama."

Daddy separated the society section from the rest of the newspaper and handed it to me. I thanked him and hid behind the first page. Catching Rusty's eye, I made a pig face at him. He scowled and looked at Mama to see if she was watching; then, when he was certain she was discussing decorating plans for the master bedroom with Au Sam, he returned the gesture.

Returning my attention to the paper, my gaze fell on a quarter-page advertisement at the bottom.

Hearing me snicker, Rusty tugged at my sleeve. "What? What's so funny?"

"Listen to this. It's an advertisement for Eau de Paris." I giggled aloud. " '... Ladies and farmer's wives will benefit equally from the scented sachets on their pillows. The fragrance is a blend of rose hips, sweetbrier blossoms, honeysuckle petals—' " I peeked over the top of the paper at the benign faces of my family, " '—and buffalo chips, well ground, sold by the pound. When dampened, Eau de Paris soothes and heals boils, carbuncles, and unwanted bunches ...' "

Jamie choked on a mouthful of toast while Rusty gurgled into his cup of hot chocolate. I caught my brothers' eyes, and the three of us dissolved into peals of laughter. Au Sam bent her head forward so only her top knot of hair and shoulders could be seen bobbing slightly. Mama covered her grin with the pink table napkin, but couldn't successfully swallow her laughter.

A dignified "Hmmph!" erupted from my father. He peered over his reading glasses and arched his eyebrows in censure, looking first at Mama, then at me. "Chloe Celeste!"

"But, Daddy, that's what it says, right here, see? In print!" I turned the newspaper so he could read the advertisement.

"Hmmph!" The grandfather clock in the hallway gonged eight. "I can't say I would want every advertisement read aloud at the breakfast table, even if it is printed in the *Boston Globe*, or the *New York Times*, for that matter." He slapped me playfully on the head with his napkin. "Just because something is in print doesn't make it appropriate subject matter for civilized dining."

"Yes, Daddy," I gurgled.

He returned his attention to the financial section of the paper, but not before I detected a twinkle in his eyes.

A few minutes passed, punctuated only by the sound of pages turning and Rusty slurping his hot cocoa.

"Au Sam, you make the best sweet rolls on either side of the Mississippi River." Jamie saluted her with the sticky pastry. "I wish I could take you back to school with me. The cafeteria's rolls make good hockey pucks."

The woman grinned and looked at the floor to hide her embarrassment. "By the way." Jamie took a second roll and slathered it with butter. "I need to head back to school earlier than I thought. I'm worried about that big test."

"I wish you didn't need to ride that contraption back and forth. Perhaps Daddy and I should consider buying you an inexpensive automobile, a Model T or—" Mama glanced toward Daddy.

"No, really," Jamie interrupted. "It wouldn't make sense to buy a car right now. When I ship out, no one knows how long I'll be gone."

"He's right, Chloe," Daddy said. "We'll save the car, son, until you return from Europe. It can be a belated graduation gift."

Mama closed her eyes for a moment. "Will you be coming back down to the Cape next weekend?"

Jamie folded his napkin and placed it beside his plate, then grinned at me. "I'll most certainly try."

Daddy laid his paper aside. "I almost forgot, CeeCee. I made appointments for auditions at three music conservatories in the city. So next weekend, plan to return to the city with me."

"Really?" I squealed with joy. "Will I get to stay at the hotel and everything?"

"No. I'll be in Washington, D.C., part of the week. Your Aunt Drucilla volunteered to have you stay with them."

My mother dropped her fork onto her plate. "You didn't tell me that part, Cyrus. I'm not too—"

"I'm sorry. I thought you knew."

She sighed and shook her head dramatically. "You know as well as I that every time those girls get together, trouble follows."

Daddy laughed. "Oh, Chloe, surely you don't blame Ashley for the problem in Boston. Julia should have known better than to take the girls anywhere near the square."

My mother's eyes widened in disbelief. "I most certainly do blame Ashley."

My father reached over and patted my hand indulgently. "Our

CeeCee is a mature young woman. She won't allow her daffy cousin to drag her into a situation she can't handle."

I smiled at him. "Thank you, Daddy."

Mama pushed her chair back from the table. "I'll hold off on the redecorating and spend the week in the city with her. It won't be a complete waste of time, since there are a number of things I need to purchase."

I cast a pleading look at my father.

"Nonsense," my father scoffed. "CeeCee will do just fine. I'll be with her as much as possible, I promise, especially for the auditions and the interviews. Besides, she's hardly a child needing constant supervision."

I grinned and nodded enthusiastically. Mama narrowed her eyes, arching one brow for accent. "It isn't CeeCee's maturity that bothers me."

"Ashley isn't all that bad," I argued.

From across the table, Jamie groaned. "Tactical error, Cricket."

Mama pursed her lips. "She's all that and worse."

Daddy closed his section of the paper and placed it on the floor beside his chair. "Well, you and I can discuss it later, Chloe. But for now, let's enjoy the rest of the day together. Rusty, this afternoon, would you like to explore a century-old whaling ship that ran aground up by Provincetown? Or would you prefer to go biking together on Martha's Vineyard?"

Grateful to have the attention diverted from my maturity or lack thereof for a while, I sipped my cocoa while Rusty and Daddy decided which activity to do this afternoon and which one to save for another.

I don't know how Daddy convinced Mama to let me go. But on the following Sunday, I returned with him to New York City, carrying a long list of Mama's regulations.

Ashley met me at the door and dragged me up to her room almost before I could kiss Daddy goodbye. "I'll be here for you at ten on Wednesday to take you to the first audition. Be sure to practice, sweetheart, or your mama will have my head."

"Don't worry, Daddy. I'll practice; I promise." I bussed his cheek and darted up the stairs after my cousin. I giggled to myself—it had been years since either he or Mama had needed to remind me to practice.

At dinner that evening, Aunt Drucilla suggested that I attend classes with Ashley the next morning. Having been out of school for over a month, I eagerly looked forward to returning to the familiar environment. I didn't learn of my cousin's alternate plans until we left for school the next day.

The moment the front door closed, Ashley bounded down the front steps and behind a large boxwood shrub. "Here," she called. "Catch!"

"Catch what?" I shouted in time to see a large carpetbag hurtling toward me. I caught it full force in the chest. "What in the world?"

She ran from behind the bush carrying a second satchel. "I dropped these from my bedroom window this morning while you practiced your violin."

"What are they for?"

"Well, you certainly wouldn't want us to tour the greatest city on earth looking like little schoolgirls, would you?" She tugged at the skirt of her school uniform.

"I beg your pardon?"

She giggled and skipped through the wrought-iron gate onto the sidewalk. "After first period, English literature class, we'll change into other clothing in the gymnasium locker room, then slip out the gymnasium door. Don't worry; we won't get caught. My friends and I do it all the time."

I stared at her in surprise. "You're going to play hooky?"

"Of course, didn't you ever—?"

She hurried down the sidewalk, past the row of identical brownstones. I rushed to keep up. "Once, maybe."

"Good. I'd hate to be the one who corrupts you." She tossed the heavy satchel over her shoulder, holding it by two leather straps, then darted out into the street. "Come on; let's beat that ice wagon."

Her plan went without a hitch. After an hour of the literature teacher reading from John Milton's *Paradise Lost* in a steady monotone, I was ready for anything, even Ashley's adventure.

Trying to look as inconspicuous as possible, I followed Ashley into the locker room, where she had earlier deposited the satchels. "Hurry! Miss Grant could come in here any time."

Charged with excitement, I fumbled with the buttons on my blouse. I had already slipped out of my blouse and started to unfasten the snaps on my skirt, when the hallway door opened. Terrified, I froze, my heart pounding to the click of Cuban heels on tile. I shot a wild glance at my cousin.

Before the person appeared around the corner of the entryway, she called, "All right, young ladies! What do you think you're doing?"

A moment later, a head covered with sleek black hair popped around the corner. "Scared ya, didn't I?"

"Oh, it's only you," Ashley whispered. Then she turned to me. "It's only Mavis. She's going with us; she knows the city."

Mavis's ebony eyes danced with excitement. "Anything worth knowing about the city, that is." The girl sauntered over to her locker. I stared, unbelieving, at the stunningly attractive girl with the almost translucent, Dresden-china complexion. "We gotta get out of here before Old Lady Pettibone takes record."

After Ashley introduced me to Mavis, I asked, "Aren't you afraid of getting in trouble?"

"What are they going to do to us? Suspend us this close to graduation? So?"

"Look." Ashley smoothed the shimmery green silk frock over her hips. "Let's talk about this later."

I removed a gray silk dress from my satchel and gasped at the delicate beauty of the dyed-to-match French lace that edged the square neckline. "Oh, Ashley, this is beautiful."

"It's Mummy's." She pirouetted in the center of the room. "So's this one. Don't you love them?"

"Ashley! Does she know?"

My cousin snorted. "Are you kidding? Do you think I asked her? I can just see it now. 'Mummy, CeeCee and I are going to skip school tomorrow, and we need a couple of dresses to wear that will make us look four years older.' Here." She tossed a pair of gray-kid heels at me. "These match your outfit."

I looked down at the delicate lace bodice, then back at Ashley. "I don't know . . ."

Mavis groaned as she stepped into a burgundy shift. "She's going to mess this up; I can tell."

I blushed at the girl's sarcastic tone, then glowered. *I don't much like you.*

Ashley tossed her blond mane from side to side, examining her image in the wall mirror, then piled her hair on her head and placed a wide-brimmed straw hat on top. "Think about it, CeeCee. We've come too far to turn back now."

Ashley's friend puckered her lips in front of the mirror and coated them with burgundy lipstick.

"Come on," Ashley urged. "You can do that once we're safely out of here."

"I forgot to bring my purse." Mavis pawed through her stack of clothing. "I have my money, but forgot my purse."

"It's OK." Ashley held up a white-kidskin clutch bag. "I brought an extra—couldn't make up my mind which one to carry." She giggled and tossed the bag to Mavis, then tossed a second one to me. "Here, this one matches your outfit. There's money inside the inner pocket. Use it however you wish."

"I can't take—"

"Nonsense! Don't be a party pooper." Ashley fluttered her hand into the air. "You'll need it all, I assure you."

I caught the bag. "I suppose the money is your mother's also?" I lathered my words with irritation. Mavis glared at me, while my cousin's delicate laughter echoed about the high-ceilinged room. "Of course not, silly."

A blend of anger and fear coursed through me as I stepped into the shoes. *I don't like this. I just don't like this.* My hands shook as I adjusted a gray-and-white straw confection on my head.

I paused, catching the reflection of Ashley's friend as she hid her sleek black hairdo beneath a tower of flowers and tulle. *And I don't much like you, Mavis.*

When Ashley's friend caught me staring, she lifted one eyebrow and the corresponding corner of her lips. Unnerved with the feeling she had read my mind, I scooped up my own clothes and stuffed them into the satchel. "Why do we have to go to all this trouble in order to tour the city?"

The two grinned at one another, then at me. "We'll tell you all about it on the way."

Warning bells jangled in my head. The more I heard about this trip, the less I wanted to go. "I am not sure this is a good idea, Ashley."

"Come on." She grabbed my hand and dragged me through the back door of the school into the alley.

We walked the four blocks to Ashley's home, stashed the satchels behind the boxwood bush, and set off for our adventure. I eyed the steps leading up to the front door longingly. *Maybe I'm being a chicken. After all, what could go wrong? It's all in fun*, I argued, as I followed Ashley and Mavis down the street toward the nearest subway station. *Besides, They're the ones truant from school.*

Once out of hearing range of Ashley's town house, I said, "It would be nice to know where you're taking me."

"Relax, CeeCee darling," Ashley laughed. "Just relax and enjoy."

At the station, I opened the borrowed purse to fish out the money for the subway ride. Stitched to the inside pocket was Ashley's name and address. *At least I'll be able to find my way home if anything goes wrong*, I thought as I studied the delicate embroidering. *Now, why did I think such a thought?*

"Here." Ashley placed a token in my hand. "Use this." She dropped three more tokens into my hand. "Keep these for later."

"Just where are we going?" I asked impatiently over the screech of the approaching train.

"To lunch," she called, leaping on the train seconds after Mavis.

I clutched my hat and ran zigzag through the waiting crowd, slipping inside the car just as the doors slid closed behind me. "Don't do that to me again," I gasped. "I'm not used to walking in these shoes!"

The train lurched forward. Nearly toppling onto an old man and his bulging shopping bags, I grabbed a leather strap that dangled from the ceiling. Ashley and Mavis laughed as I struggled to regain my balance. I glared. "What's so funny?"

"You." Ashley giggled. "You're so un-Manhattan, CeeCee."

"Really! Well, cousin dear, I could take you and your friend on a trolley tour of San Francisco."

Mavis examined her fingernails on one hand. "We do have trolleys here in New York, you know."

Not ones like ours, which travel at forty-five-degree angles, almost! I chuckled to myself. "So, what's first on the agenda, after lunch?" *I might not like the girl very much, but why ruin the day?*

Ashley shrugged. "A little shopping and—" She eyed Mavis. "And a tour of the Statue of Liberty, of course. Every tourist should visit the Lady." Except for their conspiratorial look, the plan sounded good.

We dined at a little sidewalk cafe off Thirty-fourth Street. Mavis's sense of humor kept us laughing throughout the luncheon. I'd never tried English watercress sandwiches. "Tastes like cucumbers to me!"

"How gauche!" Mavis waved her gloved hand expressively. Ashley's friend had a knack for mimicking other people's dialects and gestures. I choked on her imitation of a wealthy matron sitting with her clipped French poodle two tables from us.

By the time we finished our meal and boarded the train for Battery Park and the Statue of Liberty, I'd decided she was OK. *We got off to a bad start, that's all.*

When the train stopped at our station, we raced down the hill to where people were boarding the ferry for Bedloe's Island. I could see the wooden bar with the red stop sign coming down. Expecting Ashley and Mavis to wait for the next ferry, I slowed down. Instead, they ducked under the bar and ran on board the departing boat.

"Come on, CeeCee, you can make it," Ashley called.

Too terrified to be left behind, I shot under the bar and leapt aboard the moving ferry to the cheers of a crowd of passengers gathered along the rails. Midair, I thought, *Oh, Mama, if you could see me now!*

I landed firmly on the metal flooring and steadied myself by clutching a brass finial at the end of the iron rail. Inches below my feet, a wake of churning waters cried out for all to hear, "Stupid. Stupid. Stupid." If I'd fallen into the bay, I couldn't have blamed my stupidity on Ashley or Mavis. No one pushed me. No one made me jump.

Ashley ran to my side. "Oh, CeeCee, you were so funny."

Two good-looking sailors strolled past. "Excuse me," Mavis whispered, "but I think it's my patriotic duty to make certain America's fighting men enjoy their last sights of home before, uh, shipping out for France." She sauntered after her prey.

Ashley looked longingly at Mavis, then back at me. "Are you sure you're all right, CeeCee?"

"I'm fine. Just give me a moment to catch my breath." My heartbeat pounded in my ears. "You go ahead. I'll catch up with you and Mavis later."

Ashley nodded excitedly. "If we get separated, we'll meet back at the Battery, OK?"

"Back where?" She didn't wait to answer my question before hurrying after Mavis. I hung on to the railing until my heartbeat returned to normal. Straightening my bonnet, I brushed a stray lock of hair behind one ear, then took a deep breath.

"That was quite a sprint." A decidedly masculine voice spoke from somewhere above my left shoulder. I reddened, keeping my face turned toward the New York skyline.

The voice drew closer to my left ear. "Took quite a chance there. What if you'd missed?"

Those pesky alarms jangled in my brain again. I lifted an eyebrow and eyed the intruder. "Excuse me, sir, but have we been properly introduced?"

"No, ma'am." The man gave me a lazy grin, then tipped his hat. "Please allow me to—"

Suddenly I could hear Mama's warnings. I glanced past the young man's shoulder and spied an older woman standing alone by the railing on the other side of the boat.

"Auntie Lou," I called, waving frantically at the startled woman. She looked about her to see at whom I might be waving. "Auntie Lou, I was afraid I'd missed you." I brushed past the surprised young man and skipped across the deck to the strange woman. I threw my arms about her, whispering in her ear, "Please, pretend you know me. I need to get away from that man over there, the one with the light brown mustache."

A knowing smile filled the gray-haired woman's face. In a loud voice, she scolded, "Emmy Sue, that will teach you to dawdle so long, feeding the pigeons. If you can't keep up with me, I'll have to leave you home next time."

She took my arm and led me inside the cabin. Once inside, I turned to thank her. "There was something about that man that just didn't feel right. May I stay with you until we reach the island?"

"Of course, dearie." The woman patted my arm. "I'd enjoy seeing the sights with a sprightly young niece like you. So tell me, my dear, what are you doing touring Manhattan all alone?"

Caught in a Whirlwind

The plump lady in the brown-tweed suit introduced herself as Miss Jackson, a retired schoolteacher visiting New York City for the first time. "I managed to save up a little money for my retirement and had always wanted to see the rest of the country. One day this spring, I was watching the rain pelt my parlor window, when I decided it's now or never." The woman nodded her head for emphasis. "I packed a bag, went down to the depot, and bought a ticket on the next train out of Dodge City. If I'd been fifteen minutes earlier, I'd be boarding a cable car in San Francisco right now."

"Really? That's where I'm from, San Francisco. At least, until my dad was transferred to New York. And you know something else? My mother used to live in Hays, Kansas. Isn't that a coincidence?"

We laughed together.

"Actually, I'm here today because my daffy cousin and her friend decided to skip school. They dragged me along. We got separated when they headed after a couple of sailors." My voice drifted off uncertainly. "I wasn't too—"

"A good thing too. It sounds like your mother raised a wise daughter."

I grinned. "I hope so."

Miss Jackson and I toured the gift shop at the base of the statue, then began our ascent up the metal stairs to the top. When we stopped to catch our breath on step number fifty-three, I leaned my head back to appreciate the height of the statue's interior. Massive girders supported the iron cage surrounding the stairwell. Beyond the girders, gas lanterns revealed the folds of the Lady's green copper gown billowing in a network of trusses like a huge circus tent. The voices and the footsteps of other climbers turned the statue's interior into a giant echo.

The farther we climbed the winding stairway, the narrower the space became. We stopped again at the seventy-eighth step, then at the one hundred and second. I cast a worried glance at Miss Jackson's red face. *All I need is for her to pass out or something.* I asked her if she wanted to stop and rest again, but she shook her head. "I'll make it," she said. "I try to walk five miles every morning."

We climbed until we reached the Lady's crown, which was smaller than Bide-a-wee's kitchen pantry. One look out of the observation windows, and I forgot the tight, stuffy space. Miss Jackson glowed like a schoolgirl as she darted from one telescope to the next.

"Look, look here," she called from across the small space. I can see the Narrows from here—and the open sea. Imagine, the open sea. I've never seen—" Her words caught in her throat.

I put my arm around her. "You would love my folks' place up on Cape Cod. When I'm there, I go walking along the beach every morning." I thought of Sundance and of Thad and the delightful moments we'd spent together in the short time since we moved to Bide-a-wee.

"If I had a home on the shore, I would never want to leave it." The woman removed a handkerchief from her purse and blew her nose.

"My favorite poet, Emily Dickinson, dreamed of one day seeing a prairie."

The woman cleared her throat. "I guess the grass is always greener on the other side of the fence."

I gave the woman a gentle squeeze. "My dad was telling me about a boat ride you can take around Manhattan. You should take it before you go back home."

We chatted all the way back to the bottom of the statue. When Miss Jackson suggested we catch the next ferry back to the Battery, I looked around for Ashley and Mavis. They were nowhere to be seen, nor were the two sailors. Reluctantly, I followed Miss Jackson onto the boat, paying minimal attention as she outlined her plans for the rest of her New York stay. When she invited me to take the boat trip around Manhattan Island with her, I almost agreed, if for no other reason than to worry Ashley as she had worried me. *If anything ever worries Ashley, that is!*

By the time we stepped off the boat onto the dock, I could barely contain my anger at my cousin. I assured the kindly lady from Kansas that it would be all right if she took the boat trip without me. "I'll be fine, really. I'm sure Ashley and Mavis will be along any moment. You go ahead and enjoy yourself."

When the woman refused to leave my side, we found a park bench and made ourselves comfortable. She opened her purse and took out a small sack of bread crumbs. "One of the things I've enjoyed doing each day since I arrived is feeding the pigeons. Watch!" She threw a handful of bread crumbs into the air. Seemingly out of nowhere, dozens of pigeons descended, catching many of the crumbs before they touched the brick walkway.

"Feeding God's creatures always reminds me of how well my heavenly Father cares for me. Here, you try." The woman handed me some crumbs. "There's never been a time in my life when I doubted God's presence. Even when my William was killed in the Philippines during the Spanish-American War, I knew God was with me. We were to be married—"

"Oh, I'm sorry." *War! Why does every conversation return to that horrid subject?*

"That's all right. It was a long time ago. All I ever wanted was a farmhouse filled with children, but after William—" She sighed. "But, you know, God has filled my life with other people's children. I've been richly blessed."

She told me about a few of her favorite pupils over the years. "One of my students ran for Congress. He lost, but he had the gumption to try. That's what really counts in life—gumption! Gumption and faith in God."

As the shadows lengthened on the grassy slope above the docks, I wondered how long I should wait for Ashley to return. Foolishly, I'd left my watch in the satchel outside Ashley's town house.

"Really, Miss Jackson, you don't have to wait any longer. If she doesn't return within the hour, I'll just catch a subway uptown." I knew that finding my way back to the town house was easier said than done, since I hadn't noticed which subway lines we'd taken earlier. I glanced at the address inside my borrowed purse and the roll of bills. "Perhaps it would be better if I catch a cab instead."

The retired teacher nodded. "I'd feel better if I saw you safely to a cab."

We walked across the grass to the busy street, where a number of cabs waited. I signaled for one, then turned and thanked the woman for her concern. "Why don't you let me drop you off at your hotel? I'm sure I have enough cash to cover the cost. Please, you've been so kind to me. I insist!"

At first, Miss Jackson refused. Finally, I convinced her that I needed her presence. Reluctantly, she climbed into the cab. I had just given the driver the address when I heard someone shouting my name.

"CeeCee! CeeCee! Wait!"

I spotted Ashley running toward me. "Wait! CeeCee. It's me."

Out of breath and disheveled, the girl fell into the seat beside me. "Oh, what a terrible afternoon. I was so afraid I would miss you. Mummy would never forgive me if I lost you in downtown Manhattan."

"Lost me? I'm hardly a child whom one might lose." I examined her clothing in disgust. "Where have you been? You look a wreck."

Ashley ignored my questions and glanced past me at Miss Jackson. "You didn't need to share a cab with some stranger. You had plenty of cash."

I bristled. "I am not sharing a cab with a stranger. Ashley, I would like to introduce you to Miss Jackson of Dodge City, Kansas. She has been my companion this afternoon."

"Oh—"

I tilted my nose upward. "You haven't answered my question. Where have you been?"

Ashley went into a sulk. "You don't have to scold me, you know. I'm hurting enough!"

"Hmmph! I doubt that," I muttered.

"I met this dreadful boy from Detroit named George." Her face came alive as she reported her afternoon adventure. "After we lost Mavis and Frank, George became an animal. If it weren't for a policeman patrolling along the waterfront, I'd hate to think what might have happened."

"Perhaps that's your problem, Ashley. You don't ever think."

Ashley's lower lip protruded. "Why are you being so hateful?"

"Concerned! Not hateful. One of these days..." As I rattled on, I was shocked to realize how much I sounded like my mother.

When the cab stopped in front of Miss Jackson's hotel, I wished her well and thanked her again for spending the afternoon with me. Ashley and I didn't speak the rest of the way uptown until we were within a block of the town house. "What are you going to tell your mother when she sees us dressed like this?"

"We're not telling her anything." Ashley sighed as if she were talking to a five-year-old. "We'll grab the satchels and sneak into the house through the servants' entrance. Mummy will be in her room resting before supper."

Ashley's plan worked without a hitch. She'd obviously perfected every detail. We tiptoed through the iron gate and into the tiny walled garden, through the back door, up the back stairs to Ashley's second-floor room. Once inside, we stripped out of the purloined dresses.

"Here, let me have that." She snatched the gray silk from my hand. "I'll send both of them out to the cleaners tomorrow. They'll come back looking as good as new."

I eyed the grass stain on the back of the dress Ashley had worn but said nothing as I chose a medium blue linen dress to wear to the dinner table. Picking up my hairbrush, I began brushing out the snarls of the day. Long before, I'd discovered the restorative powers found in brushing one's hair.

As Ashley moved about the room, hiding any evidence of our day's adventure, I knew I couldn't keep quiet. "You really took a terrible chance today, going off with a complete stranger, you know."

"Oh, CeeCee, you are such a party pooper. George was a little aggressive, but I can handle men."

I shot her an exasperated look. "Women have been known to

lose more than their reputations, going off with strangers."

"Oh, pooh. What do you know about it?" She dropped to the velvet seat in front of her dressing table and started removing the pins from her hair.

"Obviously, a lot more than you." I started from the room. "I'm going down to the drawing room to practice before dinner."

"Are you going to tell Mummy and Daddy about today?" she whispered.

I paused in the doorway. "I haven't decided yet."

Downstairs in the parlor, I practiced the more difficult passages of Chausson's *Concert for Violin, Piano, and String Quartet* until Aunt Drucilla's butler called me to dinner.

I'd barely joined the family at the table, when the doorbell rang. As a premonition shot through me, I glanced at Ashley. She seemed intent upon smoothing the linen napkin in her lap.

The butler returned to the dining room. "Excuse me, sir, but two policemen are asking for Miss Ashley." Ashley and I gasped.

"There must be some mistake. I'll take care of it." Uncle Ian stood up and placed his napkin beside his plate.

Aunt Drucilla looked askance as her daughter's face drained of color. "What is this all about?" My aunt looked at me, then again at Ashley.

Uncle Ian left the room and returned within a few minutes, his face drawn and pale. "Ashley, you will need to speak with the officers in the library. It's about a purse they found with your name in it."

Both of us pushed away from the table.

My uncle patted my shoulder. "You won't need to come, CeeCee. This doesn't involve you."

"No, sir. I believe I am also involved."

Her parents and I followed Ashley into the library.

One of the policemen immediately asked, "Are you Miss Ashley McCall?"

She nodded, her face a study of confidence.

"Is this your purse?" The policeman held out the white leather purse she'd lent to Mavis.

I stared at the purse in the man's hand as though it were a rattler, coiled and ready to strike.

My cousin casually took the bag from the man's hand, opened it, then snapped it shut. "Yes, sir, I believe it is. I lost it at school about a week ago. Where did you find it?"

My mouth dropped open in surprise. The second policeman shot a suspicious glance my way. "And who might you be, Miss?"

I gulped and cast a pleading glance at my cousin. "Uh, I'm Ashley's cousin, CeeCee Chamberlain."

The first officer pointed to the purse in Ashley's hand. "Have you ever seen this pocketbook before, Miss Chamberlain?"

Ashley waved her hand distractedly. "Oh, I'm sure she has, at one time or another. I've owned the thing for ages."

Aunt Drucilla stepped forward. "Officer, what is this all about? My daughter has admitted losing the bag last week at school. And, as for my niece, she's just in from the Cape last night, so I can't see how she could know anything about the purse."

Uncle Ian stepped up behind his wife and placed his hands on her shoulders. "Let the officer explain, Dru. It seems the purse was found this evening beside the body of a woman who'd been severely beaten. Since Ashley's name and address were stitched inside the purse, they believed the victim to be our daughter."

Ashley gasped, swayed slightly, and swooned. The first policeman caught her and placed her on the leather sofa. A moment passed, and my cousin came to.

The officer continued his questioning. "Do you have any idea who the girl might be who stole the purse?"

"No one stole it, sir. I lent the pocketbook to a friend." Ashley tried to sit up with Aunt Drucilla's help.

"And her name is?"

"Her name is Mavis Bartholomew."

"You say the woman is a friend of yours?"

Ashley nodded. "She attends the same school that I do."

The second officer asked, "Do you know where this Mavis lives?"

"I don't know Mavis's home address, but Miss Agatha Hornsby, our headmistress, would."

"Something doesn't add up, Lieutenant." The second policeman shook his head. "The victim must be—"

The lieutenant glared at his partner. "I'll handle this, sergeant. Now, Miss McCall, do you have any idea what Miss Bartholomew would be doing in an alleyway down by the Battery?"

Ashley blushed. "I guess you'll have to ask her."

The lieutenant pursed his lips. "If we get the chance. I'd like you to come down to the station tomorrow for questioning, Miss McCall, when you're feeling stronger."

"She says she doesn't know anything, Officer," Uncle Ian defended.

"Look, Mr. McCall, I believe both of these young ladies know a whole lot more than they're letting on. I could take them down to the precinct tonight if you prefer." The lieutenant narrowed his eyes at Ashley and me. "By morning, we might be dealing with a murder instead of an assault."

"No, no. I appreciate the way you are taking into account the girls' ages and my daughter's health. I will personally bring them to the station the first thing in the morning, if it's all right with you."

Uncle Ian escorted the policemen to the front door. The moment the door closed behind them, Aunt Drucilla jumped to her feet. "All right, young lady, it's time you straighten up and tell me what's going on here!"

Pressing her hand dramatically to her forehead, Ashley whimpered, "Oh, Mummy, my head hurts too much to talk right now."

Aunt Drucilla snatched Ashley's hand from her forehead. "Don't 'mummy' me. I want to know what's going on—now!" She whirled toward me. "CeeCee, what happened today?"

I reddened. "I, uh, well, you see—"

"No, I don't see." Aunt Drucilla stood directly in front of me, her face only inches from mine. Tears sprang into my eyes. I swallowed hard, casting a desperate glance toward Ashley.

"Tell her, CeeCee," Ashley sniffled, "tell her how you and Mavis convinced me to skip school today."

"We convin—"

"And dragged me downtown. It's not that I didn't try to warn them. I just knew something terrible would happen."

"Dragged?" My normally alto speaking voice soared to the level of a soprano.

Ashley continued with her version of the day's events. "I mean, I couldn't just let CeeCee go off without me, could I? Who knows what might have happened to her? I did the right thing, didn't I, Mummy?"

Aunt Drucilla glared at me. "Chloe Celeste, I am surprised at you. I realize you had no way of knowing how serious this lark of yours might turn out to be, but I did take you for a level-headed young woman like your mother."

"But I—but I—" Tears ran down my cheeks unbidden. I wanted to get out of there, run, escape, before I said something I'd regret. "Excuse me, please." I darted from the parlor and up the stairs to my room.

I overheard my uncle come to my defense. "Now, Dru, weren't you a little harsh? Especially without knowing all the facts?"

I didn't hear the rest; I didn't want to hear another word. *Oh, Daddy, where are you? I need you, right now.*

A few minutes later, I heard a knock at the door. "Go away," I sniffed.

"It's Melinda, the maid," the person hissed. "I brought you some dinner, Miss CeeCee."

My growling stomach forced me to consider the practical side of events, so I opened the door.

Melinda, a woman in her twenties, carried a tray into the room and placed it on the stand next to the bed. "Here. You'll be hungry before morning. And, for what it's worth, we on the staff know what really happened today. We've each worn your shoes, so to speak."

She smiled and left, closing the door silently behind her.

I nibbled on the slice of roast and took a few bites from the volcano of mashed potatoes and gravy. What did she mean, the staff knows what really happened? How could they know?

Exhausted and frustrated, I drank the glass of milk, changed into my nightdress, and climbed into bed. I don't how long I slept before the door to my room opened, and the light from the hallway fell across my bed.

"CeeCee," the voice whispered. "It's me, Ashley. Are you awake?"

"No!" I snapped in full voice. "I'm not awake! I'm sound asleep.

Leave me alone! And I won't wake up, so don't ask me!"

"OK," she whimpered. "I'll talk to you in the morning."

"Fine!" If I hadn't been so mad at her, I would have laughed out loud. I was beginning to wonder if my cousin could help being so daft.

The next morning, I refused to speak with anyone—I'd never been so angry in my entire life. At breakfast, Aunt Drucilla tried to make small talk. I replied in monosyllables, curt enough for her to know how upset I felt and controlled enough to avoid being insolent. I knew that, regardless of the circumstances, Mama and Daddy would not tolerate any disrespect from me.

Outside the police station, Uncle Ian parked the car, then led us inside the massive gray stone building. A desk officer directed us to a small cubicle.

The first person Ashley and I saw as we rounded the corner was Mavis Bartholomew, her eyes puffy from crying, her lips in a pout, her hair disheveled, but otherwise in remarkably good health for a person who'd sustained a beating. Ashley ran to her friend.

"Mavis, are you all right? We thought you were de—"

"You silly dimwit!" She jerked away from Ashley. "Of course, I'm all right. Why did you have to tell the police my name? I was at home and asleep when they showed up at my house last night."

"But we thought you—"

"Did you ever think to ask about the person who'd been beaten before you blabbed to the coppers? The woman who snatched the purse at the subway station was a fifty-year-old prostitute, for pity sake!" Mavis's foot tapped the hardwood floor; her eyes snapped in anger.

Ashley wrung her hands. "Oh, I'm so sorry. I had no i—"

Mavis looked past Ashley at me. "And I see Miss Goody-two-shoes is safe and sound also. Did you enjoy your stroll in the park with your Great Aunt Tilly—or whatever her name was?"

Ashley shook her head. "Oh no. That wasn't our aunt. It was some lady CeeCee met on the ferry. Besides, we don't have an Aunt Tilly." She turned to me. "Do we, CeeCee? Of course, maybe you do on your mother's side of the—"

"Oh, please do shut up, Ashley!" Mavis turned and walked to the far side of the tiny office. "Because you blabbed, we've both been suspended from school. We will be allowed to march, but we'll both be stripped of all honors."

"Just for playing hooky?" Ashley screeched. "We didn't—"

Uncle Ian tightened his jaw. "Any discipline incurred will not be for what happened, but what could have happened." Then, of Mavis, he asked, "How much of this little adventure can be blamed on CeeCee?"

"That hayseed? We would have been better off without her. If she hadn't come along, Ashley and I would have stayed together. But, no, Ashley was afraid something might happen to her prudish little country cousin." Mavis shook her head in disgust.

Country? Prudish? Oooh! And to think I was worried last night that you might die. Oh, what's the use? If I have my way, I'll never have to see the little tart again!

When Uncle Ian told my aunt the entire story, she apologized to me. To make amends, she offered to take me to lunch and then shopping—a cure for all her troubles. Fortunately, I had an important audition coming up and needed to practice. Her relief at my refusal was obvious; clearly she, like her daughter, tried to avoid life's unpleasantries.

I practiced most of the afternoon, though my lack of concentration affected many of the more difficult passages. That evening, when Daddy arrived, I was still in the parlor practicing. He'd already heard about our adventure by the time he entered the room.

We talked for some time about the unfortunate events. When I finished explaining all that happened, he put his arms around me. "I'm so thankful to God you're all right. It could have turned out so much worse."

"I know. And I think, for Ashley, it might have been worse than she's letting on."

He looked into my eyes. "What do you mean?"

"I don't know exactly, except that when she ran to the cab, she was really scared about something."

He cradled my head against his shoulder, and I could hear the comforting rumble of his voice in his chest. "If you had the day to live over, what would you change?"

How like Daddy. A whimper escaped my throat. I hugged him

tighter about the waist. "I'd have refused to go in the first place. Those pesky warning bells Mama always talks about rang from the first moment we left the house."

"Good. You've learned your lesson. You're a wise daughter. Mama will be proud of you when she hears."

"Mama?" I pulled away from his arms. "Does she need to know?"

"What do you mean?" He grinned. "Hey, I can hardly wait to brag about the wise decisions you made."

"Oh, Daddy, please, no."

He took my hands in his. "I'll tell you what. I'll wait and let you tell her in your own good time. How's that?"

I nodded uncertainly.

He dropped my hands and turned to leave the parlor. "Did I tell you that Ashley will be coming back to the Cape with us on Friday? Your Aunt Drucilla thinks it will help if Ashley could spend a few days away from the city."

"Oh no."

He shrugged and exited into the hallway.

The next three days were busy with violin practice and auditions. Two of the three schools of music thanked me for applying but told me their openings had been filled two months before. The dean of the third school said I was a promising violinist and that he'd get back to me by letter.

I cried all the way back to Aunt Drucilla's place—I knew what he really meant. When Daddy tried to encourage me, I pleaded exhaustion and hurried to my room.

On Friday I awakened at dawn, eager to return to the Cape. Daddy arrived at Aunt Drucilla's place by ten. Aunt Drucilla did her best to make up to me, but all I wanted was to go home. Ashley, too, tried to make amends. Try as I might, I couldn't stay mad at my cousin. She had a way about her that wormed its way into one's affections, no matter how much one might resist.

I slept during most of the train ride north. By the time we transferred to the train heading for the Cape, my insides fluttered with excitement. I could hardly wait to see Bide-a-wee again.

Jamie, Rusty, and Mama stood beside the track, waving as our train pulled into the station. The moment the conductor slid the steps into place and opened the coach door, I bounded into Mama's waiting arms. "I missed you so much." I buried my face in her jacket collar.

"My, my, what brought this on?" She tilted my chin so that our eyes met. "I missed you too, darling. But you were gone less than a week. What happened?"

Tears stung my eyes. "I'm just so glad to see you."

Daddy tapped my shoulder. "Hey, it's my turn."

I laughed and released her. When I hugged and kissed my little brother with the same exuberance, he wriggled free as quickly as possible.

As I reached for Jamie, the sadness in his eyes stopped me for a second. "What's wrong? What's the matter?"

He wrapped me in a quick hug but didn't answer.

Mama looked surprised at seeing Ashley. But when my father failed to respond to her questioning glance, she put an arm around my cousin and welcomed her to our house for the weekend. Suddenly everyone was talking at once about the week that had passed. Jamie asked about my auditions.

"I thought I did all right, but none of the schools are falling all over themselves to enroll me." I swallowed the lump in my throat.

Jamie patted my arm. "Don't worry, Cricket. Something will turn up—you're too good a violinist to be ignored."

"That's what I told her," Daddy called over his shoulder as he drove out of the depot onto the main street. "We haven't tried any of the schools in Connecticut; Washington, D.C.; or Virginia. We've barely scratched the surface."

"You're graduating this year also, aren't you?" Jamie looked across the car at Ashley. "What are you planning to do afterward?"

She shrugged. "Mummy enrolled me in Wellesley, so I guess, Wellesley it is."

"But what do you want to study?" Jamie insisted.

I lost interest in my cousin's reply and concentrated on absorbing the charm of the Cape. When we at last turned onto Bide-a-wee's long driveway, Sundance bounded out to meet us.

I climbed out of the car and called to the dog, "Here, Sundance." The dog rounded the back of the car, pounced on my chest, and slurped his tongue across my face. "I missed you too, you big old mutt."

"He's not a mutt!" Rusty defended. "Come here, boy. I won't let her talk about you that way."

After greeting Au Sam, I took Ashley upstairs to the room next to mine and flung open the shutters to the balcony. "I know this isn't as fancy as you are used to, but the place kind of grows on you after a few days. Wait until you see the sunrise from here. It's incredible."

I considered mentioning my morning walks with Thad, but changed my mind. I wasn't sure I was ready to share that part of my life with anyone, especially my gorgeous cousin, Ashley.

Ashley turned slowly, her eyes examining the contents of the room. Though the room was clean and tidy, like the other bedrooms, it hadn't been redecorated yet. For that matter, by the mixture of furniture styles, it probably had never been decorated. "It-it's nice." She smiled uncertainly at me, her big blue eyes swimming in a pool of tears. "Thank you for letting me come home with you for a while. And for forgiving me for everything that happened. I didn't mean any harm, honest."

A battle raged inside me. I wanted to forgive her, but not until I was certain she felt as much hurt as I had. Without answering, I stepped out onto the balcony. She followed. "You do forgive me, don't you?"

I leaned against the railing and nodded. "Yes, I forgive you, Ashley."

A grin spread across her face, and her eyes danced with happiness. "Oh, goody! 'Cause you're my best friend, CeeCee, my truly best friend."

"Aw, come on. You've got a lot of friends at school—take Mavis."

"No, I don't. At least not true friends." She shook her head sadly. "Most girls I meet either hate me on sight or, because of my dad's money, want something from me. They don't really like me. You like me, don't you, CeeCee?"

I swallowed hard. "Of course, I do. You're my cousin."

"I mean beyond family."

I stared out toward the incoming tide. "Ashley, you're sweet, you're fun to be around, you're easy to talk to. Yes, I like you as a friend."

"Good! We'll have great times together while I'm here. On Monday, I'll introduce you to Chip and Rolph. I met them last summer when I spent two weeks with Grandma at their cottage. They're incredibly handsome, you know."

I stared in amazement. *After all that's happened?* I groaned and headed back inside the bedroom. *Oh, Ashley, some things never change!*

The next morning I slipped out of the house at dawn and ran barefoot to the water's edge. Sundance stayed close to my heels as I ran along the surf. I didn't care if I saw Thad or not—it was the sand and the ocean I needed most.

The wind whipped my hair about my face and shoulders as I raised my arms heavenward, responding to the joy of the morning. "Oh, dear God, I am so glad to be home. I couldn't find You in New York City. I know You were there, but somehow, You are so much more real here on the Cape."

Though I'd never done it before, talking out loud to God seemed natural. My cotton skirt billowed as I whirled in circles on the damp sand. I felt as if I could reach out and touch God's hand through the morning fog. *Ooh, I like that—touch God's hand. I should write that in my journal. Emily would appreciate the imagery.*

A Call to Arms

A wave of patriotic fervor surged through the country in the weeks following Congress's declaration of war. The villages on the Cape responded to the mood change. Flags flew from porches. Popular antiwar songs like "I Didn't Raise My Boy to Be a Soldier" disappeared from the fire department band's repertoire to be replaced by "Over There" and "Don't Sit Under the Apple Tree." Women held bandage-rolling parties instead of garden parties, and little boys played soldiers instead of cowboys and Indians. Regulars and summer people alike talked about the war with enthusiasm resembling that of college alumni at a pregame pep rally.

At our home, the sobering reality of war hit the Sunday morning Jamie announced that he and Galen had enlisted in the army and were scheduled to leave for boot camp the following Thursday.

Though my brother had been talking for weeks of enlisting, the news stunned Mama. "Oh, Jamie, oh, Jamie," she mumbled over and over again.

"What about your medical degree, son?" Deliberately, Daddy folded his newspaper and laid it on the floor beside his chair. "You're only weeks away from completing your studies."

"A group of this year's medical graduates made arrangements with the university to graduate early. I've passed all my exams, except for one I take tomorrow. Once that's over, I will be a full-fledged medical doctor." Jamie fidgeted with his fork.

"Oh, Jamie." Mama stared dry-eyed at my brother.

"Will you get to wear a uniform and carry a real rifle?" My little brother's eyes danced with excitement.

Jamie tousled Rusty's hair. "Yes, I'll get to wear a uniform, but I won't be carrying a rifle. My job is to heal people, not kill them."

"Oh, Jamie," Mama muttered.

For once, my cousin Ashley had the sense to remain silent. Daddy cleared his throat. "When do you expect to ship out, son?"

Jamie shrugged. "I'm not sure, sir. I know they're hurting badly for medical doctors at the front."

Daddy considered my brother's words for a few seconds. "Well, what's done is done. You know Mother and I wish you Godspeed. Our prayers will go with you."

Jamie nodded. "Yes, sir."

"Son, as much as I hate to see you go, I applaud you for wanting to serve your country and your God in the best way possible— saving lives instead of taking them."

Mama pushed her chair back from the table. Stifling sobs, she left the room. Au Sam, who'd silently watched the family exchange, followed Mama up the stairs to my parents' bedroom.

I didn't see either of them the rest of the morning. An hour before Jamie had to leave for Boston, Mama came downstairs to be with the family. We sat in the parlor, staring at one other. Jamie promised to write regularly and to try to bring home a supply of Swiss chocolate. When he kissed me goodbye, I asked him if we'd see him again before he left for Europe.

He tweaked my nose. "I hope so, little Cricket. I hope so."

I spent the rest of the day in my room, reading. After Jamie roared away from the house on the borrowed motorcycle, Daddy announced that he wouldn't go back to the office the next day.

That evening, the Victrola remained silent. I sat on the porch until the cold dampness penetrated my sweater. Ashley stayed with me for a while, then tired of my monosyllable replies to her prattle and headed to the guest room. Hours later, I padded out to the kitchen, fixed myself a cup of hot milk to drink, then headed up the stairs to my room.

The warm milk soothed me enough that I fell asleep quickly. I drifted off anticipating my morning walk and hoping I would run into Thad. I felt a need to talk with someone outside the family—

and I hadn't seen him since I had returned to the Cape.

By the time I awakened, Meeker basked in a pool of sunlight at the foot of my bed. My head throbbed, and my mouth tasted like I'd drunk pond scum. In my foul mood, I didn't even want to practice my violin. Putting on my robe and slippers, I tiptoed down to the kitchen to make myself a cup of hot chamomile tea, only to face Ashley's irritatingly perky chatter.

Recognizing the strain behind my parents' pained expressions, I stayed for breakfast, a repeat of yesterday's right down to the blueberry jam, except for Jamie's empty chair. I'd finished my bowl of hot cereal when Ashley suggested we go biking on Martha's Vineyard. "We could pack a picnic lunch, maybe go wading in the tidal pools. It's such a pretty day."

"I don't know—" I rubbed my forehead, hoping to ease the pressure behind my eyes.

Rusty leapt at the idea. "Wow! I'd like that! Do you think we could?"

Daddy glanced down the table at Mama, then back at Rusty. "Your mother and I have an appointment in Boston. We'll be gone most of the day." He placed his hand on my arm. "We need you to look after Rusty, CeeCee."

"Aw, do I have to?" I moaned, determined to defend my foul mood at all costs. "I have a splitting headache."

"The exercise will help relieve it."

"But Au Sam will be here."

"And she'll be busy," he reminded. "I think the outing you proposed is a good suggestion, Ashley. Don't you, dear?"

Mama nodded. "You might want to take along my sun parasol. You wouldn't want to get sunburned."

Oh, Mama, I thought you'd be on my side. Obviously, the only person on my side is me. And considering how nasty I feel, I'm not sure I'm on my side.

While Rusty helped Au Sam pack a picnic lunch, Ashley and I changed into knickers and loose-fitting blouses. Mama and Daddy agreed to drop us off in Woods Hole, where we could catch the morning ferry for the island.

"Oh, goody." Ashley clapped her hands. "We can stop at Chip's father's store, and I can introduce you to him."

My enthusiasm didn't match hers. *Just what I want to do, meet another of Ashley's conquests. Oh, well, I'll get it over with right away so as not to ruin the outing.* Daddy intercepted my snarl and smiled apologetically.

I endured the ride into town with the grace of a stoic. Holding the picnic-basket handles with both hands, I looked longingly at my parents' car as it pulled away from the side of the road. My parents waved, and I returned their wave. *Sooner or later,* my common sense told me, *Ashley is going to get me into some sort of trouble.* And I still hadn't told Mama about the New York scrape.

"Come on," my cousin called from the door of the local grocery store. "Wait till you meet Chip. You'll just love him. Maybe you can meet Rolph too. He lives on the island."

I'm sure all the eligible young men for a fifty-mile radius are lining the streets awaiting the arrival of perky little Ashley. I'd had all the perkiness I could take for one morning, and we hadn't boarded the boat yet.

"I thought we were going bike riding," Rusty whined.

"Aw, come on, it's not all bad." I couldn't believe I was saying that. "Mama gave me extra money for licorice sticks."

At the mention of his favorite candy, Rusty darted ahead of me into the store. I set the lunch basket on the floor beside the door and strode to the counter, where my brother stood eyeing the glass jars filled with jawbreakers, gumdrops, saltwater taffy, and licorice. "One stick, Rusty. That's it."

"Maybe I'll get a sack of gumdrops instead."

At the far end of the counter, Ashley batted her long eyelashes at the store owner. I strolled over to the pickle barrel, ignoring her prattle as much as possible.

"I was so hoping to see Chipper today," she cooed. "He doesn't know I'm in town." She giggled and nibbled on her thumbnail. "I've been naughty. I haven't written much lately."

The man preened under Ashley's attention. "Well, now, I'll be sure to tell Chip that you stopped in to see him. He's in school today. Gonna graduate in a few weeks, you know."

"And handsome too, like his papa." Ashley swung her shoulders back and forth, giving the man a coy smile.

I couldn't believe how her flirting affected the middle-aged store owner. When he bagged our licorice sticks, he threw in an extra stick of licorice. I rolled my eyes skyward as I strode to the door. "Ashley, we're going to miss the next ferry if we don't leave right away."

Ashley sauntered toward me, casting a long, syrupy smile over her shoulder. " 'Bye 'bye now, Mr. Adams. Tell Chipper I'll see him later."

"I'll do that." The man waved.

I thundered out of the store onto the board sidewalk. "Of all the—Ashley, you are an incorrigible flirt."

"What? Who me?" She blinked back her surprise. "I was only being friendly."

"Friendly! You had the poor man drooling all over the licorice sticks."

"Eeuuww!" Rusty stared at the piece of candy he was eating. "Did he really spit on this?"

"No, Rusty. No." I shook my head in disbelief. "I was using a figure of speech."

He squinted up at me. "What's a figure of speech?"

"Forget it." I clicked my tongue and accelerated my pace. "Ask your cousin. She's a life-size figure of speech!"

I didn't stay around to hear her retort. We made it to the boat in plenty of time, and I found a quiet corner on deck and pouted throughout the crossing. Rusty attached himself to the bow while my cousin prowled the vessel searching for her next victim. By the time we docked at Vineyard Haven and rented our bicycles, my mood had lifted.

The three of us cycled south and east until we reached the quiet little whaling town of Edgartown. As we rode past the houses, built close together and near the street, the aroma of lilacs filled the air. We continued on past the Congregational shipwright church built in 1728.

On the outskirts of town, we paused to read an epitaph carved in a headstone in a small burial plot beside the road.

ROLAND
son of
Roland and Mary Jones

> Was killed by the natives
> at one of the Mulgrave
> Islands Feb. 21, 1824
> AE 18 years
> Erected by George and Mart Lawrence
>
> Far, far from home from Friends and Kindred Dear
> By savage hands this lovely youth was slain.
> No father's pity, or no mother's tear
> Soothed the sad scene or eas'd the hour of pain.

I thought of Jamie. "Come on, let's get going!" I snapped. "We don't have all day, you know."

Ashley looked at me strangely. "Yes, we do."

"You—" I clamped my mouth shut and shoved off on my bicycle, afraid if I said more, I'd get myself in trouble.

She pumped hard to catch up with me. "I'm what? You were going to say something, CeeCee. What was it?"

Accelerating quickly, I called over my shoulder, "I can't hear you, Ashley. What did you say?"

We rode south toward Grandma and Grandpa McCall's island retreat. Though the house was still boarded for winter, the beach gave us a private place to eat our lunch. After parking our rented bikes, all three of us removed our shoes and stockings, then spread out our blanket beside a stack of weathered lumber. I opened the parasol and stuck the handle into the sand.

Out in the bay, I watched a fishing boat bob on the waves; the lone fisherman appeared to be asleep atop his nets. After we ate the lunch Au Sam had prepared, I removed my licorice stick from the bag and yawned. The sound of the ocean had soothed away my headache. "I think I'm going to take a short nap."

I adjusted the parasol and stretched out for my nap.

"Don't you want to collect shells with me?" Rusty pleaded.

"Maybe later. Why don't you get started without us?"

Ashley waved him away. "Why don't you try to catch a gull or something?"

Rusty leapt to his feet. "Fine! But don't ask for any of my shells later."

I shaded my eyes and squinted up at him. "Just be careful. Don't go in the water, understand?"

"I know. And don't turn your back on the ocean, right?"

"Right!"

The sound of the surf had lulled me into a cozy sleep, when I was shaken awake by my cousin. "CeeCee, wake up. Rusty's shouting for help."

In one motion, I leapt to my feet, bounded to the water's edge, and scanned the shore. I couldn't see him at first. He'd been pulled down by an undertow, so his head popped up fifty to sixty yards from shore. Now he was waving his arms and yelling.

"Oh, dear God, please don't let anything happen to my little brother. Please keep him safe." Before charging into the surf, I grabbed one of the shorter boards in the lumber pile. "I'm coming, Rusty. Keep your head up. I'm coming."

Focusing my eyes on the spot where I'd last seen him, I leapt through the waves. When they grew too large, I stuffed the board under my left arm and broke into a swim. The waves tossed me about like a paper sailboat. One crashed on my head, sending me helplessly tumbling in the turbulence. When I surfaced, I treaded water, searching for Rusty. But I couldn't see him anywhere.

Then I saw Ashley jumping up and down and pointing toward the left. Already tiring, I adjusted my course and swam as hard as I could but made little headway. *Hang on, little brother, hang on. I'm coming. Oh, please God, help him to hang on until I can save him.*

I knew I was in trouble when a large wave swallowed me, swirling me head over heels beneath the water until I lost all sense of direction, and my lungs threatened to burst. Somewhere in the turbulence, I let go of the board. *Oh, Rusty, I tried. I really did try. I'm sorry, Mama. I wanted to tell you, honest. Please forgive me.*

Then all went black. Sometime later I awakened to the smell of herring. I tried to sit up, but callused hands pushed me down against a hard surface.

"Just lay still, lassie," a strange voice ordered.

"Where? Where am I?" I made another halfhearted effort to sit up. Then I remembered my brother. My unexpected lunge caught my rescuer off guard, and I broke free of his grasp. "Rusty! Where's Rusty? I've got to find Rusty."

My head spinning from my sudden movement, I struggled to my feet. I could hear myself screaming, "I've got to find my brother!"

I fought the callused hands that swept me off my feet and pushed me down onto a pile of fish netting. "He's OK! Your brother's OK," the voice shouted inches from my ear.

The spinning slowed, allowing my eyes to focus. Too paralyzed with fear to fight, I stared at the weather-beaten face before me. When the man smiled, he revealed an uneven picket fence of tobacco-stained teeth. He forced me down by my shoulders. "Lassie, if I let go of you, will you promise to lie still?"

I nodded, biting my lower lip to keep from crying. "Just tell me; did you save my little brother? He was drowning, and I tried—" My voice broke into sobs. "I really did try to—"

"It's all right. Your brother is down in the galley with my son, wrapped in a blanket and trying to get warm."

"Oh, oh, oh," I whimpered, my body shaking from head to toe. "Oh, oh—"

"Don't try to talk." The man picked up a blanket and covered me. "Let me take you to see Doc Garrett. You can tell him all about it."

"My cousin, Ashley. She's waiting on the shore." I pointed in the direction I imagined land to be.

"Don't worry," he chuckled. "I sent my other son for her in the dingy. He'll bring her to Doc's place. Close your eyes for a few minutes and rest."

The sun felt warm on my face; I knew I was safe. I didn't awaken until I felt myself being carried ashore.

The doctor checked Rusty and me over thoroughly. "Well, you're none the worse for wear. But I wouldn't go pulling that stunt again. If it weren't for Ben Bassett and his sons, you would probably have drowned."

I nodded. I was too thankful to have us both alive to explain what had happened. After an hour of rest and three bowls of corn chowder, the doctor allowed us to leave for home. "Now, Miss," the doctor instructed Ashley, "see that these two go straight home to bed. You can return my blankets the next time you're on the island."

"Yes, sir." She nodded, her face drawn and anxious.

During the ferry ride back to Woods Hole, she fussed over Rusty and me, continually tucking the doctor's blankets protectively around us. *Maybe there's more than meringue in that head of hers.*

After the ferry docked, she helped us onto the dock and settled us on a wooden bench, then ran to the grocery store to get help. She returned a few minutes later. "I found Chipper. He's going to drive us home in his father's delivery wagon. He'll be here in a minute."

Relief flooded through me. I hadn't even thought about how we'd get from Woods Hole to Bide-a-wee. My relief switched to horror when our driver arrived.

"CeeCee, what are you doing here?"

I looked up into the stunned face of Thad. "Thad? What are you doing here?"

"CeeCee? Ashley?" He gazed first at me, then at my cousin.

"Thad?" Ashley repeated. "You already know Chipper?"

"Chipper?"

"Thad!"

"Thad?"

"Chipper?"

"How do you know Chipper?" Ashley asked.

"Whoa!" The boy I knew as Thad lifted his hands defensively. "Let's start all over, shall we? My name is Thaddeus Adams the third, Thad for short, sometimes also known as Chip, or Chipper."

I closed my eyes and groaned. *I might have known. The only person I knew on the Cape turned out to be Ashley's sometime sweetheart.*

"And this is CeeCee Chamberlain, my cousin." Ashley pointed at me. "How do you know Chip?"

I shook my head. "It's a long story."

Thad helped me to his father's delivery wagon and lifted me onto the wagon seat. When he returned for Rusty, Ashley climbed between where I sat and the driver's seat.

My cousin never stopped talking all the way home. She cuddled up to Thad and reminisced about all the great times they'd enjoyed together. "We didn't really get serious about one another until last summer at the Fourth of July celebrations. Remember, Chipper? You stole a kiss out behind the bandstand." Ashley wrinkled her nose and grinned foolishly. Thad reddened and hurried the horse along.

Rusty sat hunched over in the back of the wagon, silently staring out of his pinched, white face. I tried to get him to speak, but he refused.

"It's OK, honey," I coaxed. "We're both safe. It's OK."

Au Sam and Sundance ran from the house even before Thad reigned in the horse. "Missee, Missee, are you all OK?"

I smiled weakly. "I'm fine. And Rusty's fine."

"Rusty too?" The woman ran to Rusty's side.

"Take CeeCee to her room," Au Sam ordered Thad. "Ashley and I can manage Rusty."

"I'm fine," I protested. "I can walk on my own."

He didn't argue, but scooped me into his arms, blanket and all, and carried me inside the house and up the stairs. "Really, this isn't necessary. I'm feeling much better now."

"Sh!" he ordered. "You talk too much." He paused at the landing. "Which room?"

I grinned devilishly. "You said I talk too much."

He shifted my weight in his arms. "I'll just try every door until I figure out which room is yours."

Knowing I must be getting heavy, I pointed to my right. "That one, over there."

He unlatched the door and pushed it open with his boot. I sighed with relief when I discovered I'd straightened my room before I left that morning. Gently, he placed me on the bedspread, then straightened, but not before I kissed his cheek. "Thank you, Thad or Thaddeus or Chip or Chipper, whoever you are."

He blushed. "Everyone used to call me Chip or Chipper, but I prefer Thad." He stared at the rag carpet beside my bed. "I've had a crush on Ashley since last summer when she was staying with her grandmother."

I smiled sadly. "You don't have to explain."

He frowned. "I know, but I care what you think of me."

Suddenly I felt weepy. I didn't know if it was due to my near-drowning or to his tenderness. "We're just friends, remember? We barely know each other."

"Friends." His crooked grin told me all I needed to know. His hands fidgeted as he looked about the room.

"I'll be fine now. You can go."

"Yeah, well, will I see you tomorrow morning?"

"I hope so." A draft from the open window sent a chill the length of my spine.

"I'd better get out of here so you can get into dry clothes." He turned and strode to the doorway. "See ya."

I slept all the rest of the afternoon and early evening until Au Sam awakened me for supper. I went straight back to bed and slept through dawn. By the time I emerged from my room, my parents knew the story of our dangerous adventure.

When Mama reconstructed the events of the day for me, I learned that Rusty had bounded into the surf to retrieve a glass float that had broken loose from a fishing net. In the process, he found himself trapped in an undertow, from which he didn't surface until he was far from shore.

Mr. Bassett spotted him at the same time I entered the water to rescue him. We would both have drowned if it weren't for the fisherman and his sons' quick thinking.

I wandered languidly around the house most of the day, then retired early the next evening. Awakening in the middle of the night, I strolled out onto the balcony. Meeker lay curled up on one of the rocking chairs. I picked her up and walked to the railing, stroking her soft, warm fur and looking out over the lawn and beach illuminated by the full moon.

The silhouette of a person walking from the beach toward the house startled me. The flow of her white nightgown blowing in the breeze made her appear to be floating above the ground.

I watched transfixed until the figure stepped onto the edge of the lawn. "Mama," I called. "What are you doing out at this hour?"

She paused beneath the balcony. "You should be inside. You'll catch your death."

"Yes, ma'am," I turned to go inside the house.

"CeeCee? How would you like to come down for a cup of hot chocolate?"

"I'll be right down."

Seconds later, I joined her in the kitchen, where she was already heating the milk on the stove. When I asked her why she was out walking, she replied, "I needed to do some thinking, I guess. Here I was, fretting over Jamie's decision to enlist in the army and the possibility of losing him, only to have my other children almost drown. I guess I forgot that life is never a sure thing, that I can't protect my babies from every harm that may come their way."

I studied the soft curve of her cheek and chin and her gentle, caring eyes as she spoke.

"Some things, mamas must trust God to handle."

At the mention of God, I tightened my lips. "But what if Mr. Bassett hadn't been there to save us? And what if Jamie doesn't come home?"

She traced the mug handle with her fingertip. "I guess that's where a person's faith takes on a new meaning. When your real father died, I thought I would die too. If it hadn't been for loving friends, I would have."

The hall clock gonged twice. Mama took a deep breath. "I remember writing the promises of Psalm 91 on pieces of paper and pinning them all over the cabin. And every time I threatened to fall apart, I shouted the words out loud."

"Shouted?" I laughed. "I wonder what God thought about that?"

"I don't think He minded at all."

A few minutes later, Daddy staggered into the kitchen. "What's going on down here? What time is it, anyway?" He yawned and scratched his head.

Mama kissed his grizzled cheek. "You don't want to know, dear. Come on, let's go upstairs to bed."

The next morning, Thad was waiting for me when I went for my walk. We didn't talk as much as we had before Ashley entered the picture. And I didn't mention Thad to anyone.

On Wednesday afternoon we all drove to my grandparents' place in Boston for Jamie's farewell dinner. Ashley's parents were already there when we arrived. I still hadn't told my mother about the affair in the city.

Jamie brought Hershel with him, since Galen was spending the evening in Westborough with his own parents. Though Grandpa McCall did his best to keep the conversation going, even he couldn't lift the gloom at the dining table.

We returned to Bide-a-wee the next morning without my cousin. Because of the upset from Jamie's departure, Ashley's parents decided to take her home. I wondered if the near-drowning affected their decision to lift her exile.

During the rest of the week, we moved through the house like zombies. Daddy returned to the city on the Sunday-afternoon train.

A few days later, I accompanied Mama into town for groceries. We arrived in the middle of a parade celebrating the landing of the first American expeditionary forces in France. People waved flags and cheered as the noisy procession of Model T's, Pierce Arrows, Franklins, horse-drawn wagons, and fringe-topped buggies rolled past. I couldn't understand the party atmosphere surrounding the event. Everything was changing so fast, I couldn't keep up; even the parade vehicles reflected that change.

The next morning, I tried to explain my feelings to Thad. His reply was, "It's my turn—I'm enlisting as soon as possible." Knowing that whatever I said would be useless, I cut short the morning walk by feigning a headache.

The reality of Jamie's departure was not so easily avoided. At the end of his basic training, Jamie rode Hershel's motorcycle down to the Cape to say goodbye. He was scheduled to be on the troop train to New York City the following day and would ship out to France one day later. "I'll say goodbye to Dad when I get to the city," he assured us. "I already said goodbye to Grandpa and Grandma McCall. Grandma didn't take it too well."

After supper that evening, we gathered around the fireplace in the parlor—Jamie, Mama, Au Sam, Rusty, Sundance, and me. Jamie built a fire in the fireplace so that he and Rusty could pop popcorn. When the fire had burned down to glowing coals, Jamie asked if I would play a song on my violin. "You know, the one

Mama always hums as she gets ready to head upstairs for bed at night." He walked over to Mama and sat on the sofa beside her. Tenderly, he took her hands in his.

My eyes swam with tears. Relieved to have something to do, I took my violin from its case and strolled to the windows. I knew that if I saw anyone else cry, I'd cry too. Gazing outside, I slowly lifted the violin to my chin and drew the bow across the strings, producing the simple tune "Shall We Gather at the River?"

At the end of the song, Mama opened her well-worn Bible to Psalm 139. " 'Whither shall I go from thy spirit? or whither shall I flee from thy presence? If I ascend up into the heaven, thou art there: if I make my bed in hell, behold, thou art there. If I take the wings of the morning, and dwell in the uttermost parts of the sea; even there shall thy hand lead me, and thy right hand shall hold me.' " Her voice faltered. She paused to regain control. "Son, I love you so much. And I want you to know that I accept your decision to fight in this war. Most important, I am trusting you to my heavenly Father's care." She handed the book to him. "I want you to have this, Jamie. Your father gave it to me after I lost mine in the cabin fire. It's sustained me through many crises."

No one spoke. "I probably should have given it to you sooner." She traced her fingers over the gold letters in the lower right-hand corner—Chloe Mae McCall. "CeeCee will get the gold watch your father gave me, as a remembrance, but the Bible is yours. Don't merely treasure it as a keepsake; read it. Let its promises give you the strength you need whenever you feel weak or lonely."

Jamie stared silently down at the sacred book and swallowed hard.

"I've underlined the promises that have helped me through the most difficult times in my life. We may be thousands of miles apart, but the words in this book and our love for one another will bind us together."

An agonized sob burst from Jamie. Mama drew him in her arms and held him until he quieted. "Just in case things don't go so well, I want you to know, I've never regretted asking you to be my mother. My birth mother couldn't have loved me more."

Mama nodded, too choked up to speak.

Before dawn the next morning, we endured the painful goodbyes once more. *It's real*, I thought as I hugged Jamie for the last time. *It's really happening, this time.* Mama gathered Rusty, Au Sam, and me about her like a hen gathering her chicks to protect them as we waved until the motorcycle snorted out of view. I thought about it later as I sat on the balcony writing in my diary. *Emily, I think Mama needed our protection today as much as we needed hers.*

A few days after Jamie left, a letter arrived addressed to me, a letter from the Institute of Musical Arts. With trembling hands I ripped open the envelope.

"Dear Miss McCall, The faculty of the Institute of Musical Art would like to invite you to become a part of our student body. Due to the high number of young men enlisting in the war effort, we have an opening for you in our fall freshman class." The letter went on to tell me what an honor it was to be accepted by the prestigious school, especially since the faculty seldom encouraged female musicians to attend. "Over the years, we've discovered that female students tend to be less serious about their music." I stared at the letter for some time, not hearing my mother walk up behind me and ask if something was wrong.

I handed her the acceptance letter, then ran my hand distractedly through my hair. "I don't know, Mama. Through all that's happened, I'd forgotten about attending the institute."

She read the letter silently.

"I'm not sure I'm ready. Maybe I should wait a year."

She folded the letter and returned it to me. "It's up to you, dear. It's your decision." Her answer startled me. If anything, I could always depend on my mother to have an opinion. And now, when I needed it most, she told me it was my decision.

"But what do you think? I wasn't accepted for my musical talent. They really accepted me to make up for the financial inconvenience the war produced."

"You're probably right, but that fact doesn't negate the opportunity you've been given." Mama smiled. "Think about it. Pray about it. You don't need to give them your answer right away."

"But what if the war ends before I decide?"

She smiled sadly. "It won't, honey. Trust me, it won't."

Mama was right. By July 4, the first sobering casualty reports and the appalling photographs of American boys lying dead or wounded in the battlefields of Europe arrived, hitting the little town of Woods Hole, as it did thousands of other communities across the continent, with the true meaning of war.

Laughter became rarer. Shortages of soap, sugar, safety pins, and bread developed. Mama threw herself into the war effort, selling liberty bonds, rolling bandages for the Red Cross, and volunteering her services to every government agency on the Cape. Rumors of German submarines lurking off the Cape stirred Rusty to scan the waters with his telescope, hoping to spot the enemy and become a local hero.

Six weeks after Jamie left, a packet of his letters arrived. To me and to Rusty, he'd written humorous little notes about the horrid food and the strange men in his unit.

But to Mama, he painted a truer picture. Reluctantly, she allowed me to read the letter after she had finished. He began by saying, "I didn't see much of Paris. We were whisked away by train to some unpronounceable valley at the foot of the Alps where it rains continually. Rain is miserable for front-line soldiers. The water flows in rivulets through the trenches, creating an oozy, gummy mud that coats everyone and everything.

"My unit is supposedly behind the front line, a temporary hospital operating in a mud-floor tent. I see the men who are still alive. If we manage to stay their demise, the injured are transferred to the regimental hospital somewhere to the south of us."

I squeezed my eyes shut to block out the vivid images Jamie's words produced. "The bodies of the dead from both sides of the conflict lie strewn about no man's land.

"During lulls in the shelling, attempts are made to retrieve the dead behind the lines, only to produce additional casualties. In spite of everything, I am needed here. Yesterday, a French boy around Rusty's age was brought in with shrapnel in his chest. As I prepared him for surgery, he smiled up at me, took my hand, and whispered, 'Merci—thank you.' I wept because I knew he would probably die."

The next morning on the beach, I showed Jamie's letter to Thad. His lips tightened as he read it. When he finished, he handed it back to me. "All the more reason to go. They need me."

I stuffed the letter into my skirt pocket and stared out across the water. *Somewhere over there, Jamie—*

I couldn't go on; I had to think of something else. "So, have you heard from Ashley lately?"

He shook his head. "No. Not in the last two weeks. I'm thinking of catching a train to the city to see her before I go to boot camp. I want to know how she really feels about me." He hesitated. "She hasn't told you anything, has she?"

I glanced out at the water to avoid his gaze.

"I'm not the only one, right?"

"Well, you know Ashley. Her unpredictability is part of her charm." My laugh seemed hollow even to me.

Thad stuffed his hands into his pockets and hunched his shoulders. "Yeah, I guess you're right. But I still want to see for myself."

I touched his arm. "We're still friends, no matter what happens, right?"

Thad focused his steel gray eyes on me. "Absolutely. After all, who else would put up with a lovesick calf like me?"

"That's for sure!" I socked him in the arm. "And I want to hear all about the beautiful French girls you meet in Paris, ya hear?"

He glanced at me out of the corner of his eye. "Only if you promise not to run off and marry some cowboy engineer from Kansas before I get back."

I punched him again in the same spot. "Thaddeus! I should never have told you about Shane. It's not what you think."

He massaged his arm and glared. "You hit me again, woman, and I'll toss you into the ocean."

Grinning, I drew back my fist and playfully tapped his arm. "You and whose army?"

"Is that a challenge?" He narrowed his eyes, capturing my gaze for several seconds. My eyes misted, and I bit my lower lip to keep from crying.

"Take care." I reached out, but stopped short of touching his face, then slowly withdrew my hand.

"You too." He captured a stray strand of my hair in his hand and curled it around his finger. "Like spun copper." In one smooth movement, he bent forward and kissed my cheek while pressing his sketch pad into my hand. "Here. This is for you." An instant later he had turned and was walking away from me without looking back.

"No," I whispered. "I can't—" I told his retreating form as he disappeared beyond the rocky cove at the end of our beach. With leaden feet, I returned toward the house. Sundance sensed my somber mood and pressed against my leg as I walked. After stumbling up the porch steps, I dropped into the nearest rocking chair and opened the sketch pad to page after page of seascapes and sea gulls. But halfway through the pad, the subject changed. Thad had sketched pictures of me and Sundance walking along the beach, playing in the sand, closeups of me laughing, of me frowning, even one of me angry. On the last page, he had sketched my profile with my hair flying about my shoulders. A tear splattered on the sketch. Angry to be crying again, I swiped at my eyes.

"Why, Sundance? Why? Thad's too good for Ashley. I don't want to see him hurt. Oh, why should I even care? If he's too stupid—" I slammed my fist against the arm of the rocker. "Life isn't fair! When I was a little girl, I played with my dolls. I dreamed my dreams. And everything always turned out exactly how I wanted." Even as I spoke, I wondered, *Just how do you want it all to turn out? Do you even know?*

A Call to Faith

"The United States Army regrets to inform you that Lieutenant James E. McCall III has been officially declared missing in action. Further information on Lieutenant McCall will be forwarded to you as it is received." My hands trembled as I reread the sheet of yellow paper with the black border.

"No. No! No-o-o-o!" I wailed, sinking to the sandy driveway behind Bide-a-wee. A warm, moist Turkish towel of darkness slid over my face, threatening to smother me. I awakened with someone patting my face and calling my name.

"Wake up, Missee. Wake up." My eyes blinked open. Au Sam's worried face loomed over me. "What is it? What has happened?"

She helped me to my feet. "I've got to get to Boston right away. I've got to tell Mama." I stuffed the telegram into her hand and ran into the house. Au Sam, her dark eyes filled with worry, followed me into the kitchen before pausing to read the telegram.

I stopped at the kitchen sink, filling a glass with water. "How can a soldier be missing? How can the army just lose somebody?" I shouted in anguish. "Why did Mama have to drive to Boston today, of all days?"

Au Sam, thinking I expected answers to my questions, began with the easiest of the three. "Your mama had an appointment with your grandmother's eye doctor."

"I know, but why today?" I wailed, slamming the glass tumbler down on the sideboard. "What am I supposed to do? Sit here with this kind of information for an entire day until she gets home?" Doing anything would be better than waiting and doing nothing.

I glanced at the clock over the pantry. "Eight o'clock. If I leave in the next fifteen minutes, I can bike to the depot in time to catch the nine-o'clock train for Boston. I can get to Grandma's before Mama returns from her appointment. Where's Rusty?"

"Oh, Missee, I don't think that's a very—" I hardened my heart against the anxiety in her face.

"Where's Rusty?"

"He left a half-hour ago to go clam digging with the boys next door." The neighbors lived half a mile away.

"Did he take his bike?"

She shook her head.

"Good! Quick—pack me a couple of sandwiches and a few cookies while I change out of these knickers." I'd fallen into the habit of wearing the knee-length trousers almost every day.

I dashed from the kitchen and up the stairs to my bedroom. My clothing flew in every direction as I chose and discarded three different outfits. Finally I decided on a white-with-red-pinstripe cotton dress. I pulled it over my head, fastened the red bone buttons on the bodice, and tightened the matching belt about my waist. *Hair, I've got to do something with my hair.* I ran the brush through it, then braided it in one long braid down my back.

Dancing on one foot, then the other, I slipped into my stockings and shoes. *Money, I'll need some money.* I ran down the hall to Mama's room. *Please, God, let there be enough money for a ticket.* I pawed through her stack of gloves until I found the small leather change purse where she kept spare cash. *Five dollars! I can get to Boston on five dollars!*

I snatched it from the purse; dashed back to my own room, where I grabbed my shoulder-strap bag, a pair of gloves, and my white sweater; and bounded down the stairs to the kitchen.

Au Sam met me in the doorway, her face flooded with concern. "Oh, Missee, I really don't think—"

I kissed her cheek, stuffed the sandwiches and cookies into my bag, and dashed out the back door. Seconds later, I bounded back into the kitchen. "Forgot the telegram!"

She handed it to me.

"Thanks. Don't worry, I'll be fine." I charged back outside, grabbed the bicycle, and set out for the depot. *If only I can keep from getting a flat tire, I'll be fine.*

I rode through a dense fog that hid familiar landmarks and muffled the sounds, grateful that the silhouetted trees cordoned each side of the dirt road. I felt isolated in an unreal world, inhabited only by me. Usually I find the fog beautiful and mysterious. But that day, the fog penetrated my light summer sweater, chilling and disheartening me. It seemed forever before the silhouetted trees gave way to the clearing at the edge of town.

I pulled into the depot at the same time the train to Boston arrived from Provincetown. After explaining my mission to the ticket agent, he agreed to care for the bicycle until I returned. Only three other passengers were heading north to Boston at that hour of the morning—a mousy-looking woman with her five-year-old son and a denim-clad fisherman. I sank into the first window seat just as the conductor closed the doors. Amid the usual cacophony of steam and whistles, the locomotive chugged away from the station.

As the outskirts of town faded in the distance, the first doubts assailed me. *Maybe going to Boston isn't such a great idea, after all. The news would have waited, you know. You can't help Jamie or Mama by running off in a thousand different directions. You really didn't think this through very well.* "Oh, well. It's too late now."

"Excuse me, Miss. Did you say something?"

I glanced up into the conductor's questioning face. "I beg your pardon?"

He extended his hand toward me. "I need to see your ticket, Miss. You do have a ticket, don't you?"

"Oh, uh, yes. Right here somewhere." I pawed through my purse, looking for the requested item. "Here."

He took the cardboard ticket and punched a hole in the corner. Handing the ticket back to me, he touched the visor of his hat. "Have a nice day, ma'am."

After we crossed the trestle onto the mainland, the track curved northward. Soon the fog lifted, and the brilliant August sun bore down on fields of ripening crops. The train passed cows grazing in green fields and children playing in white-fenced front yards. I could almost forget the reason for my journey—almost. After what seemed like a lifetime, the conductor walked through the car, announcing our arrival in Boston.

I stepped away from the train to get my bearings. People rushed by me, avoiding eye contact and intent upon their destination. A group of uniformed soldiers, none of them old enough to have reason to shave, whistled as I swung through the door into the terminal. I wondered whether they were coming home or leaving. Considering their lighthearted attitude, I decided they were leaving.

I pushed through the crowds, following the overhead signs that directed me to the street. Finally, I emerged onto a city street, where I had to wave away the hawkers, who held their wares in front of my face. A sad-eyed little boy, not more than six-years-old, danced to the tune of a hand-cranked organ. I wanted to give him a coin, but I knew the organ grinder would take it from him.

I climbed into a waiting cab and gave the driver my grandmother's address. The cab wove slowly through the crowded, narrow streets of downtown Boston, but the midday traffic thinned once we entered the residential area. At last, the driver paused at the closed iron gate outside my grandparents' house.

After handing him the money, I ran up the driveway toward the house. But before I reached the portico, the front door swung open, and Grandma McCall rushed out to meet me. "Chloe Celeste, whatever are you doing here? I was leaving for a committee meeting when I spotted you running toward the house. Your mother didn't say you were coming to town."

She caught me in her arms. Suddenly the feeling of love and security upset my carefully repressed emotions, and I sniffed back unexpected tears. "I wasn't until this morning."

"Child, you're crying. Whatever is wrong? Come inside and tell me all about it." She drew me into the house and led me into the library. "Whatever it is, it can't be that bad."

She sat beside me on the leather sofa while I fumbled in my purse for the telegram. "Yes, it can, and it is."

Her face paled as she read the dreaded message. "No, no," she whispered. "O Lord, no!" Grandma McCall squeezed her eyes closed. "First my son, James, and now, Jamie! No, I won't allow it. I won't!"

Wanting to ease her pain, I touched her arm. "Jamie's not dead, Grandma, just missing. See." I pointed to the note. "It says he's only missing in action."

"CeeCee." He voice sounded years older. "Please help me upstairs to my room."

I took her elbow and directed her toward the staircase. In the hallway, Lawrence appeared and took her other arm. Together, we ascended the stairs. In the corridor we walked passed Rhea, her maid, without comment.

When we reached Grandma's private quarters, she dismissed Lawrence. "My granddaughter will take care of things from here." She gestured toward me. "Close the doors." I obeyed.

Of all the rooms in my grandmother's house, I loved her rosewood-paneled bedroom sitting room the most. Its large diamond-paned windows overlooked on two sides the formal gardens behind the mansion. The dusky rose accessories expressed the same elegance I saw in Grandma herself.

She paused in the middle of the room, facing the wall of gilt-framed portraits of McCalls, then turned to me. "Please stay with me."

I nodded, watching her face intently, helpless to know what to do for her. She walked over to the marble fireplace. "Why, Lord, why? What have I done to make You snatch my precious Jamie from me? Surely my little sins don't warrant such a vindictive response."

I watched with growing fear as my grandmother's face hardened, and her gaze darted about the room in anger. Suddenly, my usually composed, refined grandmother burst into a frenzy. She yanked a shiny brass poker from the sheaf of fire irons and whirled in a half circle, violent cries of anguish ripping from her throat. Terrified, I pressed against the door, afraid my grandmother might strike me.

Clutching the poker with both hands, she swung it swordlike at the collection of Dresden vases on the mantel. The artifacts crashed to the floor, leaving behind the porcelain figure of a sixteenth-century cavalier. "You defy me?" she shouted. Raising the poker over her head, she crashed it down on the smiling figurine, exploding porcelain shards in all directions.

Her eyes livid, she targeted a spindly legged table near the love seat for her next attack. The table and the collection of silver-framed photographs disintegrated before my eyes.

With Grandma screaming out her rage, I felt rather than heard someone pounding on the door behind me. I turned to open it, only to have her slam it with such violence that it bounced open again. "Leave me alone," she shouted, fleeing to the far side of the room.

A new terror grew inside me. Gently, I closed the doors, then walked toward her, my hand extended. "Grandma, come away from the windows. Hand me the poker."

Ignoring me, she continued the tirade. "God made women to create life. Why does He allow man to destroy it?" She ran her hand over the highly polished lady's secretary while shouting, "Well, I can destroy too!" The first blow hurled the lamp through the window to the brick patio below. With blow after blow, she broke the desk's delicate legs and splintered the exquisite carvings. The strenuous exertion split open the dress seams under her arms, until the dress bodice hung in sections from her shoulders. Finally exhausted, she staggered toward the bed and then collapsed, face down, on the dusky rose bedspread.

"Oh, God, I can't go through this again. I won't!" She wept into the embroidered pillow. When I offered to help her to a chair, she waved me away. I hovered nearby, uncertain of what she expected from me. After a long time, she slowly sat up and brushed the slivers of glass from her skirt. "You may go, CeeCee. I will be all right now. Please send someone to clean the room."

"Grandma, I don't want to leave you." I glanced toward the broken window.

"Your mother will be here soon. She promised to stop by after her appointment, before returning to the Cape. I don't want her to find me this way."

I bent down and picked up a large porcelain shard. "Let me help you clean—"

She grabbed my shoulders roughly and pushed me toward the door. "I want you to leave my room *now*."

Backing toward the door, I struggled with my training to obey my elders and my fear that she might try to injure herself.

"Don't worry." She read the concern on my face. "The fire inside me is out. All that's left are the ashes."

I opened the door a crack and slipped out into the hallway, where the house staff had congregated. "Stay with her, Lawrence, until my mother or grandfather get home. Use any excuse necessary, but stay with her."

"Yes, ma'am." He took a broom and dustpan from the maid's hand, entered the room, and closed the door behind him.

I staggered down the stairs to the library, where my grandmother had dropped the telegram. Collapsing into my grandfather's overstuffed leather chair, I was startled to see the hated piece of paper crumpled in the middle of the floor. *If Grandma McCall reacted so violently, how will Mama take the news?*

As if on cue, Mama entered the front door. "Yoo-hoo, anyone home? Lawrence, where are you? Did I catch you napping?"

"Lawrence is upstairs, Mama," I called from the sanctuary of Grandpa's chair.

"CeeCee? Is that you? How in the world—"

Tensely, I picked up the telegram and handed it to her. "This telegram came this morning soon after you left Bide-a-wee. I knew you'd want to know right away." I steeled myself for her outburst.

Her face paled as she read the short message. "Oh, no, no, no, no." She closed her eyes and inhaled in short, shallow breaths. "Jamie—" Her voice drifted into nothing.

Fearfully, I reached out to her, not knowing whether she would welcome the gesture. The moment my hand touched her shoulder, she gathered me into her arms. "Oh, sweetheart, I'm so sorry you had to be the one to see this first. I should have been there for you, to soften the blow."

She buried her face in my shoulder and wept. My tears soon joined hers, and we wept together for some time. Finally, my mother sniffed, dug a handkerchief from her pocket, and wiped her eyes. "Does your grandmother know?"

I gulped and glanced toward the stairwell. "Yes, she knows."

"Oh." Mama stuffed the handkerchief back in her pocket. "I should go to her—she must be devastated."

I grabbed my mother's sleeve. "I wouldn't go up there just yet."

Mama shot me a surprised look. "Why not?"

"She's resting. She took it pretty badly."

Mama tipped my chin upward. "And you, how are you doing?"

"I'm OK, I guess, but I can't understand how God can take Jamie away from us—him being a doctor and all."

"Oh, honey, God hasn't harmed your brother." My mother drew me into her arms once more. "First, we don't even know he's been hurt, let alone killed. Missing in action means missing in action. And until we receive an official message to the contrary, he's just that, missing in action."

"But Grandma said—"

Suddenly I could feel a fierceness in my mother's embrace. "It doesn't matter what your grandmother might have said in shock. I entrusted Jamie into God's hands. And until I hear otherwise, that means alive and well."

Gently, I broke free of her grasp. "Then what? What if Grandma's right and he's dead?"

Mama took a deep breath. "Then, then, I will have to trust my God to see me through the ordeal." She leaned back against the sofa and closed her eyes. Her lips moved silently, yet I knew the words she spoke. "I will say of the Lord, He is my refuge and my fortress: my God; in him will I trust."

I rushed from the room and into the formal gardens. Once outside, I broke into a run, through the rose garden to the wooden swing inside the gazebo. I'd been brave through my grandmother's and mother's pain. Now I needed to vent my own sorrow.

The swing floated gently in the breeze off the bay as I buried my face in my arm and sobbed. I awakened some time later to find Grandfather sitting beside me on the swing.

Immediately I remembered my grandmother's rampage. "I-I-I'm sorry, Grandpa. I wanted to stop her, but I couldn't."

He stroked my hair. "You didn't do anything wrong, honey. I'm just glad you were there for her."

I sat up. "But she broke—"

"The things can be replaced, unlike her heart." His face looked tired. "I thought it was hard on her when your father died, but this—I don't know."

"Is, is she all right?"

"She's resting now. Our doctor came by and gave her some medicine to help her sleep."

"And Mama?"

He smiled. "I left her in the library, reading. She asked me to check on you. She's worried about you."

"Me? I'm worried about her."

He chuckled. "That's how love works, always thinking of one another." He leaned back and set the swing in motion. "I'm sorry you had to see your grandmother like that. She's a proud woman, you know. She lashed out at her pain in the only way she knows how."

"Will she be all right?"

He frowned. "I hope so."

"Has Daddy heard the news?"

"I'm driving down to the train station to pick him up around nine o'clock tonight." Grandpa sniffed, then cleared his throat. "Hey, you must be hungry. The cook has a big potato salad in the icebox and a pot of Boston baked beans on the stove. Can I tempt you?"

My stomach growled. "I guess that's your answer, Grandpa."

Silently Grandpa and I ate together at the kitchen table where the servants regularly ate. "Umm!" Grandpa smacked his lips. "Nothing can beat a great pot of Boston baked beans. I think the secret is in the molasses."

After we finished eating, we went searching for my mother. I found her in a guest room upstairs, writing a letter to her sister, Aunt Hattie, in Pennsylvania. I didn't stay long. I sensed she wanted to be alone.

In my guest room, I cast about for something to do. I couldn't tell Emily about the day's events; she rested safely on my bedside stand at Bide-a-wee. *I wish I were at Bide-a-wee too.* Wearily I stretched out on the bed and studied the pattern on the wallpaper until I fell asleep once more. Sometime during the night, I awoke to the sound of voices. Realizing that I was still wearing street clothes, I groggily shed my dress and shoes, then fell back to sleep.

The next morning, we left for the Cape immediately after breakfast. When Grandmother didn't come downstairs to tell us goodbye, Grandpa apologized for her. Mama assured him that she understood and that we'd be seeing them again in a few weeks. "And we'll let you know the minute we hear any news about Jamie," she assured him.

"Thank you. Julia and I would appreciate that." Grandpa kissed Mama's cheek. "My son surely picked a winner when he married you."

"Thank you, James E. I love you like I love my own father."

We climbed into the Packard. When I looked toward my grandfather to wave, I saw, for the first time, an old man, his shoulders hunched, his eyes sad.

Daddy eased the vehicle through the iron gates and onto the brick roadway. "I found a place in New York the other day. Our crates are due to arrive from California next week. The ship is three weeks late because the captain had to outmaneuver a couple of German submarines."

"Praise God the ship got through at all." Mama glanced over at my father. "When can we move in?"

"As soon as possible. I've missed having my family around." He grinned at Mama. "We need to enroll Rusty in his school. And, CeeCee, I found out your classes at the conservatory start the first Monday in September."

Leave Bide-a-wee? I hadn't thought of that in weeks. "Do we have to leave the Cape?"

My mother turned in surprise. "I thought you'd be eager. We'll come back next summer."

"I suppose."

"Au Sam has asked to stay at Bide-a-wee until the weather turns cold. She'll use Rusty's old bicycle to get around until we return for her, Sundance, and Meeker at the end of October."

I leaned back and closed my eyes. There was nothing left to say. A bitter bile rose in my throat. *Jamie's gone, Thad's gone, and now Bide-a-wee too.*

Daddy left for the city the next morning, promising to contact everyone he knew in the city and in Washington, D.C. "I'll pound desks and throw tantrums, if necessary, to find out what's happened to Jamie."

Once more, I sorted through my personal belongings. There

wasn't much I wanted to take with me—my life in the city would be drastically different from that on the Cape. And I determined to keep my two worlds as separate as possible. The morning we were to start for New York, I carried two satchels out to the Packard and left them sitting beside the unopened trunk, along with a stack of Mama's things.

Halfheartedly, I stowed my violin in its case and placed my music in its leather portfolio, then paused to survey the parlor, whose atmosphere I'd helped create. Suddenly the sputter of a motorcycle in the driveway broke the silence. *Jamie! No, it can't be.*

Mama must have had the same thought, for she caught up with me as I charged through the kitchen door. We dashed around the end of the house, Sundance on our heels. Our faces fell when we spotted the rider.

"Hello, Mrs. Chamberlain," Hershel called as he set the bike's kickstand. He smiled at me and reddened. "Er, hello, Miss Chamberlain."

"Hershel, what a pleasant surprise." Mama recovered faster than I. "You must be thirsty after your long ride in the hot sun. Come on in and have a cool drink of lemonade."

"Thank you, Mrs. Chamberlain."

Mama slipped her arm into his and guided him toward the house. "So tell me, why are you here?"

Behind the car, he spotted our luggage. "Oh, are you folks ready to leave?"

"We're moving to the city. Mr. Chamberlain bought a house for us."

His face looked pained. "Oh, I'm sorry. I would have told you I was coming except I didn't know until this morning."

My mother patted his arm. "Nonsense. We're glad you came by to see us. This way, we'll get to say goodbye and thank you for loaning your motorcycle to Jamie before he—"

"That's why I'm here."

I followed them into the kitchen, where Au Sam stood canning applesauce from apples on our trees. Suspicion filled her eyes when she saw the young man. Mama introduced them, then suggested I take Hershel outside to the porch while she made the lemonade. "It's much cooler out there than in the parlor."

We sat down on the steps next to one another. Shyly, I cast about for something to say. Obviously as uncomfortable as I, Hershel replied in monosyllables. Finally, I tried the direct approach. "So, you still haven't told me to what we owe the pleasure of your visit."

He cleared his throat and studied his hands for a moment. "I came to say goodbye."

"Then you knew we were leaving?"

"No, I'm the one who's leaving. I've enlisted." He finally turned toward me.

"But I thought—"

"They took me. I guess they're getting hard up." He looked back down at his hands. "Galen came home last week. He's in pretty tough shape. It's his lungs, poisonous gas."

My hand flew to my mouth. "Oh no." The screen door slammed behind me.

"What is it, CeeCee?" Mama stood behind me, holding a metal tray of drinks.

"Galen, you remember Galen?" I could barely speak above a whisper.

"What happened to Galen?" She set the tray on a small wicker table beside the closest rocker, then sat down in the chair.

Hershel explained about the poisonous gas. "He'll have serious respiratory problems for the rest of his life, I'm afraid."

Mama handed him a glass of lemonade.

"Thank you." He sipped the refreshing liquid. "Anyway, the reason I'm here is to say goodbye. I leave for boot camp tomorrow."

She froze. "But why? I don't understand."

"Galen's one reason. And Jamie's the other. Jamie was my best friend."

My mother's voiced hardened. "I hope he still is—your best friend, that is."

Hershel's face clouded. "As you probably know, Galen and Jamie were stationed with the same medical unit." Hershel cleared his throat. "Galen said that the day Jamie disappeared, Jamie and two medics were sent out to help a badly shot-up squad

A CALL TO FAITH 225

of men. The medical team never reached their destination. Anyway, I can't sit at home and knit wool socks while my best friends give their lives for their country and for me."

Mama squeezed her eyes shut, but a tear trickled down the side of her cheek.

Hershel cleared his throat again. "I'm sorry, Mrs. Chamberlain, but I thought you should know."

Slowly, the muscles in my mother's face relaxed. "Thank you, Hershel. I want to know everything there is to know about my son."

Mama excused herself and hurried into the house, leaving Hershel and me with our glasses of lemonade. Before Hershel returned for Boston, he asked me if I'd write to him. "Every soldier needs a pretty pen pal at home, you know."

I blushed and assured him I'd be pleased to correspond with him. I wrote down our new address on a scrap of paper. "I'll write to you on two conditions."

He eyed me suspiciously.

"One, that you'll come visit us when you return home. And, two, you won't stop writing when you meet that pretty little French girl with whom you fall in love, but you'll write and tell me all about her."

Color flooded his face. "Oh, Miss CeeCee, that's unlikely to happen. I'm not the kind of man girls go for. You take Jamie and Galen—they attract the ladies."

I took his arm and led him to the kitchen. "Don't be so modest. I'm sure those black wavy curls of yours have set more than one female heart aflutter during your last four years of medical school."

He shook his head and stammered, "N-n-no, I'm afraid not."

I reached for a small jar of applesauce cooling on the windowsill. "Here, take this with you to remember me by."

He blushed again. "Thank you, but I don't need applesauce in order to remember you." His worshipful gaze unnerved me.

I gave a false laugh and tossed my head from side to side, like I'd seen Ashley do. "And I won't forget you either. It will be a pleasure adding your name to my pen-pal list."

His face clouded. "Uh, I guess I should be going."

I smiled at him. "You promised to write. I'm holding you to it."
"I will, Miss CeeCee. I will."

I walked Hershel out to the motorcycle and watched him stash the jar of applesauce in one of the leather saddlebags, then drive away. I waved until he was out of sight. With a sigh, I strode back to the house. *Another friend had left. . . .*

We Gather Together

October 11, 1917. Dear Emily, I hate school. No, that's too strong. I don't hate it, but I don't like it either. I can't settle down enough to study. And because my heart isn't in it, I practice out of habit rather than pleasure. How long will I feel this emptiness?

It's been two months since we received notice about Jamie. Two months! I went to a party with Ashley the night before she headed for college, but I left after less than an hour—bored. The best word to describe Ashley's friends is frantic. It's like they want to live as fast and as hard as possible for fear life will be snatched from them.

Everyone knows someone who has lost a loved one in the war. And everyone reacts differently to the loss. The men in the family—Daddy and Grandpa McCall—go on day after day without revealing their feelings. Mama wears herself out working at the Red Cross headquarters. She's also begun donating her time working with pregnant women at a clinic in "little Italy." Grandma McCall has become a total recluse. I went up to see her one weekend. She'd let herself go so badly that I barely recognized her. And all she talked about was Jamie. I was glad to get back home again!

As for me— I tapped my pen against the diary cover. *It seems foolish to write that I haven't been sleeping well. That's only part of the story.* I stared at the stack of letters from Hershel tied with a yellow ribbon on the corner of my desk. In the middle drawer of my desk was a similar stack from Thad, only tied with a blue ribbon. *Thad and Ashley make me feel like we're playing monkey in the middle—and I'm the monkey. In his letters he asks me if Ashley still cares for him while she vows me to secrecy regarding her latest conquests. Uncle Ian jokes about going bankrupt from paying postage for all the letters she writes to half the United States Army.*

One evening I was perched in the middle of my four-poster bed, working on a music-theory assignment, when Mama knocked on my bedroom door. "Come in," I called, barely looking up from my textbook.

"Hi there. Remember me?" She stuck her head into the room. "Haven't seen much of you lately."

"Hi. Come on in if you'd like. I'm almost finished with this exercise." I scribbled the ending notation on the score I'd transposed and put down my pencil. "What do you want to talk about?"

She ambled over to the rocker beside my bed and sat down. "Nothing much. I just needed to hear your voice and see your smile again."

I gave her a wry smile. "Not much to smile about, I guess."

She leaned her head back against the chair and began to rock slowly. "Oh, I don't know. There's still plenty I'm thankful for—you, for instance. How's school coming?"

I shrugged. *Not one of your "rah-rah" homecoming speeches tonight!* "I've been better."

"Probably so. You know, I've been thinking. How would you like to take a few days off from school and drive up to the Cape with me to pick up Au Sam and the animals?"

"Really? May I?"

Mama grinned. "Daddy thinks it's a good idea. He also suggested that I use the time to teach you to drive."

"What?" I squealed. "Really? Me? Drive?"

"I don't know why not." She continued to rock steadily. "Though it's true that most of your friends don't drive, living in the city and all, that doesn't mean you shouldn't learn, if you'd like."

"Like? I'd love it." I leapt to the edge of the bed, letting my music theory book tumble to the floor.

"Good." She stopped rocking. "Can you leave tomorrow morning?"

"You bet! What time?"

"Seven?" She rose to her feet.

"Absolutely."

My mother walked over and kissed my forehead. "We'll stay

two days before driving back. Get a good night's sleep now." She turned and left the room.

Sleep? I couldn't sleep. All night long I dreamed about driving—driving into storefronts, driving into ice wagons, driving into the East River.

The next morning I was glad Mama waited until we were out in the country, where there wasn't a storefront, ice wagon, or river in sight before giving me my first driving lesson.

After learning how to start, stop, steer, and shift, I felt confident enough to drive for a while on quiet country roads.

That noon we stopped to eat our picnic lunch at an overlook in the Berkshire Mountains, though I think the hillsides covered with brilliant red, yellow, and orange leaves nourished our souls even more than the sandwiches refreshed our bodies.

I gazed out over the ranges and thought of the Sierra Nevada in California. *So totally different. Both beautiful, but totally different.*

Mama came up behind me and put her arm around my waist. "Just look at that. Isn't God wonderful, the way He demonstrates His love for us? Makes you wish you were an artist, doesn't it?"

Thad. What would Thad do with a scene like this?

My mother continued, "I remember how much Jamie enjoyed the aspens in the fall in Colorado. When he stuffed the leaves into his pockets, he said he was collecting gold pieces."

"Mama, I haven't told you this before, but I admire how well you've dealt with Jamie's being missing. I'm afraid Grandma McCall will go insane if something doesn't change soon. Yet, you've seemed at peace with the situation—accepting, almost."

She chuckled. "Accepting? Not quite. The Lord and I have had a number of late-night conversations. As for your grandmother, don't be too hard on her. Everyone has his or her own way of coping with grief and loss."

"I've noticed that. I just wish I had your calmness, your faith."

"Honey, give yourself time. God gives me the strength, the patience, the peace to go on. He'll do the same for you, if you ask."

"I think I've been too angry at Him to ask Him for anything." I shuffled a golden leaf with the toe of my shoe. "Sometimes I've been so angry over Jamie's disappearance that I was afraid God would strike me with a bolt of lightning."

She laughed. "I can understand how you've felt. So does He."

"I don't know. It seems so hopeless."

"The only way—" My mother stepped around me to face me. "—you will ever come to terms over Jamie is to turn your pain, your anger, and your frustration completely over to God. I don't know of any other way. That's how Daddy and I do it."

I snorted. "Sounds so easy."

"It's the most difficult thing you'll ever do." She gave me a hug. "We'd better get going; we have a long way to drive."

The next day I spent every moment possible wandering along the beaches, climbing over boulders, and exploring ponds and inlets. The flower gardens were a blaze of orange marigolds and yellow mums. The deep blue of the sea framed the garnet of the red oak trees and the deep ruby of the cranberry bogs. Swamp maple and woodbine added their touch of flame to the autumn landscape.

Still restless on my last day at Bide-a-wee, Sundance and I hiked north along the eastern shore. A chilly sunset breeze rose off the tide by the time I began to retrace my steps homeward. Out on the bay, I could see the fishing boats coming in.

"Tomorrow we go home, boy." I chucked Sundance under his chin. "You're going to miss this, being cooped up in that little backyard in the city." He brushed closer to my knees, as if he understood.

It wasn't until the sun sank behind the hills that I realized I'd walked much farther than I had intended. I stepped up my pace, hoping Mama wouldn't worry much, but knowing better. None of the landmarks seemed familiar on the moon-shrouded landscape. Recurring fears niggled at my mind. *What if I can't find my way home? What if I have to sleep out here all night? What if the tide comes in while I'm sleeping, trapping me in some cove? What if . . .*

Like the unraveling of a loosely knitted sweater, my peace disintegrated, leaving my emotions naked and vulnerable. I spotted a pathway leading from the beach. *Maybe if I can get to the road, I can make better time.*

I stumbled over the rutted path until I came to an abandoned cottage. Tired, hungry, and lost, I sat down on the crumbling porch steps and cried. Sundance whined and tugged at my trouser leg, coaxing me back toward the beach.

"No, Sundance. I have to rest before I can walk any farther!"

The dog whimpered and lay by my feet, his head on his paws. I followed his example and buried my face in my arms. Memories of summer flooded back—morning walks with Thad, Jamie's weekend visits, Ashley and her antics. Suddenly I discovered I was sobbing, not crying or weeping, but sobbing from deep within myself. Sundance pressed closer and whimpered.

"God, I can't go on any longer. I'm tired of being mad at You. I'm tired of the horrid nightmares." I could hear my words echo back to me. "I'm too tired to fight You any longer. Please forgive me for all the terrible things I've said to You. Help me to find the peace I need to get past this awful experience. I need to know You still love me."

My joints ached as I straightened and opened my eyes. During the short time I'd been resting on the step, a bank of dark clouds had moved in, covering the moon, and the wind had picked up. I jumped to my feet. "Come on, boy. We'd better follow the beach."

I hadn't walked far before a rain began to fall, gently at first and then in driving sheets. On my left the waves roared and crashed against the rocks; dark pines formed a black wall on my right. I stumbled over boulders and tripped on driftwood. My feet became entangled in ropes of seaweed, yet I pressed on. *I won't quit. I won't give up. Sooner or later—*

Suddenly, Sundance yipped and bounded up the beach, then back again. "What is it, boy? What is it? Did you spot a quail?"

I rounded a bend, and there, it front of me, I saw the lights. My mother had lighted every lamp in the house. A sob caught in my throat. *Home! Mama, I'm home.*

Breaking into a run, I stumbled up the pathway, Sundance barking our arrival with every step. The moment my feet hit the edge of the lawn, Mama burst through the door onto the porch. "CeeCee, is that you? Are you all right? I've been so worried."

"Yes, Mama. I'm OK, now that I'm safely home."

She bounded off the porch and ran through the driving rain to meet me. "Let's get you inside before you catch your death. Au Sam has the water hot to make you a pot of tea. Your teeth are chattering!"

I laughed between chatters. "It's cold out here."

"I should say. Au Sam thinks it will be snowing by morning." Mama hurried me inside the house and closed the door. Five minutes later, bundled in my warmest sweater, nightgown, and slippers, I joined Mama and Au Sam in the kitchen for a mug of hot herbal tea. I told them of my adventure—all except the part about my confrontation with God. I needed time to think about that before I shared it with anyone.

When I climbed the stairs to bed that night, I had no trouble falling asleep. Whether from exhaustion or a new inner peace, I was too tired to tell.

By morning the storm had passed, and the sun shone on a jewel-toned earth. After we latched the shutters and locked the doors, Mama climbed into the passenger side of the front seat while Au Sam sat in back between Sundance and Meeker's traveling cage. I ran around to the front of the house to take one last look at the ocean. For the first time, I truly understood the cottage's name—Bide-a-wee. It was a place to find one's self, a place to heal, a place to find God.

It's time, I thought. *It's time to move on.* The honk of the car horn reminded me that I had places to be and things to do. Eagerly I hurried to the car. It was a long drive from Cape Cod to New York City.

"La-la-la-la-la-la-la-la-the King of creation. La-la-la-la-la-la-He is thy health and salvation. La-la-la-la . . ." Sundance whined at the kitchen door, begging to go out. "Sorry, boy. You're stuck until I get these last two pies in the oven."

He whined and curled up in front of the door.

This was the day before Thanksgiving, and in the morning mail Mama had received a letter from Shane Simons, asking if he could spend his Thanksgiving holiday with us, since he couldn't go home to Kansas. He'd mailed the letter several days before, but somehow the mail was unusually slow, and the letter reached us only hours before he was due to arrive.

To make matters worse, Au Sam woke up with a cold—which meant I had to help with the baking. While I grumbled a bit, I was enjoying myself more than I wanted to admit. Mama agreed to do the grocery shopping on the way home from her appointment downtown at the Red Cross.

I glanced at the kitchen clock. The first pies needed ten more minutes.

Having the entire McCall clan at our house for Thanksgiving sounded like great fun. Even Grandma McCall had reluctantly agreed to come. I'm not sure how my mother managed it, but she did. Uncle Ian and Aunt Drucilla were bringing the entree and Ashley. I wasn't too excited about having Shane in the same house with my cousin, but I didn't have much control over the matter. And anyway, it would be fun to see Shane again. I'd thought about him off and on during the past seven months.

The morning mail also brought a letter from Thad. He wrote about a family he'd met in France and included a couple sketches he'd done of them and of their home. I didn't fail to notice the sketch of the farmer's bright-eyed daughter.

Continuing to sing, I brushed the rolling pin with flour and rolled out the bottom crust on the countertop.

> Joyful, joyful, we adore Thee,
> God of glory, Lord of love;
> la-la-la-la-la-la-la-la,
> Hail Thee as the sun above;
> M-m-m-m-sin and sadness,
> la-la-la-la-la—

"Hey, anyone home?" Uncle Ian called from the front entryway.

"Out here, Uncle Ian, in the kitchen."

"Your aunt wanted me to drop off these yams for—M-m-m, what smells so good?"

I couldn't help preening. "Oh, that's the pumpkin pies baking. I'm working on the pecan ones now."

He dropped the bag of yams on the counter. "Some man is going to get a great cook when he marries you, young lady."

"I don't know about that. As Mama says, 'the proof is in the pudding; the evidence is in the tasting.' "

He took a deep breath, then tapped the side of his nose. "These olfactory nerves are seldom wrong. That's good stuff, you're baking."

"Thank you. I hope you're right."

"I'm on my way to pick up your grandparents at the station. I still can't get over how Chloe talked my mom into coming down here for the holiday. See you." He waved on his way out of the kitchen. I heard him call to me before closing the door, but I couldn't make out what he said.

"OK, see you tomorrow," I answered automatically. I held my breath as I balanced the rolled pie dough on my rolling pin and slid it into my metal pie pan. "There." I allowed myself to breathe again.

"Hi?"

The voice behind me startled me. I screamed and swung around, rolling pin in hand, ready to clobber the intruder. "Shane!"

"Hey, watch it!" Shane Simons thrust his hands up in front of his face to defend himself.

"What are you doing here? Isn't Daddy supposed to pick you up at the train station tonight at seven?"

"I'm sorry." His face fell. "I caught an earlier train out of Washington. If it's an inconvenience, I-I-I could go—"

"Nonsense." I laughed at his worried expression. "You startled me, that's all."

Shane scratched his head. "I seem to make a habit of startling you, don't I?"

"As a matter of fact, you do, don't you? Seriously, I'm glad you're here. As you can see, I can't welcome you with a handshake.

"So—" He looked at the unfilled pie pans on the table. "—tell me where to park my gear and what I can do to help."

"You help in the kitchen?" I giggled. "Thank you for the gracious offer but—"

"But? But what?" He sniffed the air. "Do I smell something burning?"

"My pies!" I whirled about, grabbed the corner of my apron, and threw open the oven door. Thanks to his nose, I'd caught the pumpkin pies just before they shifted from Thanksgiving dessert to burnt offerings for the sparrows. With my apron, I reached toward the nearest pie.

"No, wait. You'll burn yourself." He stepped in front of me, grabbed the hot pads stacked beside the stove, and lifted the first pie out of the oven, then the second, and placed them on the pie rack to cool. "My mother is always trying that stunt and is always suffering because of it. Your next pies ready?"

"In a minute. Let me crimp the dough first." I pointed toward the pan on the stove's back burner. "The custard for the pecan pies is cooling in that pan."

He washed his hands in the sink; then for the next few minutes, we worked side by side, putting the finishing touches on the two pecan pies. Shane held the oven door for me while I slid the pies onto the oven rack. I straightened and wiped my hands on my apron. "There. That's done."

"Not quite." He picked up the leftover dough and rolled it out on the floured surface. "Do you have any jam or jelly in the house?"

I nodded. "A jar of blackberry jam in the pantry."

"Great, go get it."

"Yes, sir." I snapped off a salute, then ran for the jam.

I watched fascinated as he slathered the dough with jam, then rolled it up and pinched the seam closed. "This is the best part of making pies." He opened the oven door and set the roll of dough on the top rack. "Well, second best. The best part is getting to eat what you make."

"You *do* know something about baking, don't you?"

He planted a puff of flour on the end of my nose. "Surprised, huh? I'm a man of many talents."

I laughed. "Let me wash my hands; then I'll show you upstairs to your room."

"I'm right behind you. I left my bag in the entryway."

He followed me up the stairs to the guest room. "So will I get to meet this brother of yours while I'm here?"

I swallowed hard. "Probably not. The United States Army declared him missing in action three months ago. We haven't heard a word since."

"Oh, I'm sorry. I didn't mean to—"

I smiled up into his suddenly serious brown eyes. "You had no way of knowing. Here, here's your room. Make yourself comfortable."

"Thanks." He sniffed the air. "We'd better rescue our pie-crust treat from the fires of Hades."

"Oh, you're right." We raced down the stairs and into the kitchen in time to save and to savor the treat over two glasses of milk. Our conversation seemed as natural as if we saw each other every day.

I'd just removed the last pecan pie from the oven, when the front doorbell rang. I glanced at the clock. "It's probably Mama. She sometimes forgets her keys." I hurried to answer the door. "How did your—"

It wasn't my mother. It was Mr. Tenney, the postman, making his second delivery of the day. "A letter from France for your parents and one for you too. That boyfriend of yours sure writes often enough." He thrust the stack of mail into my hands.

"Thank you, Mr. Tenney. You have a good Thanksgiving Day, you hear?"

"Absolutely. 'Bye now. See you Friday."

I waved and closed the door, absently shuffling through the letters. I found one from Thad for me and slipped it into my apron pocket. Beneath my letter was a crumpled letter addressed to my parents. I read the return address. "Mademoiselle Auriel Le Fleur." The address and the postmark were too blurred to read, but the U.S. Army seal was clear and definite. I tapped the letter against my cheek. *Who in the world is Auriel Le Fleur?*

I held the envelope up to the light but could see nothing. I tested the edges of the seal, but it was glued fast. *I want to open it so badly!* But I knew better. Respecting the privacy of others was a hard, fast rule in our family. I could no more read that letter than my mother would read any of my journals to Emily.

If my mother hadn't returned home within the next five minutes, I'm afraid I would not have been able to hold out. The moment I heard her key in the lock, I ran to the door, pulling the door out of her hand. "Here." I thrust the letter from the mysterious Frenchwoman toward her. "This just came for you. Who in the world is Auriel Le Fleur?"

"Auriel who?" She studied the letter for what seemed like ten minutes.

"Open it," I coaxed. "Open it and find out."

"Give me a chance to set my parcels down first."

"I'll take them." I snatched them from her arms and flew into the kitchen and dumped them in the pantry, then flew back in time to see her slip the letter from the envelope and unfold it. Her lips moved silently as she read the first few words. I watched as her face paled and she groped for a chair. Tears tumbled down her cheeks. "I-I-I can't—. Oh, dear God, I can't—" She clutched the letter with one hand and covered her eyes with the other.

"What? What? What's happened?" I snatched the letter from her hand and began reading. "Dear Mr. and Mrs. Chamberlain, You don't know me, but I'm writing this letter for your son, Lieutenant Dr. James McCall." *Jamie?* I stared at my mother, expecting her to explain, then continued reading. "By now, you have probably heard that he and his ambulance crew were shelled. He was knocked unconscious, and the other men were killed."

My heart pounded as I read the good news. "A higher power must have been watching out for your son, for he was soon found, hidden for six weeks, and then smuggled to the nearest military hospital. He sustained a broken leg, a severe concussion, and lacerations to his face and hands."

"Here, let me read it." Mama snatched the letter out of my hands. She reread the letter aloud. "Oh, dear Father, thank You so much. Thank You. Thank You. Thank You."

We fell into each other's arms, sobbing. I was grateful when Shane quietly closed the doors to the parlor, granting us privacy for the moment.

Mama sniffed. "The woman says she's one of the nurses who cares for Jamie. Oh, Thank You, Lord, for sparing his life and for the nurses who continue to care for him."

Of course, our Thanksgiving celebration was the most joyous ever! I'll never forget the look on my Grandmother McCall's face when Mama read her the letter. For a moment, I was afraid she'd faint.

I can't remember a time when I felt so overwhelmingly grateful for all God had done for me and my family. Several times throughout the day, I choked back tears of gratitude—and caught others doing the same. It didn't even bother me to have Ashley charm Shane into a mound of jelly. My brother was alive and safe. That was more than enough.

The clock gonged nine when Daddy gathered everyone into the parlor. "I think it would be appropriate to close this eventful celebration with a psalm of praise, don't you? And a prayer for the mothers and fathers, grandparents, and other relatives of the boys who will not be receiving a letter like ours this holiday season."

Swept away to another time
The Chloe Mae Chronicles
by Kay Rizzo

Never before have you shared the power of a dream or the emotions of young love as you will in this memorable early-pioneer series.

As Chloe Mae flees from her father's iron rule, she starts down a path of experience she never bargained for. Silence turns to love and tragedy turns to forgiveness as Chloe Mae lifts her heart to God for strength to face whatever life brings.

Four-book set: *Flee My Father's House, Silence of My Love, Claims Upon My Heart,* and *Still My Aching Heart.*

Paper. US$10.95/Cdn$15.35 each. US$34.95/Cdn$48.95 set.
Prices subject to change without notice.

Available at your local Christian bookstore

Books You Just Can't Put Down
from Pacific Press

© 1993 Pacific Press Publishing Association 489/9832b

There's no gray in a black-and-white issue

She Said No
by Kay Rizzo

From the beginning, the physical side of Heather and Josh's relationship threatened to push them over the edge of reason. Though Christians, each viewed their growing intimacy differently. When their ideas collided, two lives were severely damaged in the emotional wreckage of a criminal act—date rape.

She Said No, by Kay Rizzo, confronts a difficult subject with uncanny insight and needful honesty. Its message could salvage or help protect the lives and relationships of those who may be at risk.

Paper. $10.95/Cdn$15.35.
Prices subject to change without notice.

Books You Just Can't Put Down
From Pacific Press

Available at your favorite Christian bookstore.

© 1994 Pacific Press Publishing Association 669/9831

Why is this happening to me, God?
Nowhere to Turn
by Rhonda Graham

Ellen's blank stare followed her husband's figure as he walked out of the house and out of her life. Her head pounded with the same questions over and over. How could this be happening to a pastor's wife? To someone who "played by the rules"?

Nowhere to Turn shares the emotions of a woman going through the pain of divorce and offers hope to Christians enduring crises of faith and family.

US$9.95/Cdn$13.95. Paper.

Available at your local Christian bookstore

Prices subject to change without notice.

Books You Just Can't Put Down
from Pacific Press

© 1993 Pacific Press Publishing Association 487/9832b